DEADFALL RIDGE

BY DUNCAN McGEARY

Duncan McGeary

CHAPTER 1

Sherm Russo waited in his car, parked across from the house, looking in the rearview mirror every few seconds, his left hand hesitating over the door handle, trying to work up the courage to make the approach. It would take him some effort to leverage himself out of the seat. Anyone watching would have plenty of time to spot him.

Jennifer called him a *big* man rather than *fat,* bless her little heart, and he did mean little, because her heart was as dried up as a prune. He and his wife co-inhabited a house, both of them too dispirited to do anything about it.

Well, he was doing something now.

They might come after Jennifer, he thought. Sherm had a sudden vision of his wife tied to a chair with white-hot pokers in her face, babbling about how she didn't know *nothin'.* It gave him a moment of satisfaction, followed instantly by guilt.

He wasn't a bad man...when he had time to think about it.

The car door popped open, his hand making the decision for him. He sighed and heaved himself out of the seat, his belly catching on the steering wheel. He stood next to the car for a few moments, breathing hard. There was no one in sight. Not a sound. It was two o'clock in the morning.

Sherm didn't know who he should be looking for anyway. In the old days, he probably could have spotted his pursuers with a single glance. The old crew had a certain way about them, slow and languid, but predatory, each movement threatening to explode into violence.

These new guys? It could be hard to pick them out. They might have been his neighbor's kids, college educated, looking down at their cellphones, their fingers a blur as they texted or scrolled. At first, his new bosses had been a refreshing change. After all, the old-timers could turn on you for no reason. But then he realized the new guys, the little hipster shits, were just as unpredictable, their motives tangled up in behaviors that made no sense to him.

When had it all changed? When had the criminal enterprise become outwardly legitimate, if no less immoral?

About the time they chose that meaningless name, Airolo Corporation.

About the time I started hiding my escape stashes.

Somewhere along the line, there'd been a merger of the old and the new. Sherm's old acquaintances had started disappearing. Not retiring, disappearing. At some point, he started hearing Russian accents from those who told him what to do. Something about the cold-blooded nature of the new bosses had sent him home each night with his heart quivering. He knew too much, it was as simple as that. But he was trusted because he was loyal.

I am, he thought. *When you're loyal to me.*

But he wasn't stupid. He understood that someday the volume of illegal doings he knew about would tip the balance and his risk would outweigh his value. Or a new guy—younger, quicker, even more loyal—would take his place.

Ironically, it wasn't this startling development that got Sherm into trouble. Or so he thought. It was a simple mistake in his accounting calculations, the last thing he expected. He didn't make mistakes; he remembered everything. That's what made him such an asset...*and* a liability.

Corey Brancato, with his smug little smile, called Sherm into his office, pointed out that his error had cost the corporation several million dollars, and told him it was time to retire.

Sherm stood there for several moments, trying to comprehend what he was hearing.

"Can I see the mistake?" he asked.

"No, you're done," Brancato said. "Leave the premises, Sherm. We'll send you a severance check in a few days."

Sherm stood there desperately trying to figure out how he could possibly have made such a massive error. *Several million? How could that be?* He was as on top of things as he'd ever been.

He glanced over the partition of the corner cubicle and saw James Martinson smirking at him. His assistant was a little man you wouldn't notice if not for his bristly red mustache, which seemed to enter a room before he did.

Of course. The Cerberus merger.

He'd left the details to Martinson to finish up. He'd never expected the little bastard to betray him like this. There was nothing in it for Martinson. He was too junior, too new to move up.

But some people didn't need a reason to do shitty things.

"It wasn't me," he said. "I handed it over to Martinson."

"He predicted you'd say that," Brancato said, "but he gave us the original worksheets in your writing. It's your error, pal."

"You know how easy it is to slip in new numbers? I do all my original figures in pencil. Why would you believe Martinson over me?"

Brancato looked away, and Sherm realized his boss *didn't* believe it. It was an excuse, a setup. Over the years, Sherm had thought it prudent to squirrel away damning evidence about his bosses. He'd collected dirt on a lot of people. He never said so aloud, but hinted. Up to now, his bosses had thought it wasn't worth the risk to get rid of him.

It worked for years. But then something happened that was nearly incomprehensible.

One of his clients, a New York real estate tycoon, decided to enter politics. Sherm thought it amusing at first. Right up until the last moment he didn't think the guy had any chance of winning.

He still couldn't believe it.

Even then it might have been safe because most of his dirt was on the middleman in the transactions, a high-powered New York lawyer. It wasn't until the Right Honorable Weasel, Barton Crane, was nominated to the Supreme Court that Sherm realized he was in real trouble. Suddenly, what Sherm knew about the crooked lawyer's past, which had always been dangerous, was explosive.

What had once been leverage was now a death sentence.

"Go home, Sherm," Brancato said. "We'll send your stuff along later."

Shit. Now I'm a target. Sherm turned without another word and left the office, leaving the door wide open. Martinson ducked his head down into his cubicle, not so brave now that Sherm was heading his way.

Sherm stood behind the little man, waiting. Finally, Martinson turned, his face flushing. "It was *your* mistake."

"No, it wasn't," Sherm said. "I don't make mistakes, not when it comes to numbers. Do you realize what you've done?"

Martinson shrugged. "Hey, it was time for you to retire anyway, Russo. Long past time. You've been cock-blocking the younger, smarter guys for years."

"Like you?"

"Sure, like me."

"Do you even *know* who you work for, Martinson?"

"What do you mean?"

Sherm took a deep breath, shaking his head, disgusted. Now that it was done, he was calmer than he would've expected. "I lasted forty years here, pal. I doubt you'll last four."

"So? I'll just get another job."

"There is no other job after this one. After this one, you're done forever."

"Don't be so dramatic," Martinson said. A flicker of doubt crossed his face, but it quickly vanished.

"You've killed me," Sherm said and walked away. "Your days are just as numbered."

Sherm didn't go home. He drove around town for an hour, randomly turning down streets, buying four dollars' worth of gas with the change in his pocket, not daring to use his credit card.

To his surprise, he wasn't followed.

They underestimate me, he thought. *They think I'll be easy to dispose of. Just a tired fat old man.*

He searched his wallet and found a folded-up twenty he'd squirreled away years ago. He stopped at a Burger King and dragged out the eating of a meal until the employees started eyeballing him. Then he went to a McDonald's and did the same thing. Nerves jangling from multiple cups of coffee, he finally trudged to his car, well after midnight, when the streets were nearly empty of traffic.

He drove the long way to Greg Snyder's place. Once there, he sat contemplating his options before his left hand opted for him.

The house was nice, if humble. The kind of place someone on a janitor's salary could buy back in the '60s. Sherm checked the obituaries every morning so he was pretty sure his old friend was still kicking.

A scream stopped Sherm's hand in mid-knock. He froze.

Run away. Run away now.

He listened for footsteps, but the scream had drowned out his knocking. They didn't know he was there.

He opened the unlocked door quietly, took a quick look around, scooted to the base of the stairs, and listened. He recognized Greg Snyder's raspy voice.

"I'm telling you! My wife threw away that box years ago! It was falling apart. The only thing holding it together was duct tape," Greg was saying.

"You never opened it in all those years?" said a smooth voice.

"Russo told me not to, Mr. Samuels, so I didn't. I'm an honest man," Greg protested.

"An honest man..."

Sherm recognized the name.

It's too late, he told himself. *You can't help Greg now.*

He fingered the knife in his pocket, but his hands felt weak. It was ridiculous. Attacking a man like Samuels would be like charging a tank with a bayonet. It would be suicide. Still, he considered it for a moment, some of the old feelings coming back. He'd been in worse situations. Maybe, with the element of surprise, just maybe he could save his old friend.

Another scream interrupted his thoughts, and he felt himself shaking, his hand jittering on the switchblade.

Stop being such a coward.

No, not a coward...prudent, came a voice from deep inside. He hadn't survived the gang wars of the '70s by being foolish.

"Where's the box now?" Samuels demanded, his calm voice promising only pain.

"I...I don't know!"

Another scream echoed down the stairwell. Then Greg cried out, "You don't have to hurt me! I'll tell you anything you want, OK? Listen, believe me, I took the money and spent it. It's gone, been gone for years."

"We don't care about the money," Samuels said. "What else was in the box?"

"A floppy disk and a gun. But I threw them away."

"You threw away a *gun*?" This was a new voice, lower and less refined than Samuels's.

"I don't like guns," Greg said. "I had kids in the house."

Samuels said, "So you didn't look at what was on the disk?"

"I didn't even own a computer, man. The floppy was just trash to me. I figured Sherm would never come back for the money, and if he did, I'd say I lost the box, or that Mary threw it away."

"Where is Mary?" Samuels asked.

There was a whimper, then silence, and then, in a remarkably steady voice, Greg said, "Dead, you son of a bitch. You can't hurt her."

"Where is the floppy disk, Snyder?"

Sherm held his breath at the ensuing silence. It probably didn't matter if Greg gave up the disk now or not. He was a dead man either way. But Sherm hoped it was true that his friend had let him down and tossed it, if for no other reason than to frustrate the bastards.

When Greg finally spoke, his tone was so unconvincing that even Sherm knew he was lying. "I gave it to a friend," he said. "I told him to hand it over to the police if anything happened to me."

Samuels laughed. "I don't believe you, Snyder. I'm giving you one last chance. If you produce the floppy disk, I'll let you live."

There was a long moment of loud breathing, and then Greg spoke so quietly that Sherm could barely make out the words. "No, you won't."

When Samuels next spoke, Sherm could almost see him shaking his head regretfully. "You're right, Mr. Snyder. I won't. Do it, Jordan."

"Wait! Pleas—"

Sherm felt the knife slice across Greg's throat as if it was his own. There was a deep silence as if the Earth had been emptied of life. Then he heard a gurgling sound, the staccato rat-tat-tat of Greg's thrashing feet, and then his death rattle, going on forever and then finally, mercifully, it stopped.

Sherm's legs almost gave out. He clenched the banister to hold himself up. It took all his willpower to stumble to the door. He staggered down the steps, out onto the street, and over to his car. At this hour of the morning, no one had heard the screams, or if they had, they'd pulled their pillows up over their ears and pretended they hadn't.

Then the fear faded. An old, familiar feeling of numbness came over Sherm. He reached into his pocket as if expecting to find a gun.

He hadn't always been an accountant. Once, he'd been a soldier for the Family, following orders, no matter how dangerous. It was only after an underboss had discovered Sherm's talent for numbers that he'd been taken off the street and put into an office.

Once, he'd carried a gun, not a calculator.

He started the car without being aware of inserting the key and turned the steering wheel. The passenger side window shattered, fragments of safety glass showering down on him. His foot automatically slammed down on the accelerator. With tires screaming, the Volvo roared down the side streets and onto the freeway onramp.

The old Volvo shuddered under the strain. Sherm felt something snap, and the car slowed abruptly. He steered to the side of the road and stopped. He pulled himself out of the car, jumped over the guardrail, and ran down the rocky hillside into a part of town he didn't recognize.

He was broke. All he had were the clothes on his back. His carefully laid escape plans had been for nothing.

How did they know?

Sherm racked his brain, trying to remember when he'd last visited Greg. It had been before Mary died, at least two years ago. Was it possible they'd been following him that long?

More than possible. He, more than anyone, knew how thorough his new bosses could be. When the organization had changed from gangster to corporate, he'd been relieved at first, until he realized the organization was just as criminal and dangerous as ever, and much more efficient.

One chance remained. Without money, without a car, he somehow had to make his way across the entire country to a small town in Oregon.

What were the odds that Amanda, as she was calling herself now, hadn't opened the box years ago and taken the money? As crazy as she was, she'd always kept her word. And as far as he could tell, the corporation didn't know about her.

Or did they?

CHAPTER 2

It was my last innocent hunt.

You'd think hunting animals for sport, (and let's not kid ourselves, the Lully family wasn't there for the meat), is anything but innocent, but it is something men did long before sin, before morality, before religion.

"Can you guarantee we'll get a big one?" John Lully asked as we approached the Strawberry Mountains.

I tried not to roll my eyes. I hated that question. Some years you got lucky and some years you didn't. But that wasn't the kind of answer they were paying for. We were on a winding part of rough road, so I veered a little, running over onto a pothole, heard a *thump* and the older boy curse in the backseat. I slowed down. It was their own fault they weren't buckled up, but it wouldn't do to kill my clients.

Unfortunately, the jostling didn't take their minds off the question.

"Can you, Hart?" Michael, the younger brother, asked eagerly.

I could almost hear my father's voice saying, *"Why sure, son. We might even bag a record buck. Hell, slip me another hundred bucks and I'll show you my own private hunting spot. I tell you, I've never failed yet."*

Instead, I gave them my standard joke. "Hart Davis Hunting and Fishing guarantees…" I paused dramatically, "a nice walk in the woods."

"I just want to kill something," Jeremy said. The flat affect in his voice was chilling. He sat back and sucked the last soda out of his cup and then annoyingly, kept sucking.

I almost turned around right then and there and drove the two and a half hours back to Bend. The last thing I wanted on my hands was bloodthirsty kids.

I figured Jeremy was around sixteen years old, and his younger brother Michael looked a couple of years younger. But it was their father who was responsible, because he hadn't taught them proper respect for hunting.

I needed their money, so I kept driving.

From the highway, the Strawberry Mountains undulated across the southern horizon. Between the mountains were deep canyons, and in the spring, snowmelt ran down them. There were deer in these valleys, at least most of the time, though during hunting season, the animals tended to climb higher up. The ridges were forested almost to the top. Only a few of them rose above the tree line. In a few more weeks, snow would fall on those barren peaks, and even the lower elevations would be difficult to reach.

Bigfoot Ranch was halfway up these hills. Granger, the owner of the ranch, wasn't going to be there. He and his crew were taking a last minute vacation in the valley before winter set in. It was late in the season, and this was probably my last job. It was only a two-day-er, so I figured I could take care of the Lully's family by myself.

We pulled up and unloaded. The Lullys had the bunkhouse to themselves, while I was going to stay in the house. Dusk was beginning to fall, and I set about lighting a campfire. That was half the experience for some of the city folk. I cooked some chili (really, it was canned, but the Lully family didn't need to know that) while the two boys made *Blazing Saddles* jokes.

Their father stared into the flames silently. I had a feeling that he didn't really want be there, but had something to prove to his kids.

None of my business.

The next morning I rousted them before daylight. They grumbled, but I told them dawn was the best time to hunt deer.

We started up the trail.

The hill we climbed was too small to have an official name, but I made a point of calling it Huntsmen Mountain for those clients who could only make it that far. It made them feel like they'd accomplished something. Some of these duffers walked half a mile and acted like they'd climbed Mt. Everest. Others tried to prove what big men they were by running me—and themselves—into the ground. I wasn't sure which was worse.

John Lully propped his rifle over his shoulder, which made me wince a little but was acceptable. Both of the boys kept their rifle muzzles pointed downward and to the side. I breathed a sigh of relief. At my recommendation, they were each carrying a basic, synthetic-stocked .30-06 with a Leupold scope, a good bolt-action rifle that got the job done.

I preferred a lever-action .30-30 Winchester, since it was shorter and lighter than most hunting rifles, especially since I rarely took a shot. I had on my hunting jacket, which was an almost fluorescent bright red because my clients sometimes got buck fever and started shooting at anything that moved.

John Lully started huffing about halfway up, but I realized he wasn't going to admit to fatigue with his two sons along. I picked up the pace a little out of sheer orneriness. The Lully family annoyed me. They had too much money and attitude, not enough common sense.

We stopped and watched the rising sun. The mountains continued upward into the sunlight. From here, there was a clear vista of everything below. The rolling green of pine tree-covered hills extended as far as the eye could see. At their base, there were open fields, and glittering in the far distance was the town of John Day.

The Lullys gawked at the view. Their awe made me feel a little warmer toward them. Apparently they weren't all about shooting and killing.

A rifle cracked, and I jumped with a stifled shout. I whirled around to see the youngest boy, Michael, with his rifle still at his shoulder. "I got him!" he shouted.

The herd was barely visible in the dim light, and only because they were moving rapidly away, their white tails bobbing. Fifty yards down the hill, on the trail itself, an animal thrashed.

Michael started running. I grabbed him. "Don't run with a gun in your hands," I said.

He pulled away roughly but slowed down a little.

My heart sank when I saw what he'd shot. It was a yearling, on the small side. Its antlers were about the height of its huge ears, maybe an inch shorter, and they had barely forked. It was trying to lift its head and squealing. I looked over at Michael and saw his buck fever dissipating fast. The boy had hit the deer behind the shoulder, a good shot, but with the downward angle, he'd missed the vital organs.

I levered a shell into my Winchester and stepped forward.

Lully brusquely pushed me away. "No!" he said. "Michael has to finish it."

Michael's face paled. He showed no sign of having heard his father.

"I'll do it," I said.

"No!" Lully said. "He needs to be a man, finish what he starts. Come on, son, put the poor thing out its misery."

Michael looked down at his rifle as if he didn't know what it was. Then, slowly, he ejected the spent round and ratcheted another one into the chamber. He stepped close to the thrashing deer and placed the muzzle just inches from its head.

Careful, I almost said, but then a second shot ended it.

I sensed John Lully at my side. "Is the deer legal?" the father whispered.

"Yes, he did fine," I said. "He's fourteen years old. No one's going to make an issue of it."

"Good," Lully grinned. "Chalk up his first kill.

We carried the deer down the trail. It weighed maybe eighty pounds. I figured it was better to get it back to camp. I dressed the deer, the carcass hanging from a crossbeam.

Michael was nowhere to be seen.

That afternoon, we split up. John and Jeremy Lully headed up the trail again, while I took Michael in the opposite direction. We had walkie-talkies. With any luck, we'd drive the animals toward each other.

Michael and I hadn't gone more than a few hundred yards when the biggest buck I'd ever seen trotted up to us and stood there as if posing for the cover of *Outdoor Life*. I turned my head slowly to Michael, who was gaping at the magnificent animal.

"Take a shot," I whispered.

I watched Michael raise the rifle to his shoulder and hesitate. Then…he shook his head violently, which should have sent the buck running. Instead, it turned toward the boy as if curious.

Finally, as if getting tired of waiting to get shot, the buck turned and ran, bounding gracefully over the rocks and bitterbrush, kicking up dust.

We continued on, neither of us saying anything at first. Then Michael said, "It screamed like a hurt child when I shot it."

"Yeah, they do that," I said. I'd been about Michael's age when I'd finally stood up to my father, refusing to poach a deer, deciding not to follow my father's footsteps of dishonesty and deceit. I'd stuck to that vow ever since, pretty much.

"I don't think I want to kill any more deer," Michael continued, and I could tell he meant it, probably for life. "Don't tell my dad, okay?"

"You got it," I said. If Lully didn't ask, there was nothing to tell.

We walked along in companionable silence. I almost didn't notice when the boy veered off to the side.

"Watch it!" I shouted.

He froze, just inches from the hole. He looked down into it.

"That's the collapsed top of a gold mine," I said. "Chinese miners dug mines all over these hillsides. You have to be careful."

"Really? A real gold mine? Can we go inside?"

"We could, but it's best not to disturb the bats."

"Bats?" He took a step back.

I smiled reassuringly. "They're harmless enough. I'm more worried for them than for us. If they get bothered too much, they tend to get stressed. Bats are finicky creatures."

"Cool."

We went on. Michael surveyed the ground, hoping to catch another glimpse of a gold mine. Suddenly, he crouched over a low plant.

"Are these wild strawberries?" he asked.

"Yes," I said. "Good eye."

I was liking this kid more and more. He hadn't insisted on entering the mine, and to be honest, I hadn't been as restrained the first time I'd seen a gold mine. I'd explored it, fascinated, unaware of the danger.

We met up with the others soon after and headed back to Bigfoot Ranch.

The next day, the other Lullys never saw so much as the hind end of a receding buck, whereas Michael and I ran into two more herds, each with trophy bucks among them. It was ironic and almost funny, because by then the boy and I were making no effort to stalk quietly.

It was an uncomfortable drive back to Bend. John Lully and his eldest son weren't happy with me. I was going to get a bad online review for sure.

When I dropped the Lullys off at their hotel, I nodded to Michael, man to man, and drove off. I hoped he would be okay, that he'd grow up to be a good man, that he'd be better than his father.

CHAPTER 3

Sherm stuck to following the railroad tracks on foot. The folks in the homeless camps along the route eyed him, but his intimidating bulk kept them away. That and his lack of fear.

He still couldn't believe he'd frozen at Greg's scream. True, it would have been a stupid knife against at least one gun, but it was at least possible he could have gotten the drop on them.

It had been a long time since he'd been in that kind of situation. He'd forgotten everything he once knew. The gunfire, the very fact that he'd almost been hit, brought it all back. The old fight response flooded down his spine, along with his anger, steeling his resolve. He wouldn't panic again.

He had nowhere to run. He'd underestimated how fast and how hard they'd come down on him. In the back of his mind, he'd always thought he'd see it coming, that he'd go home, get his escape kit, and hit the road.

Greg had been his fallback plan if his home was ever compromised. That clearly hadn't worked out.

Fortunately, Sherm had another cache in his safe deposit box, but he had no doubt they already knew about that too. Samuels would undoubtedly have people watching the local bank branch.

His biggest mistake had been trusting Brancato. Like Sherm, his so-called boss had come up through the ranks. They'd once shared bodyguard duties protecting the mistress of an underboss. They had a few drinks most nights after work, laughing at the new guys.

But Brancato had adapted to the modern way of organized crime much more easily than Sherm.

Still, Sherm had felt a kinship with Brancato, and one night, after several drinks, he'd confessed his escape plan. "I've squirreled away enough stuff to bury these guys, all of them. They'd better not fuck with me."

Brancato had laughed, but it was clear now he'd ratted Sherm out. The bosses had bided their time, watching him until they'd been sure they knew where his escape packages were hidden.

Sherm still had his cellphone, but he wasn't sure he could trust it. One more call and he'd ditch it.

He called Ann Clarambeau.

The White Widow didn't seem surprised to hear from him.

"Don't worry," he said. "No one else knows where you are."

"I didn't figure," she said. "Otherwise I wouldn't be talking to you."

He attempted as best he could to tell her how important that old beat up box he'd given her years ago was. He wasn't sure she believed him, so he resorted to the old ranking system they'd come up with. "It's a Code Red," he said.

She wasn't happy, but that finally convinced her.

He hung up, dropped the phone onto the railroad tracks, and smashed it with a rock. Then he looked for a place to hide.

Sherm waited until late the next night before moving again. He spent the day under the railroad trestle, glaring at any of the transients who came near. They scuttled away.

At dark, he emerged long enough to spend his last few dollars at a McDonalds. He'd been staring at the damn golden arches all day, growing hungrier with every passing minute. He forced himself to wait until the town quieted, like a beast falling to sleep.

The railroad ran along the river until it crossed the road to the Airolo Corporation headquarters. By the time he got there it was three o'clock in the morning and the building was completely dark. He knew the cleanup crew was usually gone by midnight. He knew the night guard, Timothy Diamond, would be taking his usual hour-long break of Irish coffee in his back office.

Sherm slipped in through the side entrance and trotted up the stairs.

Inexplicably, they hadn't found the false drawer where he'd stashed a Colt revolver and a few hundred bucks. That was it. He'd have to try to get all the way across the country with barely enough money to rent a motel room for a single night and eat a few good meals.

He moved over to Martinson's desk and snagged a key at random for one of the cars in the parking lot. He'd just have to hope it was gassed up and ready to go.

At the opposite end of the room, the elevator doors opened and voices emerged.

Sherm froze for a second, cursed. He scooted over to the corner office, leaving the door open a crack.

"He can't have gotten far on foot," Brancato said.

Overhead lights blinked on. Brancato and Martinson led a crew of six other men over to Sherm's desk. They were tall and athletic and had a military bearing. Sherm recognized only one of them; Dan Jordan, who'd headed security in the main office for a couple of years. One man seemed to be in charge, slightly thinner and shorter than the others, and immaculately groomed. Blond haired and blue eyed. Surfer turned killer.

"You sure Russo didn't take anything out of here?" the leader asked.

Martinson answered, "I checked the desk myself after he left. Besides, I was watching him, Mr. Samuels. All he took with him was whatever was in his coat."

Sherm caught his breath at the name Samuels. So far he'd only heard the man's voice, known his reputation.

Samuels grunted. "His wife wasn't much help. We roughed her up a bit, but after she gave up the box, she didn't seem to know much. We scared her pretty good. I think she'll keep quiet."

Sherm almost sighed in relief. He was glad they hadn't killed her. He and his wife had been little more than roommates for years, and though he didn't love her, he had once been fond of her. The *roughing up* was a little bit of justice, though. If not for her, he would have made his escape years ago. She was the daughter of an old Mafia capo regime and had insisted he stay loyal. For all the good that did him.

"Where would Russo go for help?" Samuels demanded.

"We've already checked everywhere he could go," Brancato insisted. "I've examined every expense he's made going back a decade or two, I know his every hangout and acquaintance. There isn't any place we don't know about."

"Why wouldn't he put all that info online?" one of the other men asked.

Brancato shook his head. "Sherm's old school. He uses an old-fashioned calculator, and what he doesn't put on paper, he memorizes. He'd want something physical."

"Which is why we've been ordered to remove him," Samuels said. "We know about Russo's home cache and the one he left with Snyder, and we have to assume he's got something in his safe deposit box. Where else?"

"That's it," Brancato insisted.

"What about that Oregon thing?" Martinson said.

Brancato looked annoyed. "That's nothing."

Samuels turned to Martinson. "Explain it to me."

"Sherm kept checking the website of a wilderness guide service in Bend, Oregon. I thought it was odd because I never heard him talk about fishing or hunting."

"So?" Brancato said. "Maybe he wants a vacation."

"No," Samuels said. "Look at the dates. Russo started searching on September 3, the same day Barton Crane was nominated. Look who else he searched for...Greg Snyder."

Martinson looked up, surprised. "Is that what this is all about? Barton Crane?"

"Don't worry about it," Samuels snapped. "Show me the website."

Martinson sat at his computer and brought up the page. Sherm could see the green and red design for *Hart Davis Hunting and Fishing*, with the picture of Amanda and Hart Davis.

Sherm stifled a groan. How could he have been so stupid?

Samuels stiffened, leaned over and stared at the screen. "Well, I'll be damned."

"What is it?" Jordan asked.

"That's Ann Clarambeau."

"The White Widow?" Jordan said, nearly pushing his boss

aside to get a better look. "I thought she was dead."

"She disappeared. I guess now we know where. Do we have anyone out there, Jordan?"

Jordan closed his eyes, concentrating. "Bill Sader and Fred Carter."

"Any good?"

Jordan hesitated. "Well, Sader tends to think he's better than he is, and Carter's pretty green. But, yeah, they're competent."

"Good," Samuels said. "Call them, tell them to stake out the Davis House. But they're to hang back, not approach. *Competent* is no match for the White Widow. We'll fly out to Oregon in the morning. Meanwhile, I'll send Popov and his crew to find Russo's trail from this end. Do we have any pictures of Russo?"

Brancato shook his head. "Like I said, Sherm's an old-school soldier. He never let his picture be taken. Hell, even in his wedding pictures, he's looking away from the camera."

Samuels put a hand out and slapped Martinson's shoulder. "You're coming with us, buddy," he said. "You'll need to look over the papers, make sure they're legit."

"Me? I'm an accountant. I've never even held a gun."

"It's easy," Samuels said. "You point and pull the trigger."

He nodded to the scruffiest of his crew, who put his arm around Martinson and led him out of the room. One of Samuels's men stood behind Brancato.

Samuels waved to him, an airy swipe through the air, and walked away.

The garrote went around Brancato's neck too swiftly to see clearly. He had time for one stifled sound before the wire tightened and cut off his air. Brancato put his hands to his neck and bucked, but only for a few moments. Then he went limp.

Even from where Sherm hid, he could smell the odor of Brancato's lifeless body vacating its bowels. A puddle of urine formed at its feet. The murderer pulled a large black bag from his coat and shoved Brancato's body into it. He slung the packaged corpse over his shoulder, leaving the puddle of urine.

Sherm waited for half an hour after they left. He was numb. The old dread was returning, the feeling that someone could pop out at any moment and put a bullet through his head. In the old days, he probably would have felt nothing about Brancato's murder. He'd brought it on himself.

That's my future if I don't get to the box before they do.

He slipped out the side door, barely missing the security guard on his way up from his coffee break. He started the company car, gratified to find it was three-quarters full of gas, got onto the freeway, and headed west.

Shit. He couldn't fly, they'd be watching. He'd have drive to Oregon on back roads.

There was no way he'd beat the devil.

CHAPTER 4

When Sherm Russo called at four o'clock in the morning, Amanda Davis wasn't as surprised that he knew where she was as maybe she should have been. She figured, in his quiet and unobtrusive way, the big man knew everything about everyone. It was what made him so valuable...and so dangerous.

"They're going to kill you one of these days," she'd told him, the last time she saw him. "You know that, don't you?"

He stared back into her eyes unblinking. She had an uncomfortable feeling he was on to her even then.

Shortly thereafter Amanda did her best to disappear, as much as anyone could disappear these days, moving all the way across the country, finding a nice, if oblivious guy, and settling down. For a long time, she didn't go psycho on anyone.

She was Amanda Davis, not Ann Clarambeau.

It didn't last, of course. She was still a crazy bitch. Always had been and always would be. *The* crazy bitch. When she was manic, she was deadly. When she was depressed, she was even deadlier.

Hart Davis was just too damned good for her. He was normal, peaceful, happy with his life—until she came along. It was such a strange experience to marry him, as if meeting an alien and deciding to get hitched. Hart wouldn't walk away from a cashier with the wrong change. He picked up litter on hiking trails. He wouldn't step on ants on the sidewalk. Most of the time, she tried to ignore it, hoping his essential goodness would rub off on her.

She'd tried, oh how she'd tried to make it work. But the medications she needed to hang out with normal people made her feel dead and leaden inside. She'd stopped taking the meds. For a time, that had been cool.

Then she'd gone off her head.

She remembered standing in the middle of the living room, naked, scissors in hand ready to throw them into Hart's forehead. At the last second, she dropped the sharpened scissors, the blades had thrummed into the flooring.

Hart walked out that very night. She hadn't tried to coax him back, though she probably could have. He'd served his purpose, given her a backstory, given her a legit house even though she had enough money squirreled away to buy ten such houses. Red painted, three-bedroom, two-bath, single-story on a cul-de-sac, and a white picket fence.

The American dream.

For her, it was a nightmare.

She had to remind herself of the faces of those she'd killed to keep from spinning away. She was crazy, but she wasn't depraved. That's what she told herself. The corporation had taken advantage of her condition. She hadn't really known any better. But even crazy bitches tend to wake up when they find children lying dead at their feet.

The nagging conscience had popped out of nowhere. The more she thought, the more she remembered the terrible things she'd done. Her newfound conscience grew like an occasionally watered plant, a tiny, scared little thing.

But it *was* a conscience, fragile and blurred though it was by anger. It told her to let Hart go.

It was only after he was gone that she realized how fond she'd become of him. Not in *love,* she didn't have that in her but, well, she *liked* her former husband as much as she'd ever liked anyone.

They called her the White Widow, which was a little unfair. It wasn't her fault her first husband was also an assassin, and after all, Howard had tried to kill *her* first.

She tried to forget her past, to become her better angel, but demons tugged at her from beneath.

"I need a favor from you," Sherm told her that last time they met. He handed her a box, heavily wrapped in duct tape. "Hide this for me. Don't let anyone but me have it. It's important."

Amanda took the box rather than try to explain she wouldn't be around for him to retrieve it. She intended to throw it away, but instead tossed into the back of her Jaguar. Upon settling down in Bend, Oregon, she put it on the top shelf of the closet where they kept their old coats.

Honestly, she'd forgotten all about it.

"Hi, *Amanda*," the brusque voice said over the phone. Sherm Russo didn't identify himself, but she immediately knew who it was. He was calling her by her new name, so he must have a pretty good idea of where she was and what she was doing.

"Don't worry," he said. "No one else knows where you are."

"I didn't figure," she said. "Otherwise I wouldn't be talking to you."

Strangely, it didn't bother her that Sherm knew. He kept secrets. That's what made him tick.

He said, "You remember that package I gave you? You need to hide it. I'm coming to get it, but the others might get there first."

"I doubt it," she said. "*They* don't know where I am."

"Are you so sure?"

"All right, I'll get rid of the box."

"No! For God's sake, don't throw it away. Keep it safe. It's important, not just to me, but…well, to everyone."

"Everyone?"

"Everyone in the world, Amanda."

She laughed. "And I'm supposed to care?"

"I think maybe you should, maybe you already do," Sherm said quietly. "I've been watching you from afar. I'm very impressed. I never thought you'd be able to keep yourself under control for so long. You picked a good man, lived a good life. I'm proud of you."

Amanda felt a warm feeling wash through her, a very unfamiliar one. She'd felt it once before, when Hart had slipped an engagement ring on her finger. It was happiness, or something like it. Then it vanished as she remembered what was happening to her marriage.

"What the hell is in the box, Sherm?"

"It's a Code Red."

It was a private code they'd once shared. Until now neither one of them had ever offered the ultimate classification. Sherm didn't go for drama. If he said it was a Red, it was something big.

"You asshole, you gave me a Code Red without warning me?" It pissed her off...and it kind of excited her.

"Keep your eyes open, Amanda. Hide the box. It might keep us alive. I'll be there in a few days. I'm driving, to stay out of sight. Pack your stuff if you want to go with me. We always seemed to get along."

Get along. Once or twice, during some long stakeouts, they'd *got along.* Amanda felt her pulse quicken even more. Not quite the same thing as happiness, but it was the only kind of pleasure she'd ever known. Doing something naughty. The more dangerous, the better.

"I'll be waiting for you, baby," she said.

Sherm hung up. Amanda checked her inner gauge. She was halfway up the manic cycle, still low enough for her to appear normal if hyped, but advanced enough to keep her sharp.

She spun into a whirlwind over the next hour, packing, making notes about what she needed to do before leaving town. She wrote a goodbye note to Hart, who deserved that much at least.

Then she remembered he was coming to the house for breakfast... to sign the final divorce papers.

She'd get a last chance to say goodbye.

CHAPTER 5

I never knew whether Amanda was going to greet me at the door naked and wanting to forget we were divorcing or with a gun in her hand, ready to pull the trigger. It was fifty/fifty, with her. I'd stuck with her for fifteen years as she descended further and further into depression and mania. New stories had emerged every year, how she'd worked for the CIA, and how she'd killed people.

Like a scene from my childhood fantasies, I found myself living with a person who told wild stories and whose word I couldn't trust. I think Amanda could have done just about anything else and I would have stuck it out. The problem was, she wasn't willing to seek help. In fact, she was certain that anyone who tried to help was out to hurt her.

When she finally kicked me out in a fit of rage for not believing her, I didn't go back.

Driving to Amanda's—our—house, I felt myself tensing up. I could always gauge her mood by how much makeup she wore and how revealing her clothing was. The more femme fatale she appeared, the crazier she was likely to be.

I had to admit that, no matter how outlandish her claims about her previous life as a CIA operative might be, she could be convincing in her certainty. I'd gone so far as to investigate her past. As far as I could tell, being a security guard for a local warehouse was as close as she'd come to law enforcement.

When she stepped onto her private tightrope, she was a walking, talking menace to society.

I knocked on the door.

Amanda answered wearing jeans and a blouse, her makeup

modest, her hair combed. My tense shoulders eased and my held breath escaped through pursed lips.

"Hart!" she said, smiling. "How nice to see you!"

The signing had gone smoothly, to my relief. A cup of tea, the papers spread on the marble countertop, a nice pen I accidentally walked away with.

I nearly skipped down the steps on leaving.

By the time I got back to my office, my bones felt like rubber. My mind started shutting down. My office was little more than a one-room cubicle in the O'Kane building in downtown Bend. Magazines spilled over the desk and onto the chairs. Hunting and fishing posters on the wall were tattered and faded. As small and cheap as it was, I wasn't sure I could afford it much longer.

I lay down on the couch, intending to rest my eyes.

I woke to a phone ringing. I checked my watch; surprised I'd slept for an entire day and night, more than a day since I'd come back to the office after signing the divorce papers.

My fingers felt like putty picking up the receiver. "Hart Davis Hunting and Fishing," I mumbled.

"Hi, I'd like to book Bigfoot Ranch for the next week," came a brisk voice.

I sat up, grabbing a pen, trying to find the surface of my desk. "Sure, we'd be glad to have you. Can I get your name?"

"Peter Samuels, but I'm booking this in the name of the company I work for, Airolo Corp. It's a sort of last-minute vacation."

"It's kind of late in the season," I said. "I assume you've got the licenses and tags?"

"My company pulled some strings," Samuels said. "So can you do it? It will be worth your while. Seven people…"

"Seven?" That brought me up short. It was twice as many clients as I usually try to handle by myself. "I can't haul that many people in my Jeep."

"No worries, we've rented a 4Runner," Samuels said. "I've been wanting to take my crew on a vacation for a long time now. A couple of the guys and myself can ride with you, and the other four will take the SUV. So how much would that be?"

I did the math and doubled the price I usually quoted. Frankly, as much as I needed the money, I was tired. I was ready to take a break. If this fell through, so be it.

Samuels didn't even hesitate. "We're on our way."

"Wait..." I said, startled. "Now?"

"If you don't mind..."

I saw no reason not to head out as soon as they wanted, if I was going to do this at all. I was pretty sure Granger would appreciate the money too.

"Come on over, then," I said, but Samuels had already hung up.

Then I called Granger, who had gotten back from his little vacation, and told him we had new clients headed his way and at twice the usual rate.

"Seven guys?" He grunted. Despite his dubious tone, I could tell he was pleased by the payday. Hunting season was almost over. It was going to be a long, cold winter.

"I'll have to drive into town to buy supplies," he grumbled. Granger hated leaving Bigfoot Ranch for civilization, which in this case, meant the town of John Day, population seventeen hundred people.

A few minutes later, I met Samuels and his six friends in front of the O'Kane building. Five of them were burly types. I'm six foot, but these guys made me feel small. Had they been clean-shaven, I'd have guessed they were ex-military right off, but they wore such a variety of beards and hairstyles and clothing that it sort of disguised the fact, at least at first. They certainly looked like men who knew their way around guns. But I told myself, just because you can shoot straight doesn't mean you can hunt deer. That's where I came in.

Peter Samuels stood out even in this group. Tall and slender, his blond hair was sun-bleached, his face tanned. There were white circles around his blue eyes, as if he habitually wore sunglasses in direct sunlight.

We shook hands. I was hit with a blizzard of names that I knew from experience I wouldn't remember until they were repeated for the third time.

The sixth guy in the menagerie was short and balding, with a lazy eye and a thick red mustache. He didn't seem to fit with the rest of Samuels's crew. His name stuck with me: Martinson.

Samuels laid out a row of crisp new hundreds on the hood of his car. "Good enough?"

I scooped up the money, nodding, not bothering to count it.

"If you guys are ready to go," I said, "let's head out."

Samuels barked, "Martinson and Jordan, you ride with me and the guide here, Davis. The rest of you, follow us in the 4Runner."

"The 4Runner is a little cramped," one of the men said. Moser, was his name. "Do you mind if we unload some of our gear into the back of your Jeep?"

"Go for it," I said.

I opened the back of the Jeep and they started loading up. I hadn't asked what weapons they were bringing, but along with their high-powered rifles, I saw the outlines of something else in the gun sacks.

"I don't allow semi-automatics on my hunts," I said.

Samuels shrugged it off. "No problem. We brought a few along, but only for target practice. You know, if we don't see any deer, the boys will still want to do some shooting."

I debated on insisting that they leave the weapons behind, but the image of those hundred-dollar bills came to me and I remained silent.

The traffic was heavy all the way to Prineville, but once we started climbing into the Ochoco Mountains, it dwindled.

"We were told you were the best guide in Central Oregon," Jordan said as we approached John Day.

"I don't know about that..."

"I'm looking to bag a six-point buck, at least," Jordan continued.

"Any guide who says they can *guarantee* a trophy buck is lying to you," I said.

"Then what are we paying you for?" Jordan snorted.

I didn't answer. The guy was looking for a fight.

"But you're a good shot, right?" Jordan insisted after a brief pause, with the same challenging, mano-a-mano bullshit tone.

"I'm good enough."

"Shit... good enough ain't good enough," Jordan said. "Hanson can hit a rat's tail at a thousand yards, and most of the rest of us aren't too shabby either."

"Hunting deer isn't the same as..." Samuels voice trailed off.

"Never mind, Jordan," Samuels said, his tone shutting down the discussion.

Hunting deer isn't the same as what? I wondered. I was starting to think this whole trip was a big mistake. Usually when I didn't respond to the macho bullshit, guys tended to ease off. These guys were only getting more aggressive.

Samuels seemed to sense my mood. "Sorry. My boys are a little testy. They badly need this vacation." He turned to the back seat. "When was the last time you weren't working, Jordan? When was the last time you did shit-all?"

Jordan snorted. "Fucking never."

"See what I mean?" Samuels said. "Let's just enjoy ourselves for a few days and quit busting Davis's balls, all right?"

Thankfully, they fell silent after that. Jordan stared out the window, chin in hand. Martinson had yet to say a word. He seemed like the odd man out in this group, like a little brother tailing along.

We passed the Painted Hills and the John Day Fossil Bed National Monument, but I didn't do my usual tourist spiel. I didn't feel like it. I decided I didn't much care for these guys. They seemed to be know-it-alls.

Jordan had asked the right question. Why had they bothered to hire me?

A few miles east of John Day, we turned off onto the gravel road. The tires trilled across the first cattle grate. I almost missed the next turnoff. With a growl, I slammed on the brakes and slid to a stop in the dust.

"Wait here," I said. I trotted back toward the gate, out of sight.

Near the gate, Granger had installed a drop box; really, a hole in the ground with a plank of plywood over it. When he was in residence, he insisted I check it before driving the rest of the way to the ranch house.

"Look for messages," he'd said, not explaining. "Just in case...

In case of what, I never got around to asking. Granger didn't trust the outside world, and it wasn't for me to judge him. But I wondered sometimes if one day the FBI would stake out the place. Why, I didn't know. Just a feeling.

Under the plywood plank was a folded piece of paper with the scrawled message, *"We're here. Full crew. Come on up."*

I started to replace the plank and noticed a wrinkled yellowed sheet of paper farther down the hole. In faded pencil, it said, *"We'll be there on Friday. Noonish. Nicole."*

I held my breath for a moment, felt the quick jolt I always got from thinking about Nicole Nelson. Her Wilderness Excursions normally operated out of the Heffinger place, the next ranch over. I have to admit, I was a little hurt Granger had opened up his ranch to her. The note looked old. Maybe even from last season.

I crumpled up the note, fighting my feelings of jealousy, got back in the Jeep, and drove on.

"No Trespassing" and "No Hunting" signs were on every other fencepost along the road. The road got narrower, with more and more switchbacks. Finally, with the top of the ranch house in sight, Samuels spoke again. "You ever kill a deer out of season, Davis?"

"Nope, never."

"Right..." He grinned and shook his head. "You know, I think I've got you figured out. You're an upright guy, a straight arrow, right?"

I kept silent. How the hell do you answer that?

Samuels laughed. "It's gonna get you in trouble someday."

Jordan spoke up. "I'll bet you're divorced, Davis. Because no woman would put up with that Boy Scout bullshit."

I winced, despite myself.

Samuels looked over his shoulder. "What about you, Martinson? Are you an honest man?"

"I'm a *Certified* Public Accountant," Martinson said, his red mustache bristling.

Samuels and Jordan glanced at each other, then roared in

laughter. I glanced into the rearview mirror.

There was fear in Martinson's eyes.

As we pulled up to the ranch, I realized I'd almost forgotten my usual warning, which with these guys I was pretty sure was more necessary than ever.

"Listen," I said. "This is officially the Granger Ranch. Whatever you do, don't use the name *Bigfoot Ranch*. Granger is a little sensitive about it."

"Why?" Jordan asked.

"Because of some bullshit a few years ago. A couple of hunters swore they ran into Bigfoot. They made plaster casts of the footprints, found a tuft of black fur, the whole smear."

"So, it was real?" Martinson asked, sounding interested for the first time.

"The DNA tests were inconclusive, but I doubt it. But it didn't seem to matter. There for a few years, tourists were crawling all over these hills. So, you know, avoid bringing up Bigfoot, OK?"

CHAPTER 6

Bigfoot Ranch...that is, Granger Ranch, as I always had to remind myself...was perched on top of a hill with a commanding view of the valley. The foundations of the original pioneer house were off to one side. The new house was a red-timbered cabin with a turquoise metal roof. Granger's one concession to modernity was a solar array to the sunny side of the cabin. There were stables, tool sheds, and trailers dotting the property.

One of the sheds housed an old Harley-Davidson, hidden because it didn't fit the old-timey décor. Granger had been in a motorcycle gang once, though he wouldn't talk about it. Something bad had gone down, something that had turned Granger into a man with the appearance of a Hell's Angel and the manner of Gandhi.

Granger was waiting by the bunkhouse. He was a towering man, six and half feet tall who hadn't cut his hair or beard in years. I always got a kick out of watching my clients behold him for the first time.

His big goofy grin was a welcome respite from the tension inside the Jeep. His smile faltered a little when the crew piled out of the 4Runner. As big as Granger was, these guys were younger, a couple of them almost as tall, and in better shape.

"Namaste," Granger said, bowing his shaggy head slightly as we got out of the Jeep. Granger spoke softly; sometimes I missed his old loud-mouthed yahoo days, before he'd found his zen.

"Far out," Jordan said. "The last of the hippies."

An annoyed expression crossed Granger's face. I held my

breath. Zen or no zen, Granger spoke his mind. Thankfully, the big man decided to ignore the comment.

Granger lifted the heavy lead-lined bag in his other hand. I had no idea where he'd gotten it, but it was ever-present.

"Drop your phones in here, fellows," he said. "I don't allow the damn things on the premises. You're in nature now, so you should enjoy it without interruptions."

"What are you talking about?" Privett said. He was the shortest, about my height, and the wiriest of the men. Just about every time I'd looked at him, he was texting.

"Just do it," Samuels said. He looked at me with his eyebrows raised. I read once that you needed a Faraday cage to block all the radio waves. Lead didn't do the job. But it didn't really matter. Granger thought it worked, and that was enough for me.

Samuels must have investigated Granger's crude website, because he asked for the other guest bedroom in the house.

Granger hesitated. "I stacked a bunch of boxes in there," he said. "I figured we'd need a lot of food for this many guys."

"I insist," Samuels said.

Granger turned to me, his eyebrows raised, as if to say, *What's going on?*

I shrugged, because I wasn't sure either.

To my surprise, Granger gave in. "As long as you don't mind Conner coming in to get supplies at all times of the day or night...Speak of the devil."

Conner skipped down the steps, his arms out to give me a hug. He had Down syndrome, always seemed glad to see me, and was an amazing cook, at least when it came to ranch food. I broke into a grin, my misgivings momentarily forgotten. "Hey, Conner. How's it going?"

"I learned a new recipe," Conner said. "Baked eggs and spinach."

"Sounds mouth-watering," I said, putting my arm over his shoulder. He looked up at me expectantly. I made him wait a couple more seconds, just to tease him a little, then pulled the CD from my coat.

"Pink Floyd!" he breathed. "Thank you, Mr. Davis!"

Conner wore earphones around his neck, and one of the last

Discmans in the world still in constant use was strapped to his waist. Both Granger and I had tried to interest him in an iPod, but he loved his old CD player.

"Conner," I said, turning to the others, "is the best damn cook in the county."

The men towered over Conner, who probably didn't top five feet in height. To their credit, they didn't show any skepticism about my claim.

As usual, Kent showed up last, ambling over from the corral, drying his hands with a rag. It looked like he'd been rubbing down the horses, though it was just as likely it was his way of avoiding shaking everyone's hands. He was a grizzled old cattleman, wearing a cowboy hat that appeared to be held together by a few random straws. He had on wrinkled jeans with the worn outline of a tobacco tin in one back pocket, and a snap-button Western shirt. His face was weathered and craggy. He looked sixty-five, though he hadn't yet hit the midcentury mark.

Granger said, "If you boys are up to riding horses, Kent is your man."

"Howdy," Kent said.

"I fucking hate horses," Jordan said.

Kent turned red. He probably weighed half as much as Jordan, but I thought for a moment he was going to challenge the guy to a fight.

Martinson motioned toward Conner. "What's with the retar—Ouch!"

Kent had reached out and grabbed the man's arm, his gnarled hands whitening as he squeezed. The cowboy shook his head warningly, and then spit tobacco out of the side of his mouth.

"You boys can set up in the bunkhouse," Granger said, interrupting the dust-up. "Dinner will be ready in a couple of hours." We started unloading. Once again I felt uneasy when I saw the crew hauling gun bags, outlines of the autos clearly visible, weird black, bug-like extensions, along with boxes of ammo I hadn't spotted earlier. Granger also noticed and shot me an alarmed glance. I knew that, in addition to being an ex-biker, he'd been in the military, though he never talked about it.

The two vehicles were quickly emptied, until all that remained was a battered old file box wrapped in duct tape in the back of my Jeep.

"You guys forgot something," I said, staring at it, wondering what it was. I noticed that Samuels was fixated on it too.

Jordan stepped forward and reached for the box.

"Nah, leave it for now," Samuels said. "We'll get it later."

Jordan appeared surprised.

Samuels ignored him. He turned to me. "Why don't we start hunting now, Hart? I've always heard dusk is a good time for hunting."

"That's true," I said. "But I thought you guys might like a rest. We can get a fresh start first thing in the morning."

"To hell with that," Jordan said. "We've got tags to fill. I want my money's worth."

Samuels said, "How about taking just Jordan and me?"

They might not have been tired, but I sure as hell was. I sighed, but with what they'd paid me, I couldn't say no. "All right. We can head up the mountain a ways, see what we can see."

I took Granger aside. "Don't pull any of your shenanigans," I whispered. "I mean it. These aren't the right people, no sense of humor."

He shrugged.

I eyed him for a few more seconds, then turned to my clients. "Get your gear and meet back here in five minutes."

We started up the trail.

To my relief, Samuels and Jordan left the semi-automatics in the bags, and were carrying bolt-action .30-06's.

At the top of the hill, we stopped and watched the setting sun.

Bigfoot Ranch was cradled by three large foothills at the base of Strawberry Mountain, bordered on east by Deadfall Ridge, rimming Butcher's Cut, a boxed canyon. Massacre Creek bordered the property on the other side, and was dry most of the year.

We hunted until the shadows of the trees became deep and long and we finally headed back, disappointed.

We were nearing the ranch when a loud rustling wafted from the thick growth above us.

I held my breath. It didn't sound like deer. It could be a black bear, which, if it was a female with cubs, could be dangerous. It took too long for me to realize what it was.

A huge black shape came out of the grove of aspen trees, roaring. I recognized it.

"Wait!" I shouted as Jordan whipped his rifle to his shoulder and took aim.

He ignored me. The rifle shot seemed extra loud. The black shape fell backward. Jordan started running toward the downed creature.

I caught up to him just as Samuels produced a flashlight and sent its beam downward.

The creature was the size of a gorilla, covered in black fur from head to toes, with two arms and two legs. It had been standing upright.

"I've fucking killed Bigfoot!" Jordan shouted.

The animal moaned out loud. It sounded almost human. Jordan stepped back with a curse and raised his rifle.

"Don't shoot," I said, stepping forward, pushing the muzzle into the air.

Bigfoot put his hands to his head and twisted. The mask came off. Granger grimaced up at us.

"Why the fuck did you shoot me?" he moaned. "Damn, that hurt. It's a good thing my suit is bulletproof!"

The costume wasn't completely bulletproof, of course, but Granger had somehow gotten ahold of state of the art protection. There were light ceramic panels along the back and front, with a lighter, more experimental material along the arms and legs.

Jordan wasn't amused, but Samuels couldn't stop laughing. He nearly rolled on the ground, and every time he looked over at Granger and his Bigfoot costume, the laughter started up again.

Normally, Granger and I prepared our clients for the Bigfoot sighting, which we usually sprang on them on the last night.

Granger had obviously decided to try to scare these guys without warning.

It had been an almost fatal mistake.

CHAPTER 7

Samuels found the Bigfoot incident hugely amusing. It was the first time he'd belly laughed in years. He knew then he'd made the right decision to take his men on this little vacation.

When he'd first gotten to Bend, he'd intended to just take the package and dispose of Hart Davis after questioning him. He was glad he'd waited. He'd taken a good look at the package in the back of the Jeep and it was clear from the age of the duct tape that no one had opened it. The box was under his control, and Hart Davis had no idea what he had in his possession. So clueless, in fact, that Samuels had decided to leave it where it was rather than call attention to it.

Best of all, he wouldn't need to kill Hart, or any of his friends.

Ann Clarambeau was another story. The reward for the White Widow was too much to ignore, plus he suspected his superiors would want her gone. But that would take careful planning if she was half as dangerous as her reputation.

Meanwhile, the more time he spent in Oregon, the more the idea of a hunting vacation appealed to him.

It had been a long time since he'd hunted...for animals. But that's where he'd begun his life with guns.

He'd hated his childhood in Georgia, but rather than killing his family or his friends, he'd taken to going into the woods and killing squirrels and possum. Hell, anything that moved. He'd joined the military because it gave him a chance to hunt more challenging game.

Unlike his fellow soldiers, who hesitated when uncertain who was a good guy or a bad guy, Samuels pulled the trigger whenever there was the slightest doubt. The thing about dead targets, no one could prove they *weren't* bad guys. He advanced quickly up the ranks, finally landing in Special Ops.

After two tours, he'd hired himself out to Airolo Corporation, though at first he hadn't understood why they needed his particular talents.

Turned out, he'd landed in the perfect place. His bosses were a strange conglomeration of old school Mafia and Russian oligarchs and sociopathic white-collar Wall Street types. Samuels wasn't sure which group was worse.

It's been a long time since I had a vacation, he thought.

A wilderness trip sounded like just the thing; especially since Airolo Corp. was paying for it. His crew would appreciate it, too. It would be a good bonding opportunity. They were getting on each other's nerves these days, asked to do things they'd never thought they'd have to do. Killing Americans was only a step removed from killing Iraqi's, but it was a big one.

Their bosses loaded them down with money. There seemed to be no end to it. Men with Russian accents leaving them suitcases full of bills, odd amounts that told Samuels they hadn't even counted it, just filled the containers until they couldn't hold any more.

Killing wasn't the best way to go about things. Samuels preferred subtler methods, but they'd left it for too late.

They should have taken care of the problem long ago. Retired Sherman Russo and then let him quietly meet an accident a few months later. Same with all the old Mafia guys who knew too much.

Dmitry Kuznetsov called him, laughing.

"Barton Crane for the Supreme Court? That's like putting your Jesse James in charge of a bank."

Samuels didn't have to ask how the Russian knew about Jesse James. He'd been in Kuznetsov's office before, which was covered in Western memorabilia. "You had your West, we had our East," he'd said. "I spent my youth in the Gulag."

"What do you want me to do?" Samuels asked.

"Clean it up," Kuznetsov said. "We want no one alive who knew what Crane was doing back then. We don't care how you do it…it won't be noticed. The connections are too far back unless they survive and bring them up to date. That we can't allow."

"Kill them? Why don't we buy them off?"

"Americans like fame more than money," Kuznetsov seemed to shrug over the phone, something scratching across the mouthpiece. "We can't take a chance."

"How deep do you want me to go?"

"Anyone and everyone who knows anything."

Samuels hung up the phone shaken. If Previtt had gotten those orders, or even Jordan, there would have been a bloodbath. Instead, Samuels spent several days digging into the matter, identifying three men who he thought too dangerous to live.

One of them, Corey Brancato, had nervously informed Samuels of Russo's threat of hiding damaging information. Fortunately, there was no immediate hurry. Barton Crane's nomination to the Supreme Court had hit a roadblock with the Senate that had nothing to do with his shady past—something about his wife having had an abortion—which was delaying the confirmation hearings. Samuels had time to track down all of Russo's possible hiding spots.

Or so he'd thought.

He'd figured once he had Russo, he'd find out if he'd missed anything. But Brancato had jumped the gun, letting go of Russo a day too early.

It hadn't seemed to matter much, until now. Russo was assigned to another team.

Meanwhile, Hart Davis and the White Widow was his problem.

CHAPTER 8

Amanda started having second thoughts the moment Hart drove away. It had seemed like such a brilliant plan. Hide the box in the back of the Jeep. No one would suspect good old innocent Hart Davis.

But her mania was stronger than she'd thought. She wasn't thinking clearly. It didn't matter whether Hart was innocent. If they found him with the box, they'd kill him without a second thought.

She grabbed her phone. It was dead. The rage that filled her blotted everything else out.

She came back to herself with a broken plate still in hand, the kitchen completely destroyed. Her anger disappeared as quickly as it had appeared. She calmly went to the bedroom and plugged the phone in.

Hart should be safe at Bigfoot Ranch, which was in the middle of fucking nowhere. She'd call him tonight. She poured herself a glass of wine and sat down to ponder why she hadn't opened the box Sherm gave her long ago. The duct tape was a clever ruse. Sometimes the simplest security precautions were the best. Houdini said breaking out of a paper bag was the hardest escape of all because there was no way to hide how it was done. She wasn't afraid of anyone, but she didn't think pissing off Sherman Russo was a smart idea.

Besides, she was busy trying to make this normal life work. It wasn't as easy as it looked. Hart was such an innocent.

Hart was still her husband as far as she was concerned. He was too nice, too honest. People were always trying to take advantage of him. Sometimes she had to visit the troublemakers and set them straight. They never bothered him again after that.

The hard knock on the door startled her. They rarely if ever got visitors.

Amanda looked out the peephole, saw two hard-looking men. Sherm had warned her.

"Be right there!" she called out. She went to the bedroom, took off all her clothes and put on a bathrobe. She went to the door, put on her sweetest smile, then opened it. "Gentlemen, what can I do for you?"

"Is this the Hart Davis residence?" the taller of the two men asked. He was a good six and half feet tall. The other man was over six feet, but seemed small in comparison though both were heavily muscled under their suits. She recognized the bulge beneath their left arms.

"It's *my* residence. Hart isn't here."

"Actually, Mrs. Davis, we're here to see you," the taller man said.

Mrs. Davis. She missed hearing that. Since the separation, everyone called her Amanda these days.

"Then you'd better come on in," she said.

Not that she could have refused. The bigger man had maneuvered his boot a good six inches inside the door, which made it impossible to slam it closed even if she wanted to.

Might as well act like she welcomed the visit. She'd tied the bathrobe loosely and knew the tops of her thighs were showing. Both men looked away when she turned around, which told her that they had noticed.

"I've got some fresh coffee if you'd like some," she offered in her best, 'Coffee, tea, or me?' voice.

She started toward the kitchen, remembered the mess, and turned around, blocking the way.

The pair didn't notice her hesitation. "We're fine, Mrs. Davis. I'll get right to the point. We understand that you were holding a box for Sherman Russo. We just have one question. Did you manage to get a look inside?"

Uh, oh. They weren't asking for the box, which meant they already knew where it was.

"Call me Amanda," she said. "And you are?"

"Bill," he said. He waved at the smaller man. "And Fred."

Bill and Fred. Hell...they aren't even trying. She kept the smile plastered on her face. *Should I even admit I know what they're talking about? Best to play it straight.*

"That old beat-up thing? Never occurred to me, Bill. Why do you ask?"

Fred spoke for the first time. He seemed less confrontational, as if he was just asking for a little cooperation. "Are you *sure* you didn't open it?"

"Well, yeah. Actually, I never did get a chance to look inside it." That came out with such bluntness that Amanda could tell they believed her. "It would have been a hassle to get into."

She could also tell it wasn't enough.

"It was wrapped in duct tape," she added. She flopped into a chair, her bathrobe opening slightly, and the men couldn't stop from looking where they shouldn't.

"So you never mentioned it to anyone else?" Bill asked.

Trick question. Admit that she'd told someone and they'd torture her to find out who. Admit that she hadn't told anyone, and they'd kill her on the spot. *Orders,* she could tell. It didn't matter whether they believed her.

She got to her feet in such a fluid motion that it startled the men. But neither of them reached for their weapons. She dropped her smile. "What's this about?"

"You don't need to know," Fred said in a warning tone. He was still holding out, hoping they wouldn't have to do her. But the taller thug wasn't going to let her go, she could tell. In fact, unless she was misinterpreting his lingering gaze, Bill intended to do more than just kill her.

That decided her.

She let the bathrobe fall open and walked toward the Bill. He froze, eyes wide, just long enough for her to slam the side of her hand into his Adam's apple. Not waiting for a reaction, she spun around and rammed her knee into the nicer guy's nether regions.

Bill reached for his gun, but Amanda snagged his free hand and forced his ring finger back. He fell to his knees with a cry, the gun falling to the ground. She picked it up, placed it against his head, and pulled the trigger. Blood sprayed out across the couch as he fell back. The smell of cordite and blood was intoxicating.

Then she turned to Fred. He had both hands up. "No need," he said. "I'm just an errand boy."

"Who are you people?" she asked, aiming the Glock at his chest.

"If I tell you, they'll kill me."

"Yeah...well," she said, lifting the gun slightly.

She saw the fatalism in his eyes. Too long on the job, too many regrets. It happened to all of them, except those who had no conscience.

"You'll have to kill me, Mrs. Davis. Better you than them."

She shrugged and shot him in the chest. He died looking surprised, as if he'd somehow thought she was the same smiling woman who had met them at the door instead of the cold-blooded killer who'd shot Bill in the head.

Hart needed her.

The thought of it made her smile.

CHAPTER 9

Kent already had a fire going in the pit by the time we got back.

"Let me show you boys around," Granger said to Jordan and Samuels. He was still wearing his Bigfoot costume, the mask falling over his shoulders. Everyone else was already around the fire, staring at him.

The fire pit was between the house and the bunkhouse, surrounded by amphitheater seating made from flat rocks. Most of the ranch socializing took place there. He had an old refrigerator hooked up under the eaves of the house, filled with a dozen varieties of the local brew.

"Any time you want a drink, you can just grab one," Granger said. "All part of the service."

He sounded cheerful enough, but he was eyeballing the big men and ringing up the cost of beer in his mind.

Next to the outdoor fridge was a metal box with a big latch. "Lots of snacks in the box. Again, free of charge," he continued. "Crackers, cookies, candy, that sorta of thing. But, and this is important, you need to keep it tightly latched. If you forget, the squirrels will clean it out in minutes, and if they don't get to it, the raccoons will."

With a few big logs added to the campfire, it soon roared and crackled with life. Everyone grabbed a beer and sat down around it. Granger left to change.

Samuels proceeded to tell his men about Jordan's shooting Bigfoot.

"A toast to the mighty Bigfoot killer," Moser said, laughing. Jordan glowered.

In a while Granger came back. *"Le dîner est preparé,"* he said in his twangy version of French. *"C'est* squirrel stew, made of the finest rodents on the ranch. A special recipe created by Conner Manuel himself."

"Parlez-vous français?" Moser asked. He was the most clean-shaven of them, and his clothes fit a little better than the other men's.

"Je suis couramment," Granger answered, straightening up proudly. "Majored in it in college."

"What do you know?" Moser laughed. "An educated Bigfoot!"

"Bring it on!" one of the guys said, regarding dinner. I think it was Burton, the youngest of the crew. A little skinnier than the others, he always seemed to be in motion. He smelled of cigar smoke, though he hadn't lit up in my presence yet. "I ain't never eaten squirrel."

Of course, the stew only contained regular ground beef.

I watched the men dig in, curious about their reaction. Jordan hadn't taken more than two bites before he looked over at Conner wonderingly. "You cooked this?"

"Yes, sir," Conner said proudly. He was beaming.

Previtt snorted. "Jordan thinks he's a real foodie. Blows all his money on four-star restaurants."

Jordan stared him down, and Previtt looked away. Jordan said, "Shit, kid. You ever want a job in New York as a private cook, you've got one."

"Thank you, sir," Conner said, "but I like it here. Mr. Granger treats me good."

"Well, if you ever change your mind." Jordan finished his bowl and went back for seconds. As Conner ladled more stew into his bowl, Jordan whispered something to him that made the kid laugh. It surprised me, and made me wonder if I'd been wrong about the big man. It was another way I judged clients, by how they treated Conner.

I nursed my beer through the meal. Granger did his normal shtick, trying to get the others to sing songs around the fire, which predictably fell flat. I could see Granger getting disgusted.

"Speaking of Bigfoot," I said during a lull in the conversation.

"Granger here has actually seen him."

The men fell silent, like a crew of small boys, and turned to Granger expectantly. Encouraged by their sudden attention, Granger told them the usual story.

"I was just a boy," he began. "My pa sent me out to look for Marnie, our milk cow. She'd wandered up that very ridge right over there, and I followed her tracks.

"I smelled something foul. I looked up, and there *he* stood, taller than I am now, wide and stocky, covered from head to foot in black fur. Bigfoot, Sasquatch, the Abominable Snowman."

I watched the others' faces. Usually, clients just looked bemused, but these guys actually seemed to buy it, big, tough men though they were. I had to admit that Granger was really selling it this time. It suddenly occurred to me I'd never asked Granger if the story was true. On that night, he convinced me.

Granger continued, "Me and the creature stared into each other's eyes. I could see his malevolent intelligence. It was a full moon, and there was no doubt I was looking at something alien, something few men had seen and lived to tell about. I don't know what would have happened next, but I think it would have been bad.

"At that moment, Marnie came stumbling out of the underbrush, mooing as loudly as she could.

"Bigfoot must have jumped ten feet in the air. He let out such a howl I had to put my hands over my ears. His eyes seemed to glow red in the dark. Marnie ran into the woods, never to be seen again. The creature took a step toward me, and another, and I froze in fear. I could smell his foul breath..."

Granger fell silent for a moment, milking it for all it was worth.

"Closer and closer he came, until I couldn't breathe, until he loomed over me. He snarled and reached out with his long, sharp claws..."

Granger again fell silent.

"So what happened?" Burton asked impatiently.

"What happened?" Granger repeated. He looked at each of the men in turn.

"Yes, goddamm it! What happened?" Burton nearly shouted.

Granger's drawl was as wide as the West. "Bigfoot killed me and ate me, of course."

Kent started cackling, which was a startling sound coming from such a normally gloomy guy. Conner had almost given it away by smiling broadly halfway through. No matter how often Granger told the story, his two employees loved it.

There was a long silence as the men took in this unexpected reversal. Then Previtt said, "Shit. I want my money back." He didn't sound at all amused at the shaggy dog story. "You people are crazy about Bigfoot."

Samuels started laughing, deep and long. Tears came to his eyes. It was all out of proportion, but also reassuring. Samuels was human after all.

"Hey, the beers are free and plentiful," I broke in. "Drink up, though I warn you, we start out before sunrise."

Most of the men got up and headed for the outdoor fridge. I caught Granger's eye and shook my head. He snorted in disgust and stomped off to his room. He was done for the night. Conner sat down next to Jordan with a beer in hand. I'd never seen him drink before. The two of them seemed to be having a spirited conversation about cooking.

Previtt spoke in a loud voice. "We've got a job to do, boys. Martinson here has informed me he has never been drunk. We're going to change that."

Martinson objected, but the others drowned him out.

I grabbed another beer, even though I'd only drunk half of the first one.

As I opened it, I noticed Samuels sitting near the fire, poking at it moodily with a stick. He looked up. I realized that, despite the empty bottles around him, he was as sober as I was.

When I finally got up to go bed, half of my clients were nodding off and the other half were still going strong. Samuels got up without a word and followed me. His room was right across from mine.

He nodded at me as he went into his room, and I closed my door. I couldn't sleep. These guys bothered me...I wasn't sure why. After about an hour, I got up and opened my door and stepped out into the hall.

Samuels's door was still open. He sat up in bed and looked at me. I ignored him, went down to the tiny bathroom and came back. I went back into my room and lay down again.

CHAPTER 10

Sherm Russo made it as far as Detroit before he decided to ditch the company car. From New York, he'd driven for ten hours straight, stopping for gas only once along the way. It was a necessary detour off the freeway. He'd used the old tricks, leaving the window open to the cold morning air to stay awake and peeing into a bottle.

The car had a GPS, but Sherm had no idea how to disconnect it. So they'd know how far he'd gotten the first day, if and when they checked. But because Martinson had been in charge of the carpool, Sherm was pretty confident they wouldn't even notice the car was missing for a day or two. With any luck, he'd be long gone before they realized it.

Martinson was in deeper than Sherm had suspected. *Poor fool doesn't have a clue.*

Now, as the gas tank of his corporate car approached empty, Sherm looked for Detroit's Finest Cars, hoping he had the address right. At least, the address had been correct five years ago. He didn't remember getting any updates that Romano had gone out of business, but he could have moved.

There. It looked pretty run down, with some pathetic cars filling half the available spaces. But then, the business had always existed to launder money and didn't have to turn much of a profit.

He pulled up to the garage door and asked for the boss.

Romano came out of the garage, wiping grease off his hands with a red cloth. The old guy had always been more of a grease monkey than a salesman, which was why Sherm liked him.

His hair was as thick and shaggy as ever, but was completely gray. His eyebrows were bushy, and he wore two-day's growth of beard. He couldn't hide the look of surprise on his face, and Sherm's heart fell.

Word is already out.

Romano agreed to take in the company car and chop it up.

"I'm the only one here who knows what's going on," he said. "My people think we're legit, though how they could be that stupid, I don't know. I ain't got much selection for you, though. A bunch of beaters."

Sherm took an old Buick, a boat of a car that reminded him of one he'd owned years before. As he started the car to pull away, he rolled down the window.

"I know you'll be tempted to turn me in, Romano," he said. "I don't doubt there is a pretty hefty reward out for me, but I did your books for years, and I know you skimmed a little off the top for every one of those years. If I find out you ratted on me, that info will find the right ears."

As soon as he said it, he felt like an asshole, but his life was on the line.

The stakes are too high to be a nice guy and depend on old friendships.

Romano looked insulted, his bushy brows drawing together and becoming one long, shaggy caterpillar. "I wouldn't do that, Sherm. No matter what the reward. Get the fuck out of here, you old bastard."

Sherm pulled away, the shocks on the Buick swaying alarmingly as it went over the curb. It had been a bluff. He didn't have any proof of Romano's embezzling.

Besides, if they catch me, I won't be turning anyone in. I'll be dead.

CHAPTER 11

I was just falling asleep when I heard a strange sound, a vibration that shocked me awake. It was a buzzing sound, and it took me a full thirty seconds to figure out it was the cellphone I'd hidden beneath the mattress.

What Granger didn't know wouldn't hurt him.

Amanda's voice was so rushed she almost couldn't be understood. Mania. She was in the early throes of it, from the sound.

"Hart, you've got to get rid of the box. Hide it."

"Wait...slow down, Amanda. What are you talking about?"

"I put a box in the back of your Jeep. You need to hide it."

"What's in it?"

"I don't know," she said, sounding irritated.

"What do you mean, you don't know?"

"I took it as a favor from an old friend, and Mafia guy named Sherman Russo. Then I forgot about it. They're after it. You have to hide it."

"Hide it from who?"

"Who's with you?" she asked sharply. I heard the paranoid tone that usually hit her at the peak of her cycle.

"Some corporate guys from New York," I said, tiredly, wondering how I was going to get her to let me go. I didn't dare hang up on her. She'd go ballistic.

"Don't let them get the box, Hart. You have to hide it."

"Why? What's in it?"

"I don't *know*. But it's *important*."

Ordinarily, I'd have just figured it was her craziness talking. But there was something about Samuels and his crew that lent her story more credibility than usual.

"All right." I said. "I'll put it somewhere safe."

"Hide the box and get the hell out of there," Amanda said. "Do it now."

I walked over to the window, pulling back the corner of the curtains. Jordan, Privett, and Martinson still stood by the fire. Well, at least, Jordan and Previtt were standing—Martinson was swaying and looked ready to fall over.

"I can't just leave," I said. "What about Granger and Kent and Conner?"

"They aren't your problem," she said. "Get out of there, Hart."

I sighed. This was the real reason we'd split up. She was fiercely loyal to those she knew, but to hell with anyone else.

"They'll hurt you, Hart, to get the box. You have to believe me."

"Maybe I should just hand it over to them," I said.

"Listen to me, Hart," she said. "If you do that, Samuels will kill you anyway, just to be sure. He'll kill you and anyone who's with you. The box is your only leverage."

I suddenly believed her. I'd never once heard Amanda scared. This was something new.

"I'm on my way," she said. "Hold out until I get there."

She hung up. I stood there, phone in hand, and I wondered if I'd been sucked into her paranoid delusions again. It was as if she radiated a reality distortion field.

I peered around the curtains and checked the fire pit again. Martinson was nodding off, but Jordan and Privett were still going strong. I'd have to wait until they went to bed.

I woke at three o'clock in the morning. I didn't even have to look at my watch. It was an ability I had, estimating time. Being able to wake at a pre-appointed hour was a handy talent for an outdoor guide.

I pulled the curtains back and looked at the now-smoldering fire, half-expecting some of the men to still be there. But it was obvious everyone had gone to bed hours before.

I went to the middle of the room, silently lifted the table, and flipped back the rug.

For once, I was grateful that Granger was paranoid. There was a trapdoor in the middle of the floor. He'd pointed it out to me once, pretending it was a fire escape.

I pulled on the latch, hoping it wasn't rusty and wouldn't make noise. It opened smoothly, silently. I looked into the crawlspace, trying to ignore the cobwebs, a perfect place for black widows to breed. I shuddered at the thought of spiders crawling on my back.

I dropped down and crawled quickly toward the small exit at the base of the house.

Once outside, I crept around the house to the Jeep. I opened the rear passenger door, which I knew squealed the least. Even so, I held my breath as it ground open.

I reached over the seat and lifted the box, surprised it felt so light. My adrenaline was pumping. I doubted I'd be able to sleep for the rest of the night regardless of what else I did.

I headed down the side of the road, keeping to the rocks and grass as much as possible, brushing away any prints I left in the dirt. At the fencepost with the red shotgun shell casing, I brushed away leaves and dirt and lifted the plywood plank.

The drop box was just big enough to hold the cardboard file box. I dropped the wood plank back over it and covered it better than usual with rocks and soil.

As I walked back, I stared up at the bright Milky Way, wishing I could just get in the Jeep and drive away.

It might have been feasible to wake Granger—he had a trapdoor in his room as well—but Kent and Conner both slept in the bunkhouse. There was no possible way to wake them up without alerting the others.

Back in my room, I brushed away the cobwebs and dust, then lay on my bed, still clothed. Surprisingly, I fell asleep.

My inner alarm woke me at 5:30 a.m. as planned.

I went outside onto the porch, and clanged on the iron skillet that hung off the corner of the porch.

CHAPTER 12

Sherm managed to drive only a few miles out of Detroit before he nearly slammed into the back of a truck. He wasn't sure if he'd fallen asleep or was dazed from exhaustion. He didn't suppose it made much difference.

When did I get so old? he wondered. The memories of his days as a foot soldier were returning in full force, while his twenty years in an office were blurring into a pinpoint of time. He looked for a quiet street and pulled over. He parked under some old oaks and crawled into the backseat for a nap.

Early the next morning, before the neighborhood could wake up, he started the Buick and got back on I-80 west.

He bypassed Chicago though there were people there he could have approached for help. He didn't know how big the price was on his head, but it had to be huge. It had been twenty years since he'd seen some of his old *friends*.

Driving through the cornfields of Iowa, Sherm started falling asleep again. He cursed himself for being weak. When he was younger, he could have driven from coast to coast in less than four days. But it wouldn't help anyone if he killed himself trying to get there in time.

After ten hours, he pulled over at a rest stop outside Des Moines, climbed once again into the Buick's roomy back seat, and instantly fell asleep.

When he awoke, it was late in the morning. Alarmed at oversleeping, he pulled back out onto the freeway. He had already filled the old car with gas several times and was rapidly running out of cash. In New York, his wife drove their car while Sherm usually took the subway.

He'd had no idea gas was so expensive now and that driving an old beater might not have been the smartest thing to do. Sherm resisted the urge to step on the accelerator. He thought he had just enough gas to reach Cheyenne, Wyoming, if he nursed the fuel consumption.

I have to make it to Andriotti's place.

CHAPTER 13

I heard cursing from the bunkhouse and clanged the bell even harder.

Samuels emerged first, which I expected. I looked into his eyes and saw his usual coldness.

As long as he didn't check the back of the Jeep, I was safe.

Jordan emerged from the bunkhouse next, yawning. His eyes were bloodshot. He'd drunk more than anyone else last night. "Aren't you worried about scaring all the deer away with that clanging?" he grumbled.

"Where I'm taking you, the deer won't have heard a thing," I grinned.

"You got the keys to the Jeep?" he asked. "I left my sunglasses in there."

I raised my eyebrows. It was still pitch black in every direction.

"I don't go nowhere without my glasses," he growled.

"The Jeep's unlocked."

I watched him out of the corner of my eye as he rooted around in the back seat. Then he turned around, putting something in his pocket. I started breathing again as soon as he closed the Jeep's door and walked toward the fire pit. He hadn't looked in the back compartment.

Martinson appeared next. He made it to the bottom of the stairs before leaning over and puking. The stench of curdled beer filled the air. He straightened, wiping his mustache, and looked over at me, mortified.

Previtt skipped down the steps and slapped the smaller man on the back. "We'll make a man of you yet, Martinson!"

Behind me, Granger appeared at the door of the ranch house and surreptitiously motioned me over, giving me a hard stare. His hair and beard were combed, something he only did when he was nervous. He hadn't smiled yet this morning, which was completely out of character.

"What's going on, Hart?" he said. "Have you seen what these guys are packing? They give me a really bad feeling."

"You're right," I said. "I shouldn't have brought them."

"You're an idiot, Hart. I've met this type before. Whatever these fuckers are up to, it isn't hunting deer. They're fucking mercenaries." He turned away, heading for the kitchen, his back hunched.

Mercenaries. I realized with a cold chill that the word had been hovering in the back of my mind since I'd first met them.

I followed Granger, who now stood next to Conner, flipping flapjacks. "I'm taking them out hunting this morning, Granger. You and Kent and Conner need to pack up and get out of here."

Granger turned slowly. "Get *out* of here? Why?"

"I can't tell you," I said. "Just do it."

"We can't just leave…" Granger began, but broke off when Jordan entered the kitchen and started talking to Conner.

I pulled Granger aside. "Just do it," I repeated, trying to convey with my eyes how important it was.

Conner had cooked ham and eggs, which the group quickly scarfed up. Jordan again complimented the chef, and Conner looked more proud than I'd ever seen him.

"You're wasted here, kid," Jordan said. "If you won't let me hire you, at least give me your recipes."

It was still dark when we headed out. I watched my clients on the climb up the first ridge. Hanson had a gun I'd never seen before, something sleek and handsome. It had a rounded grip, and its metal was a beautiful grey/green color. He saw me eyeing it and presented it proudly.

"It's an AWSM," he said.

I raised my eyebrows. The acronym didn't mean anything to me. "Does that stand for *awesome*?"

Hanson snorted a laugh. "Pretty much. It's an Arctic

Warfare Super Magnum. I thought it might get cold up here, and this baby will fire in any weather."

I was impressed. I'd heard of the weapon but never seen one. The rifle was a handcrafted, precision machine, incredibly expensive and, by all accounts, had a waiting list of years.

I didn't need to worry about their firearms handling, obviously. But of the seven men, only Samuels, Jordan, and Hanson appeared to be serious about hunting. Burton, Moser, and Previtt acted as if they didn't care. They made no effort to be quiet. Martinson, meanwhile, looked like he didn't want to be there at all.

I decided to split the men into two groups, those who were serious and those who weren't.

The four less serious hunters were bunched together. I said, "Why don't you guys keep following this trail?" I said, pointing to the trail that wrapped around the mountain. Easy walking and extremely unlikely to be productive. It looped around the ridge and down into a valley, then up another ridge. About an eight-mile hike one way. "We'll meet you back here about ten o'clock. We'll take a break in the middle of the day and then try again late afternoon. Take it slow; be as quiet as you can."

"No shit." Previtt laughed. He hoisted his rifle as if it was a sword. "Come on guys, let's blast some critters."

I turned to my crew and motioned them to follow. Samuels smiled and nodded. It was clear that he knew what I'd done by separating the groups and approved. With any luck, by being thoughtlessly noisy, the other crew would push the deer in our direction.

Much more quietly and slowly, we headed in the opposite direction. We passed the mouth of a deep canyon running up the east side of the property called Butcher's Cut because some pioneer by that name had accidentally tumbled into it and died.

Jordan stopped and jerked his head toward the gully. "Why don't we try that direction?"

"It's a box canyon," I said. "It gets steeper and rockier until it's impassible. Besides, the bigger bucks stay away from the place."

Jordan nodded. "You're the man," he said. I tried to ignore the hint of mockery in his tone.

With that, I decided to take them up Deadfall Ridge, which I usually saved for the last day and only for the most intrepid of hunters. It was a steep climb, but also less hunted.

And much more dangerous.

On the maps, it was still called Ponderosa Ridge, but thirty years ago a fire had completely devastated that part of the ranch. New lodgepole pines sprouted where giants once stood. You could see the occasional charred trunk of a ponderosa sticking above them, the bark still black with spots of orange showing through, the broken branches looking like metal stakes.

At night, from Bigfoot Ranch, I occasionally heard one of the deadfalls finally giving way to the elements, crashing to the ground. Usually I didn't take my clients up here, because there was always a chance—if an extremely small one—of a snag landing pounding one of them into the ground.

The trail was dangerous at the best of times, filled with widowmakers. During storms I stayed away. Trees tilted over the trail, roots partly exposed, swaying alarmingly in the wind, branches near the bottom that seemed to reach down to clutch at unwary travelers.

The men followed me up the steep slope without complaint. It was strangely peaceful. Even the birds were subdued. Usually, we were accompanied by the raucous caws of the ravens that hung around the ranch, trying to steal scraps from the squirrels. There was not a trace of wind, which was odd in itself. Sound carried in the silence, but the men behind me had obviously stalked prey before because they were as noiseless as I was, if not more so.

Somehow, I doubted the prey these grim men had stalked were animals.

The farther we went, the stranger it became. There wasn't a trace of any kind of animal, not so much as a chipmunk or rabbit, none of the swift little lizards that usually scooted across the path. It was as if everything was on hold, as if we floated in a ghost world of possibility, and until one of us said or did something, we didn't exist.

To our right, Butcher's Cut got deeper and deeper until the trees at the base looked like shrubs. Jordan gave me a look about halfway up that acknowledged that my decision not to explore it had been wise.

The biggest widowmaker loomed as we neared the summit over the narrowest part of Deadfall Ridge, with impassable slopes on either side. There was no way past but to go under the snag.

It seemed to me that its thick trunk had dropped an inch or two since the last time I'd been there, as if it was ready to fall any moment. As we hurried under it, I noticed that the bark on the bottom had been torn off.

"Is that bear sign?" Jordan whispered.

I nodded.

"I'd rather bag a bear than a deer," he said.

"You don't have a tag."

"Shit. Doesn't matter if the bear attacks, right?"

I didn't answer. Between the four of us, our sweat and smoke was more than enough to warn most wildlife off. Including deer, unfortunately.

We crossed the narrow corridor between the steep hillside to our left and the cliffs of Butcher's Cut on our right. I figured we'd gone far enough and turned around.

The dull *thud* of a gunshot muted by the trees floated up to us, followed by several flat *booms*. I estimated the shots had come from about two miles' distance. Jordan and Hanson instantly dropped to their knees, followed a little more deliberately by Samuels, all of them unslinging their rifles in one fluid motion.

I stood there stupidly, feeling as if I'd missed something.

Samuels rose from his crouch, giving me a rueful smile. "Force of habit."

After several seconds of silence, the other men stood up also. They looked at me expectantly. I felt a chill.

"Let's keep hunting," Samuels said, as if nothing strange had happened.

The longer I kept them out here, the more time Granger, Conner, and Kent would have to get away. We descended Deadfall Ridge, and I led them to the other side of Butcher's Cut. There was a good chance the other crew had riled up the herds on the broader slope so that the deer circulated in our direction.

Without saying a word, I left the path and headed straight uphill, something I never would have done with the duffers I usually had as clients. Right behind me was Jordan, and five paces behind him was Hanson, and bringing up the rear was Samuels. I had the feeling this wasn't a new configuration for them; this was a pattern they automatically fell into when working.

The hillside was thick with brush, and loose stones rolled beneath our feet. Sometimes we were blocked by basalt outcroppings, stacked as neatly as the walls of a fortress. By the time we reached the top of the hill, I was more winded than they were, or at least, than they were willing to show. I suspected that none of them would admit weakness to the others, much less a stranger.

Though Jordan didn't look the least bit tired, he was disgruntled. "Why do we have to move around so much? Why don't we wait for the deer to come to us?"

"Jesus, Jordan," Hanson said. "You are one lazy bastard."

"I just hate climbing if I don't have to."

I said, "The deer will come to us, but only if we're in the right spot. Otherwise, why bother leaving our beds?"

Hanson snorted. "The man's got a point."

How long had it been since I was up this high? The tall cliff that boxed in Butcher's Cut was below us. I'd learned to keep clients happy by crisscrossing the hillsides instead of tackling the steep slopes directly. The main peak of the range, Strawberry Mountain itself, loomed to our right. The foothill we were on was the last before the final approach. Our view was unobstructed in every other direction.

At the base of the hills were mostly juniper trees, higher up the second-generation pine trees grew so thick that Bigfoot or any other legendary creature would have been impossible to see. Farther up, the trees got bigger, the spaces between them wider.

Mountain meadows started to appear, with white ranch houses far below, their red roofs gleaming. On the far side of the valley were more foothills, rising into snow-covered heights. There was nothing beyond them but hills and desert for hundreds of miles. Those hills didn't even have the big timber that would have made them valuable.

"I could live here," Hanson said in a low voice that didn't carry.

"Shit," Jordan muttered. "You'd be bored out of your skull in no time."

"I don't think so," Hanson said.

I nodded to Hanson. No matter how many times I came up here, the view never failed to fill me with awe.

I almost didn't hear Jordan when he whispered, "I see one."

With my bare eyes, I couldn't see what he was looking at. I sighted in with my binoculars, searching the trees below.

Jordan slowly moved his rifle to his shoulder and aimed downhill.

Halfway down the hillside, about three hundred yards away, a buck lay in the thick brush under a pine, settled in its day bed. Its head was up and alert, looking in the direction of the gunshots below. It showed no awareness of us.

It was a respectable four-point buck.

"Nice one," I whispered.

Jordan firmed up his stance and took a deep breath. It was a difficult angle downhill, but the man looked like he knew what he was doing.

"Shoot behind the shoulders," I said.

"Shit," Jordan muttered. "Don't teach your grandmother how to suck eggs."

He squeezed off the shot.

No matter how much I expect a gunshot, I always jump a little. Most people do. Not these guys. They didn't jolt a bit.

"Got him," Jordan said, standing up.

We slid down to the deer, no longer trying to be quiet. One way or the other, our hunt was done for the morning. It was a perfect shot; it had hit the buck's heart and killed it instantly. Without me saying anything, Jordan angled the deer so its belly was downhill and gutted it. The innards slid down into the dust, rolling like pastry dough in flour.

Obviously, the man had done this before.

They sure as hell didn't need me to show them anything.

What had they hired me for? But I knew the answer. For a time, I'd been so engrossed in the hunt I'd forgotten about the box.

Carrying the carcass between them, Jordan and Hanson hauled the buck down to the trail where the others waited.

"Damn," Previtt said. "We didn't see a single deer."

"What was the shooting about earlier?" Samuels asked.

"Saw a gang of wild turkeys," Moser answered. "Damn things are quicker than they look."

"Are turkeys in season?" Martinson asked.

It had never occurred to me to hunt them. "Heffinger, the guy who owns the next ranch over, feeds them. They're as tame as cats."

Jordan laughed and nudged Previtt. "Way to go, man, you almost killed a Butterball."

"I don't care," Previtt scowled. "Thanksgiving ain't that far away."

We made it back to the bunkhouse before noon.

My heart fell when I saw that Granger was still there to meet us.

What the hell?

Granger looked unsurprised at the kill. Normally, he would have made a big deal over it for the sake of the client. "Biggest trophy of the year!" he'd exclaim. Instead he just pointed toward a small shed to the side of the house.

"Hang it up in there," he said. "It'll keep cool. There's also a faucet for washing up. Oh, and check for ticks."

Moser shuddered, "Damn, I hate those things."

I pulled Granger aside. "What the hell, Granger? I told you guys to get out of here."

"You ever tried to get Conner to move when he doesn't want to? And then Kent chimes in, talking about how much he needs to feed the horses. We almost got out of here, but you came back too early."

"First chance you get, you need to leave," I said. "No excuses."

I could see that Granger didn't like me giving orders but

that he could also tell I was dead serious. Spending the day with these men had convinced me that Amanda's paranoia was justified. I now had no doubt that whatever was in the box was important enough to kill for.

"I'm taking them out for another hunt this afternoon," I said. "Be gone when we get back. These men will kill you...and Conner and Kent...without a second thought."

Startled, Granger stared into my eyes for a few moments longer, then nodded.

My clients dove into the beer fridge and settled in around the fire. I figured the hunt at dusk was probably going to be a fiasco if they kept drinking, but it would make it easier for my friends to get away. After all, I'd delivered a big trophy buck, and my clients appeared satisfied for now.

"We're done for the day," Samuels suddenly said. "We just want to relax. Right, men?"

This was unexpected. The longer they hung around the ranch, the more likely it was they'd discover the box missing. But even more importantly, it didn't give my friends a chance to escape, and until they were gone, I couldn't leave either.

"You sure?" I asked. "Dusk is the best time for hunting. I can almost guarantee you a good-sized buck."

"Guarantee a kill?" Jordan snorted. "Not just a walk?"

"The herds are moving," I insisted. "If ever there was a time..."

Samuels shook his head. "Fuck it. We've got a few more days to hunt."

I stared across the fire at Granger. *Stock up the beer,* I wanted to say. Our best chance was that these guys would get so drunk that they wouldn't be a threat. Granger nodded back as if he understood my unspoken thought.

The mercenaries didn't look as though they were going to budge from the fire or the booze. I noticed Granger taking aside Conner and Kent. They looked at the mercenaries with alarmed expressions that I feared would give it all away.

Samuels was watching me, his eyes glinting in the firelight. I could swear he was reading my thoughts. He took a sip of beer and nodded to me.

I took a big gulp of my own, then slowed down. It wouldn't do to get drunk. But *damn*, I wanted to get drunk. As long as it was daylight, as long as I was doing something, I held off the dread. Sitting there in the midst of these men, all of who I figured wouldn't feel the slightest regret shooting me, the fear crept over me.

I got up suddenly, grabbed another beer and downed it quickly. It didn't help, it just seemed to make me even more aware of Samuel's proximity and gaze.

As it approached midnight, I slipped away and went to my room, lying down on my bed still clothed. Samuels once again followed me.

The only thing I could do was wait until they all went to bed. Then I'd sneak into the bunkhouse and try to get Kent and Conner out of there.

I stared up at the ceiling, determined to stay awake.

CHAPTER 14

I awoke choking. The arm around my neck tightened. A voice, inches from my ear, said, "Don't fight it."

I bucked upward and over the side of the bed, and the arm tightened even more. My attacker landed on top of me, knocking the breath out of me. My chest and throat felt paralyzed. It was dark in the room, but it got even darker.

I stopped fighting, feeling a sense of peace come over me. A pinpoint of light appeared before me, but I knew it came from inside my mind and not outside. The light grew, and I felt myself being drawn to it.

Then I was gasping, the air filling my lungs almost painfully, as if my body had already forgotten how to breathe.

"Take him to the fire pit," Samuels' voice said from the doorway.

"Yes, sir," Jordan grunted, his sour alcohol breath rasping against my ears.

Strong hands grabbed my collar, and I was dragged unceremoniously outside, too weak to fight it.

The others were waiting, standing at attention. They were dressed in full fatigues, their hunting rifles replaced by their semi-autos. I was dumped onto the bottom row of flat rocks, uncomfortably close to the fire. I rolled onto my back, staring into Samuels's cold eyes.

"I have just one question," he said. "Where's the box?"

"Why are you asking me?" I asked. "It's in the back of the Jeep where you left it."

Samuels sighed and looked over at Jordan, then back at me. "You think you're going to resist, but I assure you, when we're done, you'll give us what we want. But we don't need to go there, Davis."

"Fuck you."

Samuels gave me a cold stare, then turned to Burton. "Where's Granger?"

"He ain't anywhere, sir. He's disappeared."

"Then go find him!" Samuels snapped. "Take Moser with you."

"You want him alive?"

"Good question," Samuels said, looking down at me. "Which will it be, Davis? Dead or alive?"

"Whatever you do, don't give them the box," I heard Amanda's voice say in my head. *"He'll kill you and anyone who's with you."*

"You're going to kill us anyway."

"You're wrong about that," Samuels said, and his voice was so matter of fact that for a moment I believed him. He turned back to Burton. "Bring Granger back alive if you can."

Samuels sat down on the seat next to me. "You can sit up," he said companionably. I struggled to push myself upright, and he grabbed my coat and pulled me the rest of the way up.

He patted me on the leg, and every muscle in my body tensed. "I don't need to kill you and Granger," he said. "You're right. Normally I would, just to be on the safe side. But I like you, and I like Granger. You're innocents in all this."

He squeezed my leg and laughed. "I really believe you didn't open the box, Davis, otherwise you'd have been dead the moment I saw it. So, right now, if I get the box back, we can simply walk away without consequence. Oh, you could report us, but what really happened here? I threatened you over some box you've never seen before? And, by the way, no one will believe that.

"But just to make sure, some of my people paid a visit to your local sheriff and convinced him ahead of time to ignore whatever you say. It's his jurisdiction. He doesn't seem to like you very much. He was easy enough to bribe, and even easier to blackmail. It appears that he's been selling the department's rifles on the black market for some time.

"So you see, Davis. I *can* let you live. So where is the box?"

I shook my head.

"This fucker must be simple-minded," Jordan said from somewhere above and behind me.

"No," Samuels said, without taking his eyes off me. "Honesty just looks that way in our world."

"Maybe *you* took it, Jordan," I answered.

Samuels shook his head. "Even if you won't save your own life, Davis, you've got your friends to think about. So far, they're out of it. They can say anything they want to the authorities. Everyone already thinks Granger is crazy and Kent is loopy, and Conner...well, who's going to believe him? So why don't you save your friends and tell me where the box is?"

It was the only thing he could've said to me that would've made a difference. I'd been an idiot to bring Samuels and his crew out here. I should've trusted my instincts. It might have ended the same way for me, but at least my friends would be safe.

Samuels saw it in my eyes. "The rest of you," he said, without turning his head, "find Granger!"

"What about Kent and that Down syndrome kid?" Hanson asked. "Davis here seems fond of them."

Samuels stared at me speculatively. "We don't have to involve them just yet, do we, Davis?"

I knew that if they found any one of friends, I'd give in immediately. I'd tell Samuels where the box was. I stared into the fire, knowing that if Samuels saw my eyes, he would see the truth.

I steeled myself, because no matter what Samuels said, he wouldn't think twice about torturing me if he had no other leverage. But neither did I believe he would let us live. He didn't strike me as the type who would take unnecessary risks.

He'll shoot us and then congratulate himself for caring.

"Why don't you save us the trouble, Davis?" Samuels said. "If we have to track down your friend he might get hurt."

It was true. Granger probably wouldn't come back without a fight, and no matter how big he was, it was tough to see how he could prevail against these hard men.

And yet, as long as Granger was free, there was a chance.

We waited in silence. My initial panic subsided, my mind working feverishly to figure out a way out of this. I wasn't bound. There was nothing to keep me from jumping up and running into the darkness, except Jordan with a rifle pointed at my back.

Even if I somehow managed to distract Jordan, I suspected Samuels had a weapon he could draw and fire before I went two steps. We sat silent for a time. Samuels's blue eyes flickered in the firelight, red and blue competing, the cold overwhelming the fire.

One by one, the other mercenaries returned.

Previtt, the last one back, spit into the fire. "They could be anywhere. They can see us coming. We'll have to wait until daylight."

"Last chance, Davis," Samuels said.

I didn't answer.

"Are you left-handed or right-handed?" Samuels asked, as if trying to remember which hand I'd favored. "Never mind... Jordan, break his right pinky finger."

Two arms pinioned me from behind as Previtt stepped down into the pit next to me. He nodded to whoever was holding me—Jordan, I thought—and my right arm was forced forward. Previtt took a hard grasp on my wrist.

I clenched my fist. Previtt pulled away my thumb first, then my forefinger, then let both go and snagged my pinky finger and, with a swift motion, pushed it backward toward my wrist. I heard and felt it *snap*, then felt pain that was beyond anything I'd ever known. I screamed, unaware for a moment that I was screaming, and the firelight dimmed, though my eyes were wide open. The shock of pain moved through my arm, up my shoulder, and exploded in my head.

"One by one, Davis," Samuels said from a distance. "You've got nine more fingers. You might very well die from the shock. That would be a shame, but I'm betting no one would ever find where you hid the box. If you and Granger are dead, I've done what my bosses wanted, eliminated the threat."

I heard his words, but they were meaningless babble. I stared down at my bent finger as if it was all of me, the only thing that mattered, and knew I couldn't leave it that way.

Somehow, I still had the guts to push it back down in one swift motion.

My mind shut off at the pain. I don't know how much time passed before I opened my eyes. I was on my back, next to the fire.

"That was really something, Davis," Jordan said, grinning down at me. "Your eyes rolled back in your head, and you fell down and started twitching."

My pinky felt as big as the rest of my body, as if everything else attached to the wounded digit was unimportant. I managed to sit up.

"You gonna live?" Samuels asked. "It doesn't have to be like this. If you give me the box, we'll drive away. Do whatever you want after that, it won't matter. We'll be long gone."

Samuels's words, Amanda's box, *my entire life before that moment* was but a small part of my consciousness. All the rest of me was pain—pain that originated in my hand but radiated into every cell of my body. Honor and honesty and loyalty: suddenly those were just words. All that mattered was my body and the pain.

If this one act could so completely eradicate what I thought was me, I knew I couldn't hold out for long.

I opened my mouth, and I'm not sure what I would have blurted, but at that moment, Bigfoot emerged from the house.

Bigfoot held a semi-automatic.

I gaped at him, and the others turned, curious.

Bigfoot strode toward the fire pit.

Even Samuels was unnerved. His mouth dropped open, and I could almost sense him trying to issue orders, but nothing came out.

"Up *contre le mur*, motherfuckers!" and though part of it was in French, I knew—and the other men knew—he'd just said *Up against the wall, motherfuckers!*

Samuels stood in a motion so fast I couldn't quite follow it. One moment he sat beside me; the next moment he was gone, fading into the darkness beyond the firelight.

The spray of gunfire from behind me was deafening, and

Granger jerked with the impact. Bulletproof the costume might be, but it had never been designed to withstand a hail of bullets at this close range.

I scrambled to one side, bumping my broken finger against the stone and shouting in pain. The other mercenaries scuttled into the darkness. Only Jordan and Previtt still faced Bigfoot. Both had emptied their magazines.

In the short lull as they reloaded, Bigfoot raised his own weapon and fired. The bullets whizzed over my head. I looked up to see Previtt's body partially disintegrate. Blood sprayed down on me as what was left of Previtt fell to his knees. He looked at me as if seeing a stranger, then toppled over.

Jordan popped a mag into his rifle, but instead of facing Bigfoot again, he turned and ran.

"Hart!" Bigfoot shouted. "Run, goddammit!"

The massive, hairy shape ran past me into the dark.

I got to my feet and stumbled in the opposite direction.

CHAPTER 15

Samuels crouched in the darkness, waiting for the firefight to continue, until realizing he wasn't facing soldiers—that Granger and Davis had fled into the night and weren't coming back. He stepped carefully into the glow of the campfire, ready to duck away, and stood over Previtt's shattered body, a cold shiver running up and down his spine. Not for the death of his man, but from the realization that he'd made the kind of mistake his employers wouldn't easily forgive.

Moser, the youngest and least cautious, emerged out of the darkness next. "Damn, I never thought I'd see Bigfoot with a machine gun!"

Jordan joined them in the circle of light. "I knew that big guy was trouble," he said. "Previtt unloaded an entire clip into him!" He went over to where Granger had emerged from the house. "There's blood here."

Their voices brought Martinson out of the bunkhouse. The accountant froze on the top step at the sight of Previtt's mangled body. Even in the dim light, Samuels could see he'd gone pale. "Oh, my God," he said. "Oh, my God!"

Burton came out of the darkness next, still looking over his shoulder; and last of all, as Samuels expected, Hanson, who was always the most guarded.

None of them seemed all that broken up about Previtt's death. None of them had liked the man much, though Samuels thought they liked that Previtt was willing to do the dirty work.

"Martinson and Burton, take the 4Runner down to the highway," Samuels ordered. "Make sure they don't flag down a car."

Burton nodded, pulling Martinson away with him.

Samuels looked out into the murk. They'd have to wait until morning to track down Davis and Granger. By the time they got organized, it would be morning anyway.

He wasn't terribly worried. His men knew how to track down an enemy. But this was the kind of mistake that could lose him assignments.

Previtt getting killed, that was one thing. Letting their prey get away was another. Now Davis was out there in the wilderness somewhere.

"I always wanted to be in on a manhunt," Burton said.

"The Most Dangerous Game," Hanson said.

"What?" Burton said, annoyed.

"It's a book. Never mind."

"Fuck you and your books," Burton said.

"It's you who gets the pages sticky," Hanson said mildly.

"Enough," Samuels said. "I want to get back to New York, so let's get this over with."

"You want them alive?" Burton asked.

"No," Samuels said, somewhat surprised at his own answer. Davis must have hidden the box somewhere in this wilderness. Chances were, it would never be found—at least by anyone who knew what it was. Which was what they wanted, after all.

He said, "Kill Davis and Granger and let's get out of here."

"What about Conner and the old cowboy?" Jordan asked. He said it reluctantly, as if he'd be sorry to have to kill the Down kid.

"Kent and Conner aren't witnesses, but keep the two of them close," Samuels said. "It will be our word against Granger and Davis…and they'll be dead."

That and a butt load of cash spread liberally around the county would take care of any lingering doubts.

"Gear up," he said. "We go after them first light."

CHAPTER 16

I ran heedlessly down the road. I could barely make out the path in the light of the half moon. After a hundred yards or so, I stopped and listened for the sound of pursuit. When my rasping breath quieted, I heard the sound of gunfire in the distance.

I sensed that none of the men had followed me, that they were too worried about Granger and his AK-47.

But they'd be coming after me in the morning. I had little doubt these mercenaries could track a human better than I could track a deer.

What a fool I'd been.

All I had were the clothes on my back. That was it. It was only luck I'd laid down on my bed with my coat and shoes still on. Luck for the time being, that is, because in the morning, my red coat would be an easy target. The inside was an unhelpful shade of yellow.

The Jeep and its keys were back at Bigfoot Ranch, my guns and knives in my room, my cellphone under my mattress.

I could keep going until I reached the highway. I gauged it to be about four o'clock in the morning. It would take me a couple hours to reach it. Even if I could flag down a car—doubtful this early and this far out—Samuels and his men could drive down the road from the ranch and get there before me. Or I could loop around, either above or below the ranch, and intersect the highway there, but I'd still be in plain sight.

But the real reason I couldn't leave was because of Granger and the others. I couldn't just abandon them.

To the left a field opened up. Beyond it was the dry bed of Massacre Creek, which meandered down out of the Strawberry

Mountains. At the top of the canyon was a spring that produced water during the spring runoff.

It was there, a few years ago, that I met Granger again, when I accidentally trespassed the borders of his ranch. He gave me his psychedelic-colored business card ("Leaf Ranch," it said and was illustrated with a purple moon surrounded by iridescent red leaves.) We'd been business partners ever since.

He'd be waiting for me there, at the head of the spring. I felt certain of it. I turned off the road and crossed the meadow, knowing I was leaving clear footprints. I descended into the dry creek bed and walked downhill for a time.

Then I turned around and, stepping only on rocks—or hardpan if I couldn't find any—made my way slowly back upstream again. The land here was red clay turned to dust in the heat, and was scattered with rocks that were stained orange. Within the rocky ground were outcroppings of orange basalt, jutting up out of the hillside like the palisades of a castle.

Strawberry Mountain was less than ten thousand feet, but the terrain was much too steep and difficult to climb vertically. The square footage of Bigfoot Ranch was misleading. The trails zigzagged up the slope, five, ten, fifteen times, each traverse another mile or two across. Only the trail up Deadfall Ridge was relatively vertical, and it was a bitch.

It was daylight by the time I scrambled halfway up. I decided I could risk leaving tracks and sped up, still trying to avoid the Central Oregon lava dust but not worrying when I left a print. If my pursuers were close enough to see these tracks, I was probably already in trouble.

The pain in my hand was a dull throb. With each heartbeat, the pain surged as if only my heart stopping would end the agony. Stopping, I took off my coat and flannel shirt. Shivering, I removed my T-shirt.

It was frustratingly difficult to tear the T-shirt. Each time I tried to pull on it, I jiggled my pinky, and it took all my willpower not to cry out. I settled on a low moan, which somehow made me feel better.

I finally managed to start a small rip in the material with my teeth, and from that I was able to tear a broad strip from the bottom. I put what was left of the shirt back on—it was better than nothing—and then replaced my outer clothing.

From the torn T-shirt, I fashioned a sling, pulling my wounded hand up near my right shoulder, above my heart. That seemed to help.

As I neared the top of the canyon, I realized I hadn't heard gunshots for over an hour. I dared to hope Granger and the others had gotten away.

There was a small band of aspen trees surrounding the dry spring. I decided not to hide my approach. If the mercenaries had followed Granger or me this far, it was over anyway. But if Granger lurked within the grove, I didn't want him mistaking me for the enemy.

I heard the caw of a raven, or, at least, what was supposed to sound like a raven, though it was more like a bird being strangled. Granger was inordinately proud of the call, which he sometimes used on hunts.

I answered him, my caw sounding much more convincing to my ears. As if in confirmation, I heard a real raven respond indignantly from a nearby tree.

Granger stepped out from the aspens, still wearing his Bigfoot costume, but with the mask hanging back over his shoulders. He had the biggest grin I'd ever seen, and that was saying something when it came to Granger.

"Hey, buddy," he said in his soft voice. "I figured you'd find me here."

I walked straight up to him and gave him a bear hug, though I had to pull my hand from the sling. I could barely get my arms around him.

He made a grunting sound, and I quickly backed away. Blood covered the front of my coat.

"You're hit?" My words sounded flat with the dread I was feeling.

"Yeah, just a flesh wound, man." Granger shrugged and then winced at the motion. "Unlucky shot hit one of the seams. Most of the Kevlar is in the chest and the back, the rest of the suit has the new-fangled material my friends smuggled out for me. Lighter—but it doesn't completely protect from rifle shots."

"Let me see," I said.

He shook his head, and I knew he was lying about the severity of the wound.

"I can't," he said. "The suit is putting pressure on the wound. Better to leave it be. Come on, let's sit down out of sight."

I followed him into the trees, not bothering to inform him I'd done nothing to hide my footprints over the last couple of miles. If Samuels and his crew did a systematic grid search, they'd come across the tracks sooner or later, but by then I figured we would have reached the Heffinger ranch.

Granger started chuckling. "Arrogant bastards didn't even realize I took one of their guns on the day they arrived."

"Where is it now?" I asked.

Granger's smile vanished, and he waved vaguely back where he'd come from. "I threw it away. Damn thing only had one magazine. The rest of their ammunition was in locked boxes." He shrugged. "Maybe not so arrogant after all."

His smile returned. "But I still have my bowie knife!"

Granger had managed to sew a cloth pocket to the costume along the hip. At first, the pouch had been a dark brown, blending with the black fur, but over the years, it had faded to a tan color. It sometimes made Granger look more like a Wookie than Bigfoot. He pulled out a gleaming knife and flourished it.

The cliché about bringing a knife to a gunfight entered my mind. "Not much use against a semi-auto—scratch that, a full automatic."

Granger was unperturbed. "An old Green Beret buddy of mine once told me, 'If you have a knife, you can get a gun. If you have a gun, you can get a bigger gun.'"

I had a feeling the *old buddy* was, in fact, Granger. He'd seemed more than familiar with the rifle.

I said, "We'd better head down to Heffinger's before they figure out which direction we went."

"What about Kent and Conner?" Granger asked, not budging.

I paused at that, feeling a little ashamed I hadn't gone back for them. I guess I'd figured they'd make their escape once the bullets started flying, since they weren't the targets. But targets or not, I doubted Samuels would leave witnesses.

"The best thing we can do for them is for us to get help," I said.

"Right," Granger said, rising and nearly toppling over. "Then we'd better get going."

I heard shouts below us. They weren't alarmed shouts or those of discovery, but the kind of noise men make to appraise each other of their locations. They must have found Granger's rifle and figured they had nothing to worry about.

"How the hell did they find us so fast?" I wondered aloud. I knew Granger was an even more experienced outdoorsman than me, and I very much doubted he'd leave an obvious trail.

"I, uh, may have left a little bit of a blood trail," Granger muttered, sitting down again. He lowered his head. When he raised it again, he was as white as a sheet, and for a moment I feared he was going to pass out.

"Take off the suit," I demanded.

"I can't," he moaned. "It hurts too much."

"We have to do it, Granger. Hurry. Give me the knife."

As Granger struggled to remove the costume, I took off my coat and shirt, then removed what was left of my T-shirt and cut it into strips. I thought I could fashion a tight bandage that might stop the bleeding long enough for us to reach the safety of the Heffinger ranch.

But not if we were followed.

Underneath the suit, Granger was wearing nothing but a pair of boxer shorts. I almost laughed despite the desperateness of the situation. He was almost as hairy without the suit as he was with it.

"Why did you bother buying a costume?" I asked.

Granger laughed, shaking his head. "Because I'm shy, dammit."

I stared at the wound, barely hearing him, my heart sinking. He'd been shot in the right shoulder, and his right arm hung uselessly at his side. Blood covered his chest, and I wondered how he was still conscious, much less walking.

I felt the throbbing from my broken finger, but suddenly that seemed unimportant by comparison. By pure luck, Samuels had guessed wrong. I was left-handed. I gingerly removed my sling and found that, if I kept the finger unmoving, I could function. I found a small branch, broke it off at the same length as my finger, and tied it tightly to my pinky as a splint.

Then I turned my attention back to Granger, ignoring the sharp, stabbing pain in my pinky.

His chest was pocked with black bruises, which he rubbed gingerly. "The damn misses hurt worse than the hit," he said.

As I finished tying the bandage, it was already soaked with blood.

Granger stood there in his boxers. Hairy or not, he was going to freeze. I took off my coat and handed it to him.

"What are you doing?" he asked.

"I've got an idea. Hurry, put on the coat."

He pulled it on, his big arms filling out the sleeves. It just covered his belly, and he could barely zip it up. But it was better than nothing.

I heard a shout that sounded like it was coming from just beyond the grove. My heart sank. There was no way we were going to get away...unless...

I took a quick look out of the blind of aspens. Below us, about half a mile away, two men crisscrossed the hillside. But they weren't heading straight toward us.

"I managed to cover up the blood the last mile or so," Granger said. "They don't know we're here."

"We might still have time to get away," I said. "At least one of us. You should be able to get to the Heffinger ranch if you leave now."

"What about you?" Granger said, not budging.

I began putting on the Bigfoot costume. It was heavy, not only from the Kevlar lining but also from the blood that soaked it. Droplets sprayed down, darkening the soil of the dry spring. I angled my broken finger into the glove, and the pain was so intense that for a few moments, I blanked out. When I became aware again, I was swaying. Granger reached for me.

"I'm good," I said in a faint voice. Now that the finger was inside the glove, the pain actually began subsiding. Immobilizing it was probably the best thing I could have done.

"I'll lead them away," I said. "If I make my tracks obvious, they might not notice yours. All you have to do is try to stick to the rocks. Can you manage that?"

Granger still didn't move. He had that mulish look on his face as if a client had asked for ketchup to smear on fresh venison.

"Either we both die or we split up," I said. "I have a better chance by leading them away than I do by staying with you."

I could see him thinking it through. He couldn't argue with the logic.

"But it will only work if you get out of sight now," I said.

Granger staggered to his feet and swayed for a few moments.

"Don't go to the sheriff," I said. "He's been bought off."

"Sheriff Black?" Granger said. "Not surprised, but I wasn't planning on going to the authorities."

"These are hardened killers, Granger," I warned.

"Yeah, well, my neighbors aren't exactly the meek type." He took a tentative step, as if testing his footing, then strode toward the far end of the aspen stand. He took one last look back at me, gave a thumbs-up.

Au revoir, old friend.

I started heading the opposite direction. I didn't make it three steps before I stumbled. The costume was huge on me, the shoulders pressing down like weights on my body. My feet felt as if they were inside buckets. I could barely walk, let alone run.

Taking a breath, I stepped out of the aspens and lurched downward the way I'd come, my huge feet obliterating the tracks I'd made getting there. It wasn't long before I understood why Granger had made such a convincing Bigfoot. The costume forced me to clomp around in an awkward way. There was Kevlar in the suit's torso, but around the thighs and shins, and around the biceps and forearms, there was something lighter, more flexible. Even though there were cloth hinges at the ankles, knees, elbows, and shoulders, I still felt like Frankenstein's monster lurching down the trail.

Eventually, I fell into a rhythm that seemed to work, leaving giant footprints. I was suddenly glad to be wearing the costume.

With any luck, the mercenaries would believe they were still following Granger.

I looked behind me and saw droplets of bright-red blood, and the sight of it spurred me on. Granger needed a head start. There was a good chance he'd make it if blood loss didn't kill him first.

I didn't hold out much hope for myself, with or without a bulletproof Bigfoot costume.

CHAPTER 17

Halfway down the dry Massacre Creek, near the same spot where I'd stopped trying to hide my tracks, I realized my blunder.

I was walking into a trap.

If I succeeded in drawing away the two men chasing Granger, then they were behind me and probably gaining on me. It was likely that other trackers had followed my original trail and were heading toward me from that direction. My guess was that at least a couple of men were assigned to that job. And if Samuels was smart—and I didn't have much doubt about that—he'd hold back a couple of men to watch the road and the house.

The Bigfoot suit got heavier with every step. It was hard to see how it could get much worse. Immediately upon thinking that, I grabbed a broken branch from the ground and snapped it in two. Knock wood.

Too late. I felt something cool and wet strike my cheek.

The forecast for the week had been mild fall weather, highs in the fifties and lows at night in the mid-thirties. There had been some dark clouds on the horizon the evening before, but I hadn't thought much of it. I figured they'd most likely blow over before morning.

I looked up into skies that appeared mostly blue, but that didn't mean much in these parts. I'd seen rainstorms appear out of apparently clear skies before. Another drop hit me squarely in the eye, removing all doubt.

Good. A rainstorm will wash away my tracks.

I turned left, away from the dry canyon, picking my way

carefully so that even the huge footprints of the Bigfoot costume wouldn't leave a trace. I reasoned that from here, it should be fairly easy to lose my trackers, especially if it did start raining hard.

It was slow going, but if I could get far enough away from the creek bed, I could jettison the suit and loop back toward the Heffinger ranch.

The rain started pouring down, and I urged it on. The water trickled down my neck and started filling the suit, my feet sloshing. I looked for a place to hide it.

The first snowflake landed as I approached a dead juniper with thick branches. I realized it was starting to get cold. It would be bad enough if the temperatures plummeted, but if I was soaking wet too, I was in real trouble. It wouldn't take long for hypothermia to set in.

Thick, fluffy flakes swirled down around me, quickly accumulating on the ground. A snowstorm in early October, just my luck.

I sat at the base of a tall pine, watched one of my deep footprints, and estimated that the snow was thick enough to capture my tracks, but not to cover them. While the rain might wash away my footprints, the snow would highlight them.

I was shivering already, and as much as I wanted to be free of the Bigfoot costume, I realized that without it, I would be even more exposed.

I pulled the mask on and pondered the situation. With the suit sealed, I could feel myself warming up, slowly but surely.

Would my trackers continue on in this weather?

Of course they would. These guys had probably spent winters in the mountains of Afghanistan. They could bundle up and keep on going. They could start campfires. They could spell each other.

I heard footsteps behind me. Someone whistled a Beatles tune.

The mask's eyeholes were an inch too high for me to see out of. I pushed down on the top of the mask to align them properly and surveyed my surroundings through the narrow slits.

I noticed tennis shoes first, and then blue jeans, and suddenly I was certain it wasn't one of my pursuers.

Without thinking, I jumped up and moved away from the tree.

An older man stared at me from a dozen yards away, his mouth open in shock. He wore a brown, wide-brimmed hat with chinstraps, white hair, and a long goatee. He wore a light coat, carried a backpack, and was holding a long walking stick.

He let out a primal scream, not high and shrill, but deep and warning, as if confronting a nightmare he could disperse with sound. Only then did it occur to me that what the poor guy had seen was a giant, hairy creature pop out onto the trail in front of him.

"Wait!" I shouted, my voice muffled by the costume. Even to my own ears, it sounded like a growl. I reached up, desperately looking for the zipper on the mask, but my fingers were clumsy with pain, and all I did was wrench the mask around until I couldn't see.

I heard a high scream and footsteps pounding away. I stumbled after the man shouting. "Wait! It's a costume! I'm not Bigfoot!"

I finally wrestled the mask off. Just as the hiker seemed as if he was going to leave me in his dust, he tripped. Instead of landing on his face, he managed to roll. I was impressed.

I caught up to him and stood over him. He looked up at me as if expecting fangs and claws to rip him to shreds. Instead, all he saw was a weather-beaten human face.

"What the...?" he asked. He got up and, to my surprise, got right in my face.

"So it's all a scam," he said. "I fucking knew it."

I was offended, though the accusation was ridiculous. "This is private property," I said. "You aren't even supposed to be here."

"I paid for it," he said. "Nelson Wilderness Excursions."

"That's the next ranch over," I said. Actually, now that I'd said it, I wasn't so sure. We might very well be within the bounds of the Heffinger property. "You need to go back," I finished, a little less forcefully.

"I sure as hell am," the guy said. "And I'm going to demand a refund. You thought I'd fall for this?"

I didn't point out that, until I'd removed the mask, he had in fact fallen for it. Despite the danger, I was annoyed. This was the kind of client I dreaded, and I felt sorry for Nicole.

"Are you saying Nicole *promised* you a sighting of Bigfoot?" I asked.

"No," he admitted, "in fact, she told me it was all nonsense. But she took my money anyway."

"Well, it's not like you were going to find Bigfoot by whistling 'Sgt. Pepper,'" I said.

He looked down and brushed the dust off. "I know that," he said. "I was just out for a walk. It's not like I haven't been in the wilderness before."

It was getting dark. I'd been intent on getting this guy out of here, but now I realized there wasn't time. The men hunting me would probably shoot anything that moved.

"You need to come with me," I said. "We need to find cover."

"Like hell. I'm not going anywhere with you. I'm like half an hour from the ranch."

"People are trying to kill me," I said without thinking. "They might mistake you for me."

The guy looked at me with a different kind of fear than before. This was the fear of the crazy. "That's all right," he said, moderating his tone as if he was afraid he was going to trigger me. "I'll just head on back."

"Wait," I said.

I grabbed for him, but he pulled away. He ran, and I knew I couldn't catch up. Within a few hundred feet, all that was left of the hiker were his tracks and there, abandoned on the ground, his walking stick. I leaned over and picked it up, then swooshed it through the air a couple of times. It was made of hardwood and had some heft.

I looked down at the man's tracks, which were obvious, but even as I watched, they blurred. In a few minutes, they would be no different from the tracks I'd left getting to this spot.

To my left was a rock outcropping, which the snow rapidly was melting off of. I jumped as far as I could toward it, landing in the mud at its base. I climbed onto the rock, reached down with my Bigfoot gloves, smoothing the footprints away. From there, I climbed as best I could along the rocks and repeated the process.

It was slow going, but within a few minutes, I'd made steady progress. The big tree I'd sat under was out of sight. The snow had stopped falling, but it wasn't melting either. I found a crevice in the rocks and hunched down into it, resealing the mask, hoping it would be enough to warm me up.

Gunshots sent me sprawling deeper into the crevice. It sounded like the flurry of shots from only a few yards away.

They weren't shooting at me.

I didn't poke my head up, but I found myself praying the innocent, if annoying, hiker was safe. The silence continued. It was now so dark that I could only see a few feet.

I pulled out the bowie knife from the Bigfoot pocket and tried to cut into the end of the walking stick. The knife slid right off. Trying again, I pressed down harder on the blade, doubting Granger would tolerate a dull knife. Though the wood was dense, the blade took a bite. Once I had a start, the rest of the shavings came off easier. I started carving a point, the activity calming me down. Anything was preferable to just sitting there waiting for them to find me.

As I whittled, it got darker and darker until I could no longer see what I was doing. I clutched the stick in my arms and leaned back, closing my eyes. I felt almost warm, the blanket of snow on the faux Bigfoot fur insulating me.

A strange noise woke me.

I sensed rather than heard the presence of something above me. I reached up slowly and unzipped the mask. With the cloud cover, it was too dark to see anything. I held my breath, waiting for the sound that woke me to repeat itself.

It was completely silent, and slowly, I began to breathe again, wondering if it had been a dream.

The cloud cover drew back for a moment, letting the light of the half moon silhouette the animal crouched above my head. The mountain lion's head was down, its back slung low, and its tail whipped from side to side as if it was still trying to ascertain where or what I was.

I rose to my feet, spear in hand, and shouted a guttural cry. It was pure instinct, but it seemed to work. The creature's tail switched back and forth a few more times and it stood up, but after a couple of moments of hesitation, it turned and slunk off.

I shouted again, trying to reproduce the primitive noise I'd made upon rising to my feet.

It seemed to me that in the distance, another cry answered me. It was louder, deeper, and there was an otherworldly sound to it. I held my breath and waited for it to come again, but the world remained dark and silent.

I sat back down, cradling the spear, telling myself it had been an echo.

But I didn't fall asleep again.

CHAPTER 18

Amanda called Hart three times after cleaning up the mess she'd made of her visitors. They'd bled all over the new rug, which sucked. Then again the new rug was perfect for dragging them into the backyard, where she dug a shallow grave under the turned-over boat Hart used for fishing.

She didn't leave a message for Hart. You could never be sure who was going to listen to a recording. Then she remembered that Granger didn't allow cellphones because he was paranoid, almost as paranoid as she was, though as far as she could tell, without any reason. But then, no one believed her either.

She grabbed her overnight bag and headed out to her Mustang. But somewhere between the door of the house and the car, she changed her mind about her destination. There would be no end of hired guns going after Hart and his precious box. Besides, he knew the wilderness better than her. He'd be able to lose them.

Better to find out who was behind it and resolve it with them instead.

She sat in the driver's seat, still within reach of the house's Wi-Fi, and looked up the Airolo Corporation. The nearest office was in Portland.

Three hours later, Amanda was in Portland and crossing St. John's Bridge. When she got to the Airolo offices, she found they were surprisingly modest, which only made her more suspicious. In her experience, outside of New York real estate tycoon politicians, most real wealth tried not to call attention to itself, especially if there was something shady about where all that wealth came from.

Amanda sat in the car trying to decide her approach. She knew Sherm Russo worked for Airolo Corp. and that he had information they wanted—and were willing to kill for—but that was about all she knew. Normally she would have researched it more and contacted some of her old friends, but Hart was in the Strawberry Mountains with stone-cold killers and she needed them called off.

A direct approach was usually best.

Stop bothering my husband or I'll kill you.

There was a beefy man at the desk, a security guy posing as an office assistant. He watched Amanda appreciatively as she approached. His nametag said, Joseph Turow.

"Hey, there any jobs here, Joe?" she asked casually.

"You have to kill to get a job here," he said.

Oh, you have no idea. "Can I talk to your boss?"

"Sure…if you can tell me who *that* is."

"You don't know?"

"Well, I report to Barry Anderson, but I doubt you'd want to talk to him. Who Barry reports to, you'll have to ask him."

"Where is he?"

She could see him resisting the urge to look over his shoulder. She brushed past him and headed for the door behind the desk.

"Miss?" the guy said. "Come back here, please." Despite the "please" there was no politeness in the demand.

Amanda turned. He was pointing a Taser at her. She dropped her smile. "You aren't being paid enough for this, Joseph. Go home, forget you ever worked here."

For a moment he looked like he was considering it. Then again, he probably *had* killed to be there.

She dove aside as he pulled the trigger, and she heard the two prongs fly over her head with a buzz. She rolled, kicked out, and slammed her foot into the guard's right knee, which bent backward at an unnatural angle. He screamed and dropped sideways to the floor, his head hitting the desk with a fatal-sounding *thud*. She examined the desk and found a pistol in a cubbyhole near the chair.

Amanda turned toward the door. It began to open. A trim, bald man came out, gun in hand but down by his side. He stopped cold, his eyes narrowing at the sight of the man on the floor, whose head floated in a pool of blood. He started to raise his pistol. Amanda shook her head and pointed her weapon between his eyes. That always got their attention. He let the gun drop.

She leaned down, pulled the keys from the guard's pocket, and backed up to the front door. She locked it without taking her eyes off of Barry Anderson. "Who's your boss, Barry?" she asked.

He hesitated. She let him see her fingers tighten on the gun. "Janet Montgomery."

"Who does she report to?" Amanda asked, knowing that in this kind of organization, a woman wouldn't be the ultimate authority.

"You really don't know what you're taking on here, do you?" Barry asked. He seemed offended that she was so stupid that the reputation of his bosses hadn't kept him safe.

"No. Why don't you tell me," she cooed.

He shook his head. "It's *all* of them, lady. They're all under one umbrella now. We're all one big happy Family. Money from Russia, muscle from the Balkans, brains from…well, that's the only thing I don't know. Who's at the top."

"Family," she said slowly, enunciating each syllable. "If you're Family tell me who your capo is."

"Peter Samuels. It's no secret. You can look it up on the company masthead. Head of Security."

"What about Sherman Russo?"

Amanda saw the knowledge pass behind his eyes.

"Who?"

She lifted the Taser from the floor and examined it. There were two more prongs in it. She shot them into Barry's midriff. He tried to fight it, standing for a moment, then with a yell of pain and frustration, he dropped to the floor, writhing.

"Fuck!" he said, when he could speak again. He got on his hands and knees. "I've told you everything."

"Not about Russo. What do you know about him?"

"Nothing, only that they want him and he might be headed this way."

"You mentioned a masthead with Samuels' name on it. You got something with that?"

"In the drawer, lady. It's our orientation pamphlet." He glanced at the dead man. "You killed Joe on his third day."

"Good thing for you," she said. "He wasn't very good at his job. Are you good at your job, Barry?"

He stared into her eyes and seemed to sense that the answer was important. "I like to think so," he said.

"And your bosses can keep thinking it, if they're told Joe's death was an accident. Nothing happened here that you have to report."

He nodded. "I suppose not. No harm done…except to Joe."

"So I won't have to come back?"

"No," he said. "You were never here. I don't know who the hell you are anyway."

Amanda turned to leave, but kept an eye on Barry in case he decided to make a move. She figured there was a fifty/fifty chance he'd go for his weapon. Instead, he shot off his mouth.

"You psycho bitch!" he yelled as she unlocked the door. "You didn't learn anything that you couldn't have found out in five minutes of Googling."

She turned back around, and Barry saw the anger in her eyes. He lunged for his gun and she shot him twice in the head.

Just as well, she thought. *He wasn't very good at his job either.*

As she drove back to Bend over the Santiam Pass, Amanda wondered whether to keep going on to John Day. Sherm Russo was on his way west, that was clear.

Should I wait for him?

Amanda wasn't sure why she'd done that favor for Russo all those years ago. She'd barely known him. She'd been loaned out to the Family, since they were helping out the Agency in a situation overseas. She hadn't minded. It was better than sitting around waiting for the gutless president at the time to decide to take action. They'd been in a couple of gunfights together. He was a good but unimaginative soldier at the time.

And there was that time…

She blushed at the memory. The first and only time someone

had gotten the drop on her, Russo had come to her rescue. The big guy had never said anything about it, but they both knew it was why he'd thought he could ask a favor of her.

Turns out, Russo wasn't just a thug. He was damned smart. By the time she was ready to disappear, he was in a different line of business.

"I'm an accountant now," he said.

"An accountant..." she said, looking up and down his stolid body. He looked like a fireplug.

"Yep, but for the same bosses. Which is why I'm here. I've got to have insurance. These new guys, they're nothing like you remember. You're lucky you're getting out."

Now, it appeared that instead of getting out, she'd dragged an innocent man into her world.

When Hart had driven away, unaware of the box in the back of the Jeep, he'd smiled at her. She'd treated him like shit and still he smiled.

Stupid, stupid, stupid.

It was her fault he was in trouble. She stepped on the accelerator, pushing her old Mustang to its limit.

CHAPTER 19

The snow melted in the morning sun, leaving the soil muddy and soft. My feet sank an inch into the mud with every step; there was no way to hide my trail. The sky was bright blue, and the sun was beating down. But I knew the weather could change without a moment's notice.

The damned suit weighed me down. I thought about shedding the costume and trying a route over the rocks and through the bushes, but I couldn't be certain I wouldn't need its fur again. I hadn't eaten for over a day. The water I'd drunk from a depression in the rock had been filled with grit. No matter how much I spit, I couldn't completely get the taste out of my mouth.

The snowfall of the night before, along with the plunging temperatures, unnerved me. It was possible that it had been an anomaly, but it was equally possible that winter was starting early. The fur of the costume, the very thickness that had so bothered me in the daytime, had probably saved me from freezing to death.

I realized that my pinky no longer hurt. I tried to wiggle it inside the glove, but it didn't seem to want to move. I reached over with my left hand and touched it.

Numb. That can't be good.

It was too much trouble to take off the costume to check on it. In a way, I was relieved at the lack of feeling, though the thought of losing my finger, perhaps even my hand, scared the hell out of me.

Since I couldn't hide my tracks, I decided to simply go where I knew the trackers had already gone. Chances were they wouldn't retrace their steps, but would seek new ground to search.

I should try to get out of the search zone as fast as possible. Six men could cover a helluva lot of territory. I could try to reach one of the nearby ranches, nearby being relative, for all of them were hours, even days away on rough trails.

Or I could try for the highway.

If I hitched a ride out of the area, I could at least seek help. I doubted Samuels would give up on the search, but I'd much rather face him in my own territory back in Bend, armed and fortified with allies.

The hiker I'd scared had followed a winding deer path down through the foothills. His footprints were overlain by the tracks of two other men. They headed downhill, toward the highway. I tried to stay silent, but I also took long strides. The sooner I reached the road, the better.

I noticed an odd shape in the path as I came around a dark boulder. Sprawled on his back across the trail, his empty eyes staring up into the morning sun, the hiker lay sprawled across the trail, his head slightly downhill, stuck to a drying pool of blood. The astonished look in his face would follow him to the morgue and probably to his grave.

I'd never seen a dead man before. Oh, Previtt had died just a few feet from me, but that hadn't seemed real. The mercenary's body had barely hit the ground before I was running.

But this was death without the cover of darkness, stark and still. The man's skin was stretched across his cheeks as if already shrinking. His eyes were cloudy as if under a film of rancid milk. He had the "uncanny valley" effect of looking like a human, but seeming more like a broken mannequin.

I stood over him, and the apology spilled from my lips. "I'm sorry. I'm so, so sorry. Oh, my God, I'm so sorry this happened."

With effort, I stopped the outpouring of remorse. It wasn't doing him any good or making me feel any better. Tears came to my eyes. I'd only seen the man alive for a few minutes, and he'd been superficially annoying, and yet now it was as if I knew him: a doting grandfather with a plump, white-haired wife waiting at home, a man who'd spent his life working in a store and retired to Eastern Oregon so he could go hiking in the woods.

Dead because of me.

The shame that infused me was overpowering, and again I started to apologize out loud. None of this would have happened if I'd just given up the box in the first place, or if I'd turned down the money for the hunt, a subtle bribe. If I'd done either of those things this man wouldn't be dead, and Granger wouldn't be wounded, perhaps even dead himself.

Suddenly, concern for anything else, for the box or for my own safety, disappeared. I needed to know that Granger had reached the Heffinger ranch and that he was out of danger.

"I'm sorry, whoever you are," I said, dropping to my knees and searching the dead man's pockets and backpack. There was nothing. The killers had taken everything. I thought about taking his blood-drenched coat, but I couldn't bear to touch the dead man's body.

I stood up. A couple of shadows passed over me, and I looked up to see several ravens circling far overhead. I knew I couldn't leave this man exposed to the world.

It took me a good hour to cover him with rocks. I didn't think the barrier would be completely effective against scavengers, nor would it last long but it might help. I looked around for a landmark so I could find the place again. On a nearby hill, I saw a single large pine tree with the top sheared off.

It would have to do.

I turned and headed uphill again, no longer trying for the highway. If I didn't stop along the way, I could reach the Heffinger ranch by noon. Once there, I'd throw myself on the mercy of the local authorities. Sheriff Black might be corrupt, but I didn't think he'd shoot me.

I saw the flickering red and blue lights before I reached the bluff that overlooked the Heffinger spread. The urge to run toward the lights was overwhelming. Instead, I forced myself to slow down as I reached the crest of the bluff. I got on my hands and knees and looked over the edge.

An EMT van was parked in front of the old three-story ranch

house, along with a police cruiser. The despair I'd felt moments before lifted. In a few minutes it would all be over. I'd hand over the box and let the powers that be deal with it.

It would be Granger's and my word against those of six strangers, who no doubt had highly suspicious backgrounds. I was pretty sure I knew how a local jury would decide, if it ever went that far. As least, I hoped so. The people of John Day might not like me much, but I didn't think they'd convict an innocent man.

I stood up, looking down at the hillside, searching for a path down through the rocks. Below, I heard people laughing. The door of the house opened, and a wheeled stretcher bounced down the steps, a woman in an EMT uniform at one end and another EMT at the other.

Granger lay unconscious, a bright white bandage with a spot of blood on his shoulder, an IV hooked into his arm. Something metal flashed on his wrist, and I realized he was handcuffed to the gurney.

That made me pause; just long enough for the door to open a second time. Sheriff Black came out, followed by my competition in the outdoor wilderness guide business, Nicole Nelson.

I crouched down again and reconsidered.

When Nicole had first started up Nelson Wilderness Excursions, I'd gone out on a "date" with her. The date—a meeting, really—had been her idea. I could tell she was trying to size me up. She'd recently set up her base at the Heffinger ranch.

Running a guide business was a sideline for me, but it had always been in Nicole's future. Her father was a legendary character in these parts. Cameron Nelson had been a firefighter, a sheriff, a rancher, and finally an outdoor guide who had more or less written the book on Eastern Oregon. (His *Eastern Oregon Habitats* was sold in every local bookstore.)

I remember watching a locally produced TV show that featured Nicole following her father around. She'd been about sixteen years old then, a smaller version of her adult self, with the same blonde pigtails and rugged clothing. She was short, with clear blue eyes, a little bit chubby, and as far as I could tell, almost always cheerful—in other words, the exact opposite of my ex-wife in every way.

I met her at a pizza parlor in Bend. "Thanks for coming," I said.

"I had to," she said. She had to climb the rungs to sit on the tall stool opposite me. "I was curious to meet the man everyone hates so much."

"Oh," I said, "not everyone." My eyelid twitched a little, and I was suddenly at a loss for words. I resisted tapping my finger.

"Don't worry." She smiled brightly. "I just want to hear your side of the story."

I hesitated. My past wasn't something I talked about much. Then something about the open look on her face emboldened me.

As I told her what had happened, it occurred to me I hadn't told anyone about it in years. My wife had become bored halfway through the story and said, "So they're jerks," and that was that.

"I grew up in John Day," I began. "In the late 1980s my father went into business selling solar panels. It was pretty lucrative at first. John Day has lots of days of sunshine."

Nicole snorted. "Yeah, three hundred and fifty days of sunshine, according to the local Chamber of Commerce."

I nodded and continued. "I began to hope that my father was finally growing up. Yeah, I know how strange that sounds. I was in high school. Mom had left a few years before, and I thought maybe the shock of it had finally gotten to him.

"I remember even being proud of him. He paid his crew high commissions. I worked for him for a couple of summers, going from house to house, business to business. Turned out I was pretty good at selling things. I bought a new car and new clothes. For the first time in my life, I was popular, though I didn't realize it was because I was spending money on my new friends.

"But then I began to notice that other than that first year, my father didn't seem in a hurry to install the solar panels. 'The more contracts I get, the cheaper it will be,' he explained to me.

"You can probably guess the rest. We started getting

complaining phone calls, which my father fielded, and he was so convincing in his explanations for the delays that even I believed him, and I knew his past better than anyone.

"Despite my doubts, I kept selling contracts. By then, I'd gotten used to the money."

I broke off from the memory and found Nicole listening intently.

"You wouldn't have liked me back then," I said.

"Who says I like you now?" She laughed at my expression. "Don't worry, I don't dislike you either. I'm still trying to make up my mind."

"My father disappeared a day before the police knocked on the door. How he knew they were coming, I never discovered. We'd sold far more contracts than I'd realized. It was almost enough to bring down the local economy. Several people were sent into bankruptcy."

I paused and looked her in the eye. "I suppose you know about old man Heffinger's son, Sam?"

She nodded.

"He spent all his families' money investing with my father. He was so ashamed that he tried to rob a grocery store. Idiotic, because everyone in town knew who he was, mask or no mask. To make an example of him, the district attorney asked for the maximum penalty. He's still in prison."

"Ernie hates your guts with a passion," Nicole said.

"It didn't help that all charges against me were dropped. I truly didn't *know* what was happening, but I suspected. I tried to make up for it. I sold my car; I gave up what little money I had. Our house had more than one mortgage and was underwater. Eventually, I went off to the University of Oregon, and then moved to Bend.

"But you couldn't stay away," Nicole said.

"I didn't really have any choice. When I started selling outdoor tours, the place I knew best was my old stomping grounds. I just sort of stay away from John Day as much as possible."

Nicole glanced around, looking worried.

"What's wrong?"

"I just realized. I shouldn't be seen with you."

I stared at her in surprise. She winked at me. I think I fell a little bit in love with her at that moment.

"What about Granger?" she asked.

"He was my best friend in high school. After graduation, he went into the military. It wasn't until years later that we hooked up again. He offered to let me use his property.

"To this day, we've never talked about his time in the military."

"A true friend," Nicole said. "You're both weird enough to deserve each other."

I laughed.

She squinted at me, cocked her head to one side. It was so cute that I wanted to reach out and pat her cheek. "You know, Ernie gets an anonymous check every month. You've been paying them back all this time, haven't you, Hart? That's why you're always short of money."

I couldn't meet her eyes. I had decided a long time ago that a penance that everyone knew about wasn't a penance at all. It would probably take my entire lifetime to pay everyone back, but I was going to try.

By the time we left the pizza parlor, Nicole was friendly, and not just in a surface way. I think she liked me.

I kissed her good night, but we never went out again. I never asked her. It would have felt weird to, because she was my competition. And to be honest, Nicole scared me a little. She was a little too sharp for me.

But she always seemed happy to see me.

Now, I decided it was probably a good thing she was here as a witness to my surrender.

I rose to my full height, intending to call out and wave my arms. The doors to the house opened again, and old man Heffinger stepped out, his cane clanking against the screen as it closed. Beside him was a trim man whose blond hair flashed in the afternoon sun.

The two men turned to each other and shook hands.

I dropped to my belly, breathing hard, closing my eyes in frustration. I'd come so close to clearing it all up.

I could still stand up and surrender.

But I suspected that Samuels wouldn't hesitate to kill all the witnesses if it meant he got what he wanted. Sheriff Black and Nicole, the EMTs, old man Heffinger, and even Granger, unconscious though he was.

What if I yelled a warning?

I doubted Black would understand or react instantly, but I had little doubt that Samuels would.

I ducked behind some bitterbrush and poked my head over the bluff again. Samuels surveyed the hill, and it was as if I could sense his penetrating blue eyes pinning me down, though I thought it was unlikely he could see me, any more than I could actually see the blue of his eyes.

Samuels turned to the sheriff and slapped him on the back, laughing.

I ducked down again. If old man Heffinger, who had no love of government, especially the police, was willing to give up Granger, what chance did I have with any of the other ranchers?

The box and I were on our own again.

Somehow, I had to use the box to expose what was happening.

I just had to hope that whatever was in it was important enough to save us.

CHAPTER 20

I found my way back to the main path and hurried down it, my resolve slowly growing.

I wouldn't give Samuels the box, no matter what. It was a true test. There wasn't much chance I could defeat these hardened killers, but I could expose them, if I could stay alive long enough.

I swung the walking stick through the air, wondering if it would work as a weapon.

Halfway down, a creeping sensation ran down my back as if someone had centered a scope there, and once that feeling came over me, I couldn't shake it. I wondered if I'd feel it when the bullet entered me, wondered whether I'd hear the shot.

I was covered by a bulletproof costume, but that didn't make me feel safe. My head was exposed, and I suspected that by now, my trackers had figured out the costume's unusual attributes and that none of them would have any trouble hitting their target.

Never before had I been so aware of my body and its vulnerability. I veered to one side of the trail, under the cover of a big juniper tree, trying to shake the feeling off. The suit was stifling and sweat ran down my arms and legs. I didn't dare take it off. I would need it again in the night, and it was too unwieldy to carry. I hadn't had anything to drink since that morning. All the moisture from the snowfall was gone, with not so much as a tablespoonful in the rock depressions.

The walking stick in my hands seemed pathetically inadequate. I threw it like a spear at a tree. It spun lazily in the air, striking the target sideways. I picked it up again. It was better than nothing.

I summoned the images of Granger handcuffed to the gurney and of the hiker lying sprawled on the trail, and my determination slowly returned—at least, enough for me to move again. But now I stayed in the shadows of the trees, moving stealthily from cover to cover. It wasn't that different being the hunted than being the hunter, I realized. It required staying out of sight, being silent, going unnoticed. No difference at all.

Except for the fear.

I finally reached the borders of the Granger ranch, which was surrounded by meadows and pasture. If I stuck to the path from here on, I'd be completely exposed. To my left was Massacre Creek. Very little runoff flowed down this far, even during floods, so the channel wasn't that deep. But I figured if I crouched down, I should be able to stay out of sight.

I scooted across the pasture and descended into the ravine, which headed due north and eventually reached the highway. It was also parallel to the road that led to the Granger ranch so I could watch out for pursuit from that direction.

I would hide by the side of the highway and spring out when I saw a vehicle. Bigfoot would thumb a ride.

Crouching low, staying near the bank, I reached the first barbed wire fence and eyed it. It was half falling down, but was still too tall to climb over. There was no way to crawl under it. I'd have to hold the strands apart as best I could and slip between them.

As I'd feared would happen, I was halfway through the maneuver when I felt myself caught by a barb. I paused there for a second, trying to figure out how bad it was. I'd torn more than one hunting coat doing this, and this costume was far bulkier.

No amount of maneuvering disentangled me, so I finally forced myself through the fence, feeling and hearing the fur on the costume tearing.

I rubbed my shoulder. There was a bald spot there, and I could feel the shiny surface of the Kevlar. Two of the barbed prongs had tufts of black hair stuck to them, and I reached over with my clumsy gloved hands and tried to remove them. But no matter how hard I pulled, a few black hairs remained.

I buried the handful of fur under a rock and kept going.

The second fence was a little easier to get through, and I managed not to tear the suit further. At the last fence, there was a stump close enough so that I could climb onto it and jump over.

I landed harder on the other side than I expected, feeling dust and twigs grinding into the costume when I rolled. I had a feeling that I was going to regret the added wear and tear. But I was close enough to the highway that I started to get my hopes up.

It wouldn't be long now.

A familiar engine whine rose up behind me. I crouched down—realizing as I did that I'd been walking upright, though the ravine that was shallower than ever—and scrambled to the bank. I peered over the edge.

My old Jeep barreled down the road, past one fence and then another. Clearly, the gates weren't closed.

Granger won't like that. Then I realized how ridiculous that was. Escaping livestock was the least of our worries. The Jeep approached the first cattle guard and didn't even slow down. Burton drove, wearing his camouflage hat, a big cigar in his mouth, as if he didn't have a thing to worry about. I could hear my CD of Bruce Springsteen's "Born to Run" blasting away, rattling the speakers.

The Jeep rattled across the metal barrier, swaying slightly to one side, and then it was gone around the corner.

If that son of a bitch blows out my speakers...

You'd think that being threatened, tortured, and hunted, that seeing my best friend shot and an innocent man murdered, would have brought me to peak anger. But seeing my poor old Jeep abused was what really pissed me off. Sometimes it seemed I spent as much time in my Jeep as I did in my own home. It burned me to no end that that yahoo Burton treated it like it was a piece of shit. Which no doubt it was, but it was *my* piece of shit.

I looked down the remainder of the dry canyon to where it met the highway and realized it would no longer provide enough cover. Nor was it a good idea to be so near the entrance to the ranch. Obviously, Burton patrolled the nearby roads.

Crossing the channel, I climbed up the narrow bank and jogged toward a stand of junipers. Once there, I made my way west, parallel to the highway, close enough to see the pavement but not so close I could be seen.

I worked my way down one canyon and up another until I was pretty sure I was far enough away from the road to Bigfoot Ranch not to be seen.

A ditch ran along the highway, blocked by a rock that had fallen from the cliff on the other side of the road and rolled across it.

I crawled to the back of the rock, pulling out some old sagebrush along the way, and created a crude blind. Then I sat back, listening for the sound of traffic.

A half hour went by, and then an hour.

My heart sank. This part of Grant County was sparsely populated, but not so much so that a car didn't come by every few minutes or so, at least during the late afternoon.

Something was wrong.

I closed my eyes, wondering if I was just unlucky.

The mask hung down my back, like a pillow. I just wanted to rest.

My eyes popped open, thinking I heard a car.

I laughed, suddenly realizing it might not be a good idea for Bigfoot to jump out onto the road. And yet, I was reluctant to take the costume off. It had become part of me, a lucky talisman.

The SUV was nearly past me before I heard it. I almost jumped up, but at the last second, I poked my head out instead.

It was a white sheriff's vehicle, traveling slowly, almost coasting, which was why I hadn't heard it. Sheriff Black swiveled his head from one side of the road to the other, and I was lucky enough to see him before he saw me.

I hadn't been surprised when Samuels told me Don Black was corrupt. Of all my tormentors in my last year in school, he'd been the worst.

He would need no convincing that I'd murdered someone.

The sheriff's car continued down the highway. It became hauntingly silent again. Another half an hour went by without a car passing by, and it was then I knew: the highway was barricaded on both ends.

What were they saying about me? That I was some kind of murderous desperado? Did they have orders to shoot first and ask questions later?

I stood up, wondering what to do. Looking into the ditch alongside the road, I saw that the boulder I'd been hiding behind had trapped some of the previous night's snowfall, the shadow protecting the water throughout the day. I slid down the bank and grabbed a handful of snow. I hadn't realized how dry my mouth was until it nearly squirted saliva in anticipation. A painful ache radiated along my jaw..

Below the snow was a muddy puddle, and I crouched down and sucked it up, trying to filter out the sand and dirt. I retched at the taste, but managed to keep it down. A little road oil and some insects were mixed into the liquid, but I knew I had no choice but to drink it.

The way was clear for me to cross the road and head north, except for a high cliff too steep to climb that ran along the highway for miles in either direction. Even if I managed to surmount the cliff, there was no purpose to it. There were no dwellings, no roads, and most importantly, no water for many miles.

It was only now, when I had three different directions open to me, that I realized how boxed in I was. In theory, I could avoid the ranch, but to the north were the cliffs and desert, and to the east, the cliffs continued, along with Henderson Gorge, which was nearly impassible. Even if I managed to cross both barriers, the next water was another twenty miles of rough terrain away. I didn't think I'd make it.

The way west was alluring. It was much more populated, with busy roads. But if the alarm was out, I was pretty sure it wouldn't take long before I was spotted and reported. I didn't think many of the citizens of John Day would take my side. They'd believe the worst.

Samuels had apparently done his research. The trap was neatly closed.

Which left only one direction to go where I knew there was both water and a chance to get out of Grant County. To the south, from which I'd just escaped.

Above Bigfoot Ranch, at the summit of Deadfall Ridge, was the old Forest Service road, which looped around and approached Canyon City, directly to the south of John Day. As close as the two small towns were, the residents of the smaller town didn't consider the John Day folks to be their neighbors, but their rivals. Over the years, I'd made friends there who could care less about my father's swindling in John Day.

They might smuggle me out.

What's more, I knew there were several springs along the way. Years ago, I'd followed the Forest Service road in my Jeep, but decided halfway over that the road was too rough to risk.

I also knew it wasn't on any maps so Samuels wouldn't know about it. All I needed to do was get to the summit of Deadfall Ridge through the gauntlet of Samuels and his men.

That's all.

CHAPTER 21

I turned around yet again. It was as if I was in a cage and everywhere I turned, there were bars.

If I'd headed straight for Canyon City in the first place, I might have gotten there by now. But of course, that would have left Granger easy to track. In the end, it'd been pointless, but I hadn't known that at the time.

I'd lingered too long in the area, thinking all I needed to do was get to the highway. Now I had to find a way to climb the foothills without being spotted, locate the old road, which the Forest Service purposely obscured, and survive the long trek to Canyon City.

Once again, I felt completely exposed, though I stuck close to the dry canyon's banks. The trackers would eventually figure out where I was hiding so the ravine wouldn't remain a safe place for much longer. It was midafternoon. I thought I might stand a good chance if I hid out somewhere and waited for nightfall.

The ravine passed near the fence where I'd hidden the box. I decided to risk a quick look. I crawled over the side of the embankment, crouching down low in the sagebrush, and made my way as close as I dared.

The hiding place was undisturbed, as far as I could tell. Rocks and twigs covered the spot. Above it, I could see the small red shotgun shell I'd attached to the fence. The cattle guard was just a little beyond it.

I began to turn away, but something flashed in the corner of my eye, and I turned in time to see a chipmunk's fluffy tail disappearing between the rails of the cattle grate.

Before the idea was fully formed, I was up and walking toward the fence. The grate's rails were far apart, difficult to walk across. I'd noticed that the hole beneath was deep, almost a yard down. It was full of rocks and leaves and sludge. The maintenance crews must need to open the grate occasionally to clear it out.

I could hear the Jeep in the distance returning, and decided to take the chance.

Reaching down tentatively, I pulled on the grate. It didn't budge an inch, and I hadn't really expected it to. I examined how it was attached. Two of the corners had metal hinges, which I'd never noticed before. If there were hinges, it meant the grate could be lifted.

I quickly surveyed the other side. The latches were rusted, but when I smashed down on them with the butt of the walking stick, they came loose.

Once again, I tried to lift the grate. It shifted a few centimeters to the side, but I couldn't get it higher than an inch or so—whether it was because it was stuck or because it was too heavy, I couldn't tell.

Shoving the sharpened end of the stick into the gap, I rolled a rock under it, and tried to pry it farther open. The stick, as hard as it was, bent alarmingly. Then there was a small *crack* and the wood shivered in my hand. The grate popped up a couple of inches just as the end of the stick broke off.

With my gloved hands I grabbed the grate and lifted. It came up as if greased, and I heaved it as hard as I could. It flopped to the side of the road. I teetered for a couple of moments on the edge of the hole, flailing my arms, then managed to fall back.

The startled eyes of a chipmunk looked up at me. It leaped out of the hole, its flicking tail disappeared into the sagebrush.

I should follow his example.

I crawled to the nearest bushes and lay down. It wouldn't do to be too far away when it happened.

The familiar refrains of "Jungle Land" reached me first, and then the high whine of the Jeep. It sounded as if Burton was still in first gear, as if he didn't know he should shift to a higher gear. Or didn't care.

He came flying around the corner, the back end of the Jeep
swiping at the nearby bushes, and barreled toward the guard.
I had a moment to regret what was about to happen to my old
Jeep.

The Jeep went flying. I held my breath. It looked as if the
Jeep's momentum would carry it across the gap. Then the Jeep
dipped, and the front tires slammed into the far side of the
hole. The vehicle stopped so abruptly that my eyes kept going
forward to where my brain expected the Jeep to be.

It smashed into the trap with a loud crash. The windshield
popped out, and the top of the steaming engine poked through
the hood. The engine whined for a few seconds more, then froze
with a loud screech. The sound sent shivers down my back. The
silence was broken by steam rising from the engine block.

I scrambled to my feet, wondering if I had enough time
before Burton recovered.

Burton watched me approach with a strange look on his
face. He didn't reach for his weapon. He didn't pop the door
and get out. I slowed as I came closer, uncertain what was going
on.

He was pinioned against the seat, the steering wheel
penetrating so far into his chest that he looked as if he'd been
pinched in half. He coughed blood as I reached the broken
window. His bloodshot eyes blurrily tried to fix on me.

I looked inside the car and saw the Springsteen CD shattered
on the dashboard. The rifle was on the floor. The scope had
broken off and was lying on the seat.

I went around to the passenger's side and pulled on the
door. It felt warm, and I suddenly realized I could smell both
gas and smoke. The fuel line had ruptured, spraying the inside
of the Jeep with gas, and Burton's cigar had ignited it.

I wrenched the door open and reached through the smoke
for the rifle. Burton's feet suddenly kicked out, hitting the rifle
and shoving it into the flames at the base of the steering wheel.

I tried to unfasten Burton's seat belt so I could pull him out.
He slammed his fist into my arm.

"Fuck you, asshole," he coughed. Then he grunted, and the
grunt turned into a low scream as the fire caught his pants and

raced up to his chest. His hair flared and his face blackened, and the scream grew louder.

I grabbed the broken scope and ran. Behind me, the ammunition in the rifle exploded.

It sounded like a war.

CHAPTER 22

Utterly stunned that I'd killed a man, I was back at the hiker's makeshift grave before I came to my senses, reawakening to the dangers around me. Burton's screams had scraped my mind clear of anything but pure, unreasoning panic.

The most I'd expected was that Burton would be stunned long enough for me to get the drop on him. I'd forgotten how old the Jeep was, and that it didn't have airbags, and I'd completely underestimated the damage it would cause.

But as the panic faded, I found a savage joy rising within me, an atavistic response to combat. Until that moment, I'd expected to be killed at any time, and there hadn't been a thing I could do about it. They were out to kill me.

Got one of the bastards!

The euphoric feeling faded almost instantly. With two of Samuels' thugs out of action, I reconsidered my options. I knew these woods. The mercenaries were in my territory. But I wasn't sure I had it in me to kill them deliberately, even in self-defense.

But it wasn't only about me anymore; there was Conner and Kent to think about. I knew that if it came down to it, I'd do what I had to do to protect them.

I moved into the shelter of a large, broken juniper and became aware of the weight in my hand. I'd grabbed the scope from the Jeep's front seat by instinct. It was oddly shaped, like no scope I'd ever seen, thicker and with a wider lens. I looked into it, and it seemed normal enough, but there were extra knobs on it, and one of them was labeled "N.V."

Night vision. My enemies were equipped with night vision scopes. Not only wouldn't I be able to slip by them in the darkness of night, it would actually make it easier for them to hunt me.

I still had the walking stick. The tip was broken, but I could sharpen it again. I continued hiking upward, reaching the rock crevice where I'd spent the previous night. The moment I saw the shelter, I realized it was pure luck I was still alive. The rock shelter had kept me out of sight.

The hiker hadn't been so lucky.

The sun faded below the mountains to the west. With reluctance, I squeezed my way into the cleft. I'd have to lay low for one more night. In the morning, I'd make a run for it.

The sandy soil was flattened where I'd slept the night before. Tufts of Bigfoot fur still littered the ground. As I sat, my stomach growled, and kept growling, as if it wasn't going to shut up until I ate something.

My nervous energy dissipated, and my body filled with a thick lethargy. It was as if I was waking up from surgery, my limbs numbed by drugs, my mind struggling to shake off the stupor. I was thirsty, hungry, tired, and sore.

But I was still alive.

I lay there for a few minutes, looking up at the darkening skies. I wondered if the cougar would return, and if it did, whether it would be so easily scared away this time. I leaned the walking stick against the rocks, took out the bowie knife, and held it in my hand. It seemed such a meager weapon.

It wasn't going to be dark for another hour, and I realized that I couldn't just wait. I needed to do something, anything. I climbed to the top of the lava outcropping, carrying the scope, and examined the hillside above me. The magnification was startling.

In almost any other part of the Strawberry Mountains, I could have hidden in the thick stands of trees, though hunger and the elements would eventually have driven me out. But Granger's father had logged the hillsides above the ranch. Instead of innumerable tree-covered hills and glens, there were three prominent hills with a clear view of the surrounding territory. As long as Samuels posted guards on the hillsides, I was trapped.

Did they know I was still in the area? How did they know I hadn't escaped?

But of course, they'd know about Burton. They'd know the cattle grate hadn't been flipped by itself. They were probably communicating by walkie-talkie. In time, they might tighten the cordon, but it wasn't necessary. All they had to do was wait me out while I became hungrier and thirstier.

Despite the loss of two of their comrades, they were still overconfident. They made no effort to conceal themselves. I was unarmed and they had the upper hand.

The mercenaries were positioned at the highest points above the ranch, arrayed in such a way that between them, they could see everything below. To the east of Butcher's Cut was Hanson, his fancy rifle in his lap. He raised binoculars lazily and swept the terrain, and I almost ducked down when he appeared to look directly at me. But I realized that in the dwindling light, the Bigfoot costume blended in with the rocks I was perched on. As long as I didn't move, I was safe.

At the western edge, Moser stood still, nearly blending with the trees behind him, directly below the Massacre Creek wellspring where'd I'd met Granger the morning before. It was fortunate I spotted him.

I swept the scope due south to the center hill, and as I expected, Jordan was there, pacing impatiently. There were two horses on the flat ridge beside him, and I could see Kent's scrawny frame as he quieted the animals. Apparently, Jordan's laziness about climbing hills had overcome his dislike of horses. Kent wouldn't have gone along willingly, I realized with a sinking heart. For one thing, he wouldn't have voluntarily exposed his animals to the steep, rocky terrain.

Until then, I'd hoped Kent and Conner had gotten away. Kent being in plain sight was a clear warning. And if Kent was still under their control, what about Conner? Did I have any right to endanger them?

For a moment, I felt a strange sense of relief. The decision was out of my hands. I would have to surrender to save them. Then the realization hit me. They were probably only alive because I was still free. I doubted that Samuels would have any compunction about killing them once they were no longer useful.

The mercenaries wore full camouflage gear, heavy coats, and hats, prepared to spend a long, cold night waiting for me. The rifles they carried weren't bolt-action .30-06s, but semiautomatics, except for Hanson, who still carried his sniper rifle.

They had all escape routes covered. Meanwhile, I didn't doubt Samuels and Martinson, along with the sheriff and all his deputies, were below me. There was no way to get past them, day or night.

For the next half an hour, I swiveled from watcher to watcher, but their vigilance never wavered. Kent finally quieted the horses and sat down on the rocks, his head bowed, the top of his battered white hat showing.

I activated the night vision of the scope and a green glow around the lens began to fill the edges, not quite turning into clear vision, but it was a warning for me to get out of sight. I slid back into my hiding spot and tried to ignore my protesting stomach and the dryness in my mouth and throat. I'd slept very little the night before. I expected to sleep even less tonight.

I felt something scrabbling on my cheek and brushed it off. A big tick landed on its back in my lap, struggling to regain its footing in the thick fur.

I shuddered. God only knew how many ticks I had on me. The suit was probably infested with them, because I was hiding in the same types of places that deer hid in, and for the same reasons.

After that, it was difficult to even close my eyes. In my imagination, every little itch was an insect burrowing into my skin. I shook myself, the costume sliding over my body, hoping to dislodge the little bastards.

Eventually, despite everything, I fell asleep.

I woke to full darkness.

It wasn't the first bite that woke me, or even the second. I could feel the after-stings all over my shoulders. I yelped despite myself and instinctively slapped at the outside of the suit, feeling the insects drop away. I stood, reaching for the zipper behind my back, and then hesitated.

I felt a bite on my forehead and, as I brushed my hands over my face and hair, more insects dropped away, but through my panic, I felt bites under the suit.

I'd fallen asleep with the scope still clutched in my hand. I put it to my eyes and looked down.

Roiling, illuminated insects covered the costume, squirming over each other to reach my bare skin. I brushed them away frantically, killing some; others clung to the fur with their mandibles. I started to calm down. It was almost reassuring to realize they were common red ants.

I scoped the surroundings, and my calmness evaporated. Ants were pouring out of the crevices between the lava rocks, summoned to battle the giant intruder.

I couldn't stay here.

A few ant bites were discomforting, but there was enough venom here to kill me if I let them swarm me. On the other hand, if I left the shelter of the rocks, I'd be exposed to the night vision scopes of my enemy.

There really wasn't any choice. A bullet to the head and it would be over quickly at least. At that moment, waiting to be stung to death by ants was the worst nightmare I could imagine.

I crawled out of the shelter, wondering if I should run or try to hide in the shadows. There were rock formations all along the slope. I just needed to find one big enough to hide in.

I felt a slight whiffle of air near my neck, then the report of a rifle. I started running before I could think about what to do next. I barely dodged a tree in the darkness and stumbled over a fallen branch. I lifted the scope and could make out some of the terrain, enough to get by.

My arm flew out from my side, and the scope went spinning away. The impact of the bullet spun me completely around, and I fell backward, my head striking soft soil, thankfully. For a moment, the pain was so bad that I was sure I'd been wounded.

I lay there stunned, then, with a surge of fear, I moved. A puff of dust rose where the next bullet hit, exactly where my head had been. Then I was on my feet, dodging in the dark, hoping I wouldn't go off a cliff. I felt something fly off my shoulder and realized that a bullet had torn off some of the fur along the seam there.

It was only a matter of time before one of the bullets struck a weak spot or my bare head. I tripped and rolled, and it probably saved my life, for another whizzing sound energized me again. I ran blindly in the darkness.

The ground dropped out from under me. I closed my eyes, waiting for impact, but to my surprise, I only fell a few feet before landing on soft sand. Then I tumbled down a slope, landing on my face on something wet and squishy.

I turned onto my back, disoriented. Above me, the quarter moon was shining through a round hole; then a cloud passed over the moon, and I was in complete darkness.

Something brushed against my face, and then something else, and I heard faint squeaking sounds and rustling. A dark fear overcame me, and I took a gasping breath and exhaled.

The bats were harmless. I was safe inside the womb of the Earth itself.

Covered in bat guano.

CHAPTER 23

I may have felt safe in the darkness of the mine, but I knew I was anything but. With their night vision, the mercenaries would have watched me drop out of sight and known that I'd gone to ground (if not underground.) The only question was: would they try to track me down in the dark or wait until morning?

Either way, I was trapped. The moment I showed myself, they'd have me in their sights. I stood and climbed up the little sand dune under the cave entrance. My hands barely reached the rocky rim. I thought I'd probably be able to pull myself up. The walking stick lay extended into the opening above, and I reached up and pulled it down. Somehow, amid all the panic, I had managed to keep hold of it.

If bringing a knife to a gunfight was a joke, I wondered what bringing a stick meant. Still, it made me feel slightly safer, even with the sharpened end broken off.

The sky became lighter outside. Probably false dawn, but true dawn would soon follow. I'd needed to decide what I was going to do soon.

Yet, I stood paralyzed with indecision as the sky became brighter and brighter. I stepped down a couple of paces to let the light come through the hole.

Something struck my left calf, and I almost reached down to see what it was. The snake's rattle warned me off at the last second. A huge rattler was attached to the fur of the costume, and venom squirted out against the Kevlar beneath. To the right of the pile of sand, I saw squirming, and I realized that I'd fallen into a nest of rattlers.

In the light, I could see the rattler twitching back and forth, wrapping and unwrapping itself around my leg. I closed my eyes and forced myself to breathe deeply, fighting the gibbering fear rising up my body. My right hand, numb pinky extended, held the walking stick, and I instinctively started to swing it, then held back at the last moment.

I was in a bulletproof suit, and if it was bulletproof, it had to be snakeproof. Right?

Carefully, I reached down with my gloved hands. I wasn't sure the fabric around the fingers, which were free of Kevlar for easy movement, would withstand a strike. The snake was intent on sinking its fangs into my leg, however, and I managed to take hold of it by the back of the head. I pulled it away and up toward my face, the venom running down my arm.

The snake didn't need venom. The look of hate in its eyes was almost enough to paralyze me.

"I don't blame you," I muttered. I'd invaded its home. The snake was thrashing frantically, almost pulling out of my hands.

Then it quieted for a moment, and I wondered if it had heard my words or my tone, but of course, it was just tired, resting before redoubling its efforts. I could grab it by the tail and dash it against the rocky walls of the cave.

"What am I going to do with you?" I asked aloud.

The other snakes left the nest, wriggling toward me, struggling for traction on the sandy slope. I *thought* I was safe, but I had a sudden image of a dozen fangs seeking defects in the Kevlar. The toe and ankle area had seams to allow movement.

I prepared myself to drop the snake and leap for the cave entrance. It was fully light outside now. I was lucky, the mercenaries having apparently decided to wait for morning, secure in the knowledge I had nowhere to run. But it was probably only a matter of minutes before they arrived.

I heard loud shouts from outside the cave. My pursuers made no effort to be quiet. They had semiautomatic rifles. There was nothing I could do to fight them. I doubted they'd find my hiding place right away, perhaps never, because they'd only know within a radius of a quarter mile where I'd disappeared. I'd hunted this hillside for years and hadn't known this mine entrance existed.

A breeze lifted my hair. I realized it wasn't coming from the opening above me, but from below. It was a strong breeze, not the kind of airflow that would come from cracks in the rocks, but from a larger opening.

I examined the chamber I was in. It was about ten feet wide and twenty feet deep. I stepped over the wriggling snakes, still holding the biggest one, and made my way to the back of the cave. As I got closer, I could barely make out a chest-high opening to the left.

But it didn't matter. I couldn't stay. If the snakes didn't get me, the lack of water would.

I lifted the rattlesnake and looked it in the eyes. "Don't follow me," I said, willing it to understand. Then I tossed it across the chamber onto the sand dune. I had just enough time to see the other rattlers swarming before I ducked into the darkness.

I was able to scramble about twenty feet, the walking stick over my head, before the stick clattered against the roof. It sent a shock down my hand, and my pinky started throbbing. The pain was reassuring. It meant the finger still had some circulation and the nerves weren't dead yet.

I got on my hands and knees and kept going. I expected my hands to land on a snake's dry skin, or to hear a rattle in front of me, but it was as quiet as a tomb. I doubted there were snakes this far in, or that the snakes I'd disturbed would follow. I'd probably interrupted them as they were settling into winter hibernation.

The walking stick kept catching on the rocks, and I resisted the urge to abandon it. It was like a talisman to me now, if I lost it, I would be diminished.

The breeze got stronger. The morning winds in this part of the Strawberry Mountains usually came from the east, which was the direction I sensed I was headed, though without markers, it was only a feeling, but like my sense of time, my sense of direction was usually reliable.

The passage became narrower and narrower with every few yards, but I managed to squeeze through without getting hung up. If I caused a rock fall, I'd be stuck here forever.

After a few hundred feet, the mine opened up again, and as

I stepped on solid rock, I heard echoes. It was pitch black, but I sensed that the chamber was huge. The Chinese miners had cut into a natural cave, it appeared.

I kept to the wall, following it until my hands met empty space, except for a strong draft against my palms.

To my surprise, moisture ran down my face. The cave was cool, but I didn't think it contained enough humidity to feel it. Then I realized the water was coming from above, trickling down the sides of the cave. The lava terrain above was porous, soaking up the rain. But it had to have been raining hard for the water to already reach these depths.

Outside I suspected it was just warm enough to be rain, not snow. Or the snow was rapidly melting. I wondered what I'd find outside, if I ever made it out.

I licked the moisture off my hands, and my tongue soaked up the droplets like a sponge. I reached out and cupped my hand, palm upward, against the wall, felt the water fill it, and brought it to my mouth, again and again.

The water was enough to keep me going. I ducked into the new passage and held my stick in front of me, suddenly aware that not only could the roof come down to block the passage, but the earth could fall away beneath me. But the passage was straight for a time, cut by human hands, as if I walked down a hallway.

At first, the illumination appeared to be something manufactured by my own light-starved eyes, but the pinprick of brightness grew until it was dazzling. I crawled the last few yards, almost afraid to know where I was.

I cautiously poked my head out of the narrow opening.

I'd come out on the sharp cliffs on the western side of Butcher's Cut near the bottom of the gorge, a short distance above jagged rocks.

On the other side of the cut, the eastern slope beckoned.

CHAPTER 24

Samuels' phone rang near the peak of Strawberry Mountain. Amazed that he had reception, he answered without checking to see who it was. But then, it could only be one of a very select number of people, none of whom he wanted to keep waiting.

"Barton Crane wants to meet you face to face," Kuznetsov said.

"He also wants me to catch this guy, doesn't he?" Samuels answered. "I can't leave here."

"He wants both, he wants everything," Kuznetsov said. "But you have your men in place, do you not? Your target will not get away?"

The Russian always sounded so casual, but Samuels wasn't fooled. It was a dangerous question, for which there could be only one answer. "Of course he won't get away," Samuels said, and he believed it.

It was surprising Davis had evaded capture for two days now, but Samuels was certain that the man was still contained on Bigfoot ranch or close by.

Samuels hadn't tried to hide the escape to his bosses.

"What were you thinking?" Kuznetsov had asked.

"I was thinking my men needed a vacation."

He'd held his breath, wondering if he'd done the right thing reporting it. But he also knew if bosses had found out about the escape some other way he'd have been in even bigger trouble. Samuels was good at his job, despite this setback, and the situation called for backup. Though the new administration wasn't yet in power, favors were called in, the Deep State responded in a reliably Pavolvian way to reports of "terrorism."

A tight ring of police and federal agents surrounded the area. Hart Davis was now the "Strawberry Mountain Killer," whose political motives for killing three innocent tourists were being slowly revealed by fake news planted throughout social media. The mass media had picked up on it, and in response, the police from every surrounding county had showed up to help. If Davis somehow managed to be captured outside the immediate area, he would be transported to the Grant County jail, where an accident could be arranged.

But Samuels had so far managed to keep Bigfoot Ranch under his authority. It was so much easier to take care of problems when there weren't any witnesses. Somewhere below him in the little valleys that ran between the mountains, Hart Davis had gone to ground. But he must be cold and hungry and tired and scared, and that made him easy prey. His men would take care of it.

"Where does Mr. Crane want to meet me?" Samuels asked.

"He'll be in Portland this evening, giving a speech," Kuznetsov said. "The media is quite puzzled by it. The two senators in Oregon have already announced that they will vote against him, but Crane is pretending it was a previously scheduled event. He'll meet you in his private jet at the airport."

"Does he realize how far I have to go?" Samuels said. "It's a six hour drive from here!"

"You and I know about the Western U.S.A," Kuznetsov said, "but the Right Honorable Barton Crane neither knows or cares. I grew up in the gulag, my friend, which makes even your great high desert look small."

Samuels could almost see the Russian leaning back in his chair, his feet on the desk, looking up at his photograph of Monument Valley.

He heard the squeak of the chair as Kuznetsov leaned forward, suddenly serious. "You can pick up Popov and his men at the same time. They'll be waiting."

"I've got this," Samuels said. "I don't need help."

"You've lost, what, two men? Seems to me that you very much need help. Besides, Popov is wasted chasing Russo. The guy is in the wind, somewhere between Kansas and Oregon. He's obviously heading your way because the package Mr. Davis has is important. Find it, or take out everyone who knows about it, one or the other."

"Yes, sir," Samuels said. Davis taking out Burton in the Jeep had been a big surprise. Maybe it wouldn't be so bad to have a few more men. He'd worked with Popov before; the man took instructions.

"I still think it's a waste of time to drive all the way to Portland," he said.

"Burton thinks he can get his way by bullying everyone. Easier to bully someone in person than over the phone."

"But he isn't the boss, is he?"

"Boss?" Kuznetsov didn't laugh like Samuels expected. "Crane is not the boss but he thinks he's the boss and our boss wants him to think he's the boss so he's the boss, understand?"

"Yes, sir. I'd better get going. I'm on top of a damn mountain."

"I envy you," the Russian said. "I really must check out this Bigfoot Ranch when I get the chance. Maybe I'll buy it. I assume it will need a new owner soon…"

CHAPTER 25

Sherm Russo knew he was in trouble when he saw the sign that said, "Next gas, 90 miles."

The Buick sputtered to a stop at the side of a road in the middle of a vast, dry plain. Brown rocks and dirt with sparse underbrush and a few scattered trees were all that was visible. Sherm had exited I-80 a few hundred miles back, leaving behind the endless fields of corn, preferring country roads. There wasn't a building in sight.

He sat clutching the steering wheel, feeling numb. He was out of gas and money and ideas. All he had left was the clothing he wore.

I've got my revolver, he thought, but immediately rejected the idea. He wouldn't rob anyone. He'd been honest for twenty years now, aside from a few accounting tricks. He'd never had an appetite for violence, and any crime he committed with a gun could turn violent.

I'm never going to make it to Oregon in time. All I've done is put Amanda's life in danger.

No other cars came by in the ten minutes he sat there. It was dusk. He climbed over into the back seat and closed his eyes. He'd think of something in the morning. His stomach rumbled from hunger.

It may come down to begging or crime, and I'm not sure which is worse.

A truck rumbling by woke him the next morning. The sun was barely over the horizon. It was surprisingly chilly.

Begging it is, he thought.

He stood by the road and waited for the next car to come by, expecting to be ignored. The last time he'd hitchhiked had been with friends, so long ago that it seemed like an innocent scene from a movie, and they'd begged him to get out of sight because his presence was so intimidating.

To his surprise, a young woman pulled up in a battered pickup. She was a heavy-boned blonde girl in jeans and a cowboy hat. He started toward the pickup bed in back, but she leaned over and pushed open the passenger door. "Get in, if you're heading to Cheyenne."

He climbed in and muttered, "Thank you."

"You're welcome," she said. She didn't add *old man*, but she might as well have. "I can take you to the nearest gas station, but I've got to get to work, so I can't bring you back here."

"Actually, if you'll drive me all the way into Cheyenne, I've got a friend there who can help me."

"No problem," she said. "I've been stuck out here myself a couple of times. This old pickup eats gas like a son of a bitch. I swear, I'd save enough money at the pump to pay for a new car, if I only had the down payment."

"What's your name?" Sherm asked.

"Hayley," she said.

"Your last name?"

For the first time, she looked a little worried. His bigness hadn't scared her, but his attempt at familiarity was starting to.

"Hayley Hawkins," she said reluctantly.

"Hayley Hawkins of Cheyenne," Sherm repeated, filing it away amid all the other names and addresses he'd memorized.

They made small talk the rest of the way to Cheyenne.

"Where do you want to be dropped off?" she asked as they passed the city limits sign.

"You ever heard of the Rumpus Bar and Grill?"

She glanced over at him curiously. "I guess you're tough enough to handle it," she said cryptically. They drove down Capitol Avenue, passing by modern office buildings as well as old downtown Western facades.

Hayley turned left before they reached the capitol building. They bounced over some railroad tracks and into a neighborhood that looked almost deserted. But on one corner was a large building lit up with neon, with crowds of people outside.

"A lot more popular than I remember," Sherm muttered.

"But just as rough," Hayley said. "If you don't mind, I'm going to drop you off here on the corner and head back. I can't get stuck in traffic. My shift starts in ten minutes."

"Thank you, Hayley. I wish I had some gas money to give you, but I'm all tapped out."

"No problem," she said cheerfully. "I hope your friend can help you."

Haley Hawkins of Cheyenne, Wyoming. When this was all over, if he survived, she'd get an anonymous cashier's check in the mail, enough money to buy the most fuel-efficient car she wanted. Assuming, that is, that he ever got access to his safety deposit box.

Sherm slowed as he neared the old bar. He remembered the Rumpus as rundown and full of old drunks day and night. Now he watched a young couple enter, though it was barely noon. They eyed him curiously but didn't seem to think he was out of place.

In fact, the man at the entrance looked a whole lot like a younger version of Sherman Russo.

The guy tensed, narrowing his eyes, sizing up Sherm. Then he relaxed, apparently deciding the newcomer was too old to be a threat. But that didn't mean Sherm couldn't be important. Wiseguys who were still in the business at his age almost always were.

"I'm looking for Don Andriotti," Sherm said.

"Mr. Andriotti passed away a couple of nights ago," the bouncer said. He must have seen Sherm's look of surprise, because he added, "In his sleep."

Sherm shook his head. It was one hell of a coincidence. The new Supreme Court nominee, Barton Crane, had gotten his start as a mob lawyer in Chicago under Don Andriotti's patronage before moving on to New York and joining one of the high-powered firms there. Could it be that Don Andriotti had known too much?

If they were willing to take out a Don to protect that information, they'd do just about anything. Then again, it *could* be a coincidence. The old man had to have been at least ninety years old.

Sherm tried to remember who the underboss was. "Is Max Marino here?"

"Yes, sir, in his office. I'm going to need to pat you down."

Sherm held up his hand, then removed his Colt and handed it over. The bouncer took it and then gave Sherm a quick search.

"Go on in, sir," he said finally. "I'll hold your weapon for you until you're ready to leave."

Some kind of music Sherm had never heard before nearly blasted him backward when he opened the door. He forced his way through the wall of drum sounds to the bar in back. He leaned over to the bartender.

"I'm looking for Max," he shouted.

"Who?"

"Max Marino!"

"Oh, Mr. Marino!" the bartender nodded, as if he'd never heard his boss's first name before. "Who do I say is here?"

Sherm hesitated, looking around. In the old Rumpus Bar, he probably would have withheld his name, but everyone in sight looked like they were barely out of high school. They wouldn't know him.

"Sherman Russo," he said.

The bartender picked up his phone and spoke into it. After a couple of seconds, he motioned Sherm toward the door at the side of the bar.

Sherm stood there for a few minutes, waiting. Time enough for Max to make a few calls.

The door finally opened, and there stood his old partner, looking twenty years younger with his tailored suit and immaculately groomed hair. Max closed the office door behind them, cutting off the sound from the front.

"I can't stand that noise," Max said. He turned and gave Sherm a hug. "What's going on, pal? Word is out about you. In fact, you've probably made trouble for me just by showing up. I mean, what am I supposed to do, turn you in?"

He laughed, but Sherm wasn't reassured. The old Max wouldn't have thought twice about turning in his own mother if it benefited him. He doubted the new Max was any better.

So why is he pretending?

Doesn't matter as long as I get enough money to get out of here.

"Doesn't concern you, Max," he said, not even pretending to be friendly. "I need a thousand bucks and a car that can't be traced."

Max sat down behind his desk, which was a modern sculpture of glass and metal bricks. He motioned for Sherm to sit down opposite him.

Damn. He's trying to delay me.

"I wondered about you when I heard Barton Crane had been nominated to the Supreme Court," Max said. "Suddenly, all that stuff we know about good old Bart is dangerous. Don Andriotti was on his deathbed already, so he was safe enough. And as for me, my memory sucks and everyone knows it. I was just a dumb foot soldier when that all went down. But you had to be the genius who figured out how to save our people all that money."

He wants to reminisce about old times?

"Just give me the thousand bucks, Max," Sherm said. Then he invoked the words that he could only hope Max would honor. "You *owe* me."

Long ago, Don Andriotti's young wife had taken a shine to one of her husband's bodyguards. Sherm had lied for Max more than once to protect his adulterous ass. By the code they had once lived by, Max couldn't deny him a reasonable request.

Max sighed and reached into his pocket. He pulled out a thick bankroll. He hefted it a couple of times in the air, as if weighing it. "My guess is...nine hundred and twenty-five bucks." He tossed it to Sherm. "What do you think?"

Despite himself, Sherm mimicked Max's motion, feeling the weight of the money. "Nine hundred twenty," he guessed.

"Oh, right!" Max said, looking delighted. "I got some coffee on my way to work." He reached into the coat that was draped over his chair, pulled out a keychain, and separated out an electronic key. "You can take my car."

Sherm got up immediately, wondering if he'd misjudged his old comrade in arms. Max came around the desk and gave him another hug. "We even, pal?" he asked.

Sherm nodded. He went out the front door, collecting his gun from the bouncer. He checked to make sure it was still loaded. In the back parking lot, he pushed the button on the key, and a brand-new Cadillac Escalade chirped. The car was immaculate: not a grain of dust, not a candy wrapper, nothing of a personal nature. The glove box contained the owner's manual, the registration, a box of tissues, and an insurance form. That was it.

It was also worth seventy times the money in Sherm's pocket.

No way Max will let me get away.

The thousand dollars? It was just barely possible that Max would let go of that much money to cancel an old debt, but a new car? And the no doubt sizeable reward for Sherm's head? It was extremely doubtful.

Still, Sherm saw no sign of pursuit on the way out of Cheyenne. An hour later, he passed through Laramie and started to breathe easier.

As bad as the old days had been, there had once been understandable rules. Sure, the rules had been broken as often as they were followed, but they had existed, and sometimes there were consequences.

It wasn't until Sherm slowed down for the last traffic light in Laramie that he saw the other Escalade following him.

Damn. They've probably been tracking me from the moment I left the Rumpus Bar.

He slowed down suddenly. The tail crept up on him inadvertently, coming into closer view. Max was behind the wheel, accompanied by at least three men.

Sherm had known Max when they'd both been at the bottom. While Sherm had worked his way up the ranks by using his brains, Max had used his driving skills. He'd been the personal driver for the consigliore, and then for old man Andriotti and his wife. It had always been a joke to most of the other wise guys that the Don ran the Midwest operations out of such an out-of-the-way place. But there was no arguing with success. Andriotti was one of the few old Dons who hadn't ended up in jail.

No doubt the Rumpus Bar had been Max's reward.

Just outside of Laramie, I-80 passed by the small town of Elk Mountain, with its namesake peak looming behind it. Sherm shot down the exit, drove quickly through the scenic little hamlet, and turned off at the first road that promised to go upward toward the mountains.

There was no way he could win a gunfight with four armed men, especially since all he had was a revolver. But he could still try to lose them.

As the pavement turned to gravel, Max zoomed up behind him as if admitting that there was no point in hiding anymore. No matter how fast Sherm went he couldn't shake Max. The gravel turned to dirt and the road narrowed even more, it got steeper, and the bottom of the Escalade bounced off rocks. Sherm envisioned oil and gas flowing out of ruptured tanks, but Max would be having the same problems. Maybe Sherm would get lucky.

Max roared up on him suddenly, striking the right rear side of Sherm's car, and he felt himself sliding sideways toward the steep cliff that opened to one side. He managed to control the skid, then stomped on the accelerator.

Surprised that Sherm had survived, his pursuer fell behind for a couple of moments. Sherm came around a sharp corner and slammed on the brakes. The dust still flying in his face, he leapt out of the car, revolver in hand.

Max came around the corner at full speed. The soldier in the passenger seat had propped his rifle out the window, resting it on the side mirror. When he saw Sherm, he fired a panicked spray of bullets.

Sherm fired a single shot. He couldn't tell where the bullet hit, but Max's car jerked toward the embankment on one side of the road. Despite his skills, Max overcorrected, and the Escalade shot back across the road. Bullets from the AK-47 whizzed over Sherm's head. He felt the shock of something striking him in the shoulder but managed to stay on his feet.

The Escalade slid past within inches of Sherm, who stood unmoving, his revolver still extended. He saw the white faces of the two men in back and the hunched-over shape of Max desperately trying to gain control, and then the car was gone.

Sherm closed his eyes and held his breath. He didn't count, but he thought it was at least three seconds before he heard the crash.

The pain started to hit him, at first a dull warning and then a searing agony as if someone had taken a screwdriver and slammed it into his shoulder. His left arm wouldn't respond. He holstered his revolver, reached up with his free hand, and touched the wound. Strangely, despite the pain, he couldn't feel the touch. His hand came away drenched in blood.

He stumbled over to the open door of his car and sat down heavily. Gingerly taking off his coat, he reached into the glove compartment, wadded up half the box of tissue, pressed it against the wound and held it there. He could feel it having an effect. When the blood slowed, he put his coat back on. The makeshift bandage seemed to stay in place.

It took Sherm an hour to climb down to the wreckage. Whenever he pushed his body too hard, he felt more blood soaking the bandage. Halfway down the slope, blood started dripping down his arm again.

He sat on a rock above the wreck, revolver in hand.

One of the men in the back seat was still alive and groaning, and there was such fear in his eyes that Sherm looked away. A few minutes later, the groaning man fell silent. The other two passengers had been ejected, their bodies broken on the hillside.

In the front seat, Max's head had been obliterated by the crash, but his body looked almost untouched. Sherm reached gingerly into the dead man's pocket and pulled out his wallet. Max's driver's license showed a beefy, white-haired old man. *Close enough*, Sherm thought. To most people, they would probably look the same.

He looked for Max's gun, but it must have spun away in the crash. The Escalade's shattered remains covered the hillside. Sherm realized he didn't have the time or the strength to crawl around looking for weapons.

He slowly climbed back up to his own vehicle, trying not to put stress on the wound. The bandage was completely soaked by now. When he got to the car, he grabbed another wad of tissue and pushed it against the wound, holding it against the flow, feeling himself almost losing consciousness.

Salt Lake City is five hours away, he told himself. Despite his own desires, he'd intended to bypass the city and drive straight to Bend. But there was no way he was going to make it to Oregon without help.

Gina...

Will she slam the door in my face? Will she call the police?

It might be worth it just to see her again.

He started the car and turned the wheel with his good arm. The road was so narrow, he almost couldn't get turned around, at one point nearly slipping over the edge of the cliff himself, but eventually, he got the car pointed downhill.

At the base of the mountain, he stopped, finally letting what had happened wash over him. It wasn't fear or anger that overcame him, but sadness. Max had been one of his last friends from the old days. He probably hadn't had any choice but to pursue Sherm. Their bosses would have expected it.

Max had never had a chance at another kind of life. He hadn't been as lucky as Sherm, taken off the streets and allowed to live an everyday life without the need to be constantly armed and vigilant.

Sherm stopped at the one grocery store in Elk Mountain, pressed his hand against the wound, and got out of the car. His coat was dark. If the clerk wasn't paying attention, he might not notice the blood.

Sherm bought aspirin, a first aid travel kit, a box of tissue, a tube of antiseptic, and a six-pack of bottled water. The only extra/extra large T-shirt on the rack featured a neon elk advertising Yellowstone. Hanging over the counter were hoodies, all in bright colors. He asked to clerk to bring down the least obnoxious of them, a mustard yellow one. At the last second, he grabbed a map. He paid for everything with three fifty-dollar bills, though the total was only a little over a hundred bucks. A drop of blood landed on the counter, and the clerk looked up at him in surprise.

"Keep it," Sherm said when the clerk tried to give him the change. He figured it was fifty/fifty whether the clerk would call the police.

In the parking lot, he removed his coat and shirt, wiped the blood away from his shoulder with water and tissue, and swabbed the bullet hole with antiseptic. The wound just oozed blood now, and he wasn't sure if that was a good sign or a bad one. He managed to tear his old shirt into strips and bind the wound. The pain, which had been so unendurable at first, had now become a dull throb.

He munched down a handful aspirin.

The map showed no large towns west of Laramie for hundreds of miles, so Sherm turned back east.

In Laramie, he traded in the Escalade for a green Toyota Camry, which he'd once read was one of the most common cars in America. The salesman didn't look at his ID too closely, though he eyed Sherm's neon T-shirt and yellow hoodie with raised eyebrows. He was obviously delighted to trade a old Toyota for a SUV without a title that was worth twice as much.

As darkness fell, Sherm looked for other Camrys on the street, finally finding one that was a brighter green, but close enough. He exchanged license plates, hoping the other car's owner wouldn't notice for a couple of days.

This time, he didn't stop to sleep when it got dark. He found I-80 again and pushed the car to eighty miles an hour. The pain started to surge again now that he wasn't doing anything but sitting.

The agony kept him awake.

CHAPTER 26

The other side of Butcher's Cut was barely visible through the curtain of rain. The skies were pouring an ocean of water onto the parched Eastern Oregon soil. It was as if the earth itself was surprised, for instead of instantly being soaked up, the water ran off the rocks and sand, gathering in the low places.

Butcher's Cut was the lowest place of all. Water from miles around would run toward the steep gash, in rivulets at first, then in streams, and then in a flood. I didn't want to be caught this far down the ravine.

I scrambled out of the cave, and at first the rain felt refreshing. The bat guano washed away, a white and brown runoff. I rubbed my glove against the costume to help the water cleanse the fur. Dead ants, leaves, twigs, bat shit, and yes, a few ticks fell to the ground.

A stream swelled in the middle of the cut, getting broader and faster with every second. I carefully made my way down the rockfall, sliding a couple of times, catching myself by grabbing small trees that sprouted along the sides of the seasonal overspill.

The stream nearly knocked me off my feet, but the extra weight of the waterlogged costume kept me upright. I waded across and scrambled onto the rocks on the other side. Looking upward, I saw no sign of my hunters. By pure luck, I'd emerged in a blind spot. If Hanson remained at his post, he couldn't see me, but he would spot me the moment I emerged on the ridgeline above.

Maybe the rain drove him away. Maybe he joined the others searching for me on the other side of the hill.

But even as I thought it, I knew it was a long shot. These men were disciplined soldiers. They wouldn't abandon their posts over a little rain.

Still, the rain provided my best chance to escape so far. I needed to get by just one man. Hanson would know I'd disappeared on the other side of the hill, far from Butcher's Cut. He wouldn't expect me to have made it so far from my last sighting. The rain and the dim light would provide at least a little cover. If I made my way up the ridge along the tree line, I thought there might be just enough room to get past the sentry without being seen.

If he is half asleep and drunk.

If it had been the western edge of the canyon I needed to climb, I doubt I could have done it, especially in the Bigfoot costume, but there were spots on the eastern side that could be traversed. A few hundred yards uphill, a small gully cut the side of the ravine nearly in half. A waterfall already poured over the edge. I made my way toward it.

The sky burst with light, and a sharp crack of thunder sent me sprawling behind the low sagebrush. The skies above Strawberry Mountain were as dark as night, the sheet of rain a solid gray curtain.

A deluge headed my way, merging and gathering speed.

I scrambled up the bank to the cleft. It was about ten feet wide at the base, lined on both sides by nearly vertical walls of squared lava rocks, piled on top of each other like battlements. Water coursed down the middle, but a shelf along one side provided access and I stepped up on it.

I looked back and saw something black flapping in the wind.

Jordan stood there, a black poncho over his shoulders.

I'd been worried that Hanson might be able to see me, but from this angle, it was Jordan who had a clear line of sight through the trees and rocks. It was purely bad luck. He'd settled on the only place on the opposite side of the canyon where I could be spotted.

Jordan was looking the other way, sweeping the hillside with binoculars, his posture radiating impatience and anger. They had no doubt expected to track me down within hours, not days.

He'd tied a tarp between two trees. A pair horses stooped beneath the covering, their heads hanging miserably. I could see the top of Kent's dirty white hat huddled down next to them.

Moving swiftly but smoothly—at least, as smoothly as the costume would allow—I moved farther up the cleft, out of sight. After two sharp turns, the gully ran long and straight up to the top of the ridge. This ravine was a collapsed gold mine, I realized, much like the hole from which I'd emerged a few minutes earlier.

The roots of a huge juniper of at least twelve-foot circumference had pushed out the rocks, creating right angles in the gulley. For a hundred years or more, the tree had won the war between rock and wood, splitting the lava wall apart. But in the end, the rocks had won. The tree was dead, its branches drooping over the gully like a shattered roof, providing cover as I ducked under and kept going.

The ravine narrowed near the top, and the torrential flow nearly swept me away. I stepped over the stream, my head finally above the edge of the ravine.

Hanson stood steadfast in the rain.

He probably would have seen me, but lightning struck just uphill, sounding like cannon fire, and he looked over his shoulder. I ducked out of sight.

I slipped, tumbling down the coursing water. I reached out desperately, to no avail, but fortunately the suit snagged against a rock and halted my fall. I found a small ledge that could hold me and I climbed up onto it. I closed my eyes, the thunder filling the world, the lightning flashing through my eyelids. I was wet and tired and cold. My hunger was ever-present. It had become part of me and now I hardly noticed.

At least the thirst is gone, I thought, and laughed. No one would hear my laughter through the downpour.

There was no way I was going to get past Hanson.

CHAPTER 27

The rain whipped against my face, blown by sudden gusts of wind. I didn't seek protection from it. What did it matter? I'd reached the end of my strength and abilities.

The stream at my feet rose, splashing against the black fur on my legs. Sitting up on the small ledge, I watched the fur sway in the current. In all my sporadic attempts at meditation over the years, I'd never emptied my mind of thoughts as much as at that moment.

And then the urge to rise to my feet, to march unyieldingly toward my enemy, became almost overpowering. I wouldn't wait for them to find me, cowering. I looked down at the splintered walking staff I still carried. I brought out the bowie knife and started whittling.

With the activity, my mind churned again, and slowly, a plan developed. I tried to remember the traps and snares that Granger had taught me, but which I had never used. I was adept at leading my clients to fishing holes and deer ranges, knowing what lures and bait to use, which weapons were appropriate for which animals, but that didn't mean I was a survival expert.

I'd been an outdoor guide for years, I'd read up on stories of survival, but damned if I could remember anything now. What I knew was this: most of survival is in the preparation, making sure of adequate clothing, supplies, and shelter in advance. If you did that right, the survival tricks should never be necessary. Next to my bed, back at the ranch, was the backpack I always carried, which contained everything I needed to survive until a search party could find me.

I'd never expected to be trapped in the wilderness without

resources. I'd never conceived of being chased by armed men.

The simplest of all traps was a deadfall, rigging something heavy to fall on the unwary prey. But even the most basic of deadfalls usually required a rope. I looked around me. From where I sat, I could see piles of rocks of all sizes. If they could be rigged to fall, they would do some damage. I would need something to hold them up, but most of all, I would need something to trigger the trap.

Having the trap work would depend on everything going my way, and even more unlikely, my opponent doing what I predicted—or rather, hoped—he would do. Which, of course, never happened in real life. Predicting someone else's actions was impossible, no matter how much I might try to envision it. Most traps depend on time. The longer the trap is in place, the more likely the prey will stumble into it. Even then, more often than not, the trap is never sprung, or sprung too soon or too late.

I'd have to lure Hanson away from his sentry post, but to do that, I'd have to show myself. If I did that, he'd be suspicious and wary, which would make triggering the trap successfully all the more difficult.

I looked down at the walking stick. I'd almost cut too far, like forcing a pencil down in a sharpener for too long. The point was needle sharp.

One way or the other, I'd go down fighting.

The rain started to let up, though the volume of water streaming through the channel continued to grow. I looked up at the summit of Strawberry Mountain far above me. A lightning bolt briefly illuminated the dark clouds; patches of early-season snow gleamed brightly. A few moments later, thunder cracked dully against the curtain of rain. The thunder had echoed the entire time I was sitting there, but somehow, what had seemed so frightening at first was fading into the background.

I got to my feet, swaying uncertainly. Over the last day or so, the lack of food had been secondary to my thirst. Now my hunger had come to the fore, demanding my attention.

"Unless you want me to eat bugs," I muttered to my stomach, "shut the fuck up."

I picked my way carefully back down the ravine. As the channel widened, I was able to find a path that avoided the torrent. I reached the umbrella of branches from the dead juniper tree. It didn't provide much in the way of shelter, seeming to just gather the rain into larger droplets, but I wasn't there for shelter.

The tree had been dying for years. Some of the branches still had some of their springiness, and there were still needles on the smaller tips. Most of the needles broke off as I stripped the branches away, but the small offshoots still provided a latticework of twigs.

Most of the branches were too stiff to break or too thin to be useable, but I managed to find two that I thought might work. I examined the rocky wall. The deadfall would need to be out of sight until the last moment, which meant it needed to be placed just beyond the point where the roots of the juniper had pushed the wall out.

I leaned the two branches against the side of the coulee. Climbing the rocks was more difficult than I'd expected but, eventually, I found my way to the top. I placed the first rock on top of the lattice of small branches, which fanned off from the larger branch. The rock held for moment, then fell, taking the branch down with it.

I restrained a shout of frustration. I climbed down and propped up the larger branch. This time, I held onto it while I placed the first rock. The twigs bent and then held. Slowly, I built up the number of rocks, and though three or four fell through the latticework, I managed to get enough rocks in place to anchor the branch. From that point, I didn't need to stack the rest of the rocks so that they pushed against the branch, only so they would tumble when the lower rocks were removed.

Holding my breath, I slowly let go of my trap.

It was clear to me that I wouldn't be able to pile up enough stones, or large enough stones, to really do much damage. But I was pretty sure that an avalanche of rocks would surprise Hanson, at least.

I climbed down carefully.

If I was going to ambush my enemy, I'd needed a place to conceal myself. There was only one place where I could get out of sight, and it was on the uphill side of the trap. Beneath the base of the dead juniper tree, some of the roots had rotted away. I was able to pull apart other roots, leaving enough room for me to crouch down and hide.

I'd left the most difficult part for last.

Slowly, I peeled away the costume. As I extracted my fingers from the gloves, the pain of my broken pinky nearly dropped me to my knees.

I stared down at the rushing stream at my feet. If I fainted, I'd be swept away.

I avoided looking at my hand for now, afraid of what I'd see. I removed the rest of the costume and laid it carefully on a ledge above me.

Which should I use? Pants or shirt? Shirt or pants?

As I shivered, exposed to the elements, I realized I had no choice. I took off my shoes and socks carefully, wrung out the socks, and set them aside. I removed my jeans, and then quickly put my socks and shoes back on.

Only then did I look at my right hand.

It was a dark purple, not just the finger, but the entire hand all the way up to the wrist. And yet, it wasn't as bad as I'd expected. The bruise appeared to be fading around the edges, which I thought probably meant healing. The broken finger was at an odd angle and twice its normal size, but when I tried to move it, the pain told me that it was still alive. God only knew what it would look like when it healed, but I thought perhaps I had been extremely lucky. I wasn't going to lose my hand, like I'd feared, I might even keep the finger.

But like a screaming child who was suddenly noticed, the pain in the finger demanded my full attention. Everything else—my enemy with his sniper rifle, the trap I was laying, the rain and thunder—all of it faded away.

I lay there, concentrating on my breathing, waiting for the world to return. The rain slowed, and that seemed like a sign to me.

I started to put on the costume again, first the legs, then my left arm, and last of all, my right arm. Gingerly, I ran my right hand down into the costume, desperately trying to avoid jostling my pinky. When I reached the glove, I didn't hesitate, but quickly shoved my hand down into the fabric.

I sat down in the water, holding my head up with the last of my consciousness. Somehow, I stayed aware, the pain surging through my body, tightening all my muscles.

Then the pain faded. *Faded* was a relative term, for I didn't doubt the pain I was feeling at this moment would have been enough to stagger me a few hours before, but compared to the pain of inserting my hand into that glove, it was almost pleasant.

I examined my jeans, looking for seams. With the bowie knife, thankfully still sharp, I cut strips down the legs, and then tied them together. I estimated that I needed at least ten feet of length overall.

With my makeshift rope, I knelt before the deadfall branch, trying to figure out how and where to tie it.

I should have tied the branch first.

Never in my life, not in my calmest moments, had I concentrated as much as I did then. I tied a loop at the end of the rope, then delicately wound it around the branch without touching the wood. I slipped the other end of the rope through the knot and slowly tightened it.

I backed away, leaving plenty of slack in my fabricated rope. By the time I reached my hiding place, the line had played out, but I still had enough cloth left to tear off another strip, which I tied to the end.

The deadfall, such as it was, was ready. Now all I needed to do was to entice my prey into passing under it.

I looked at the makeshift trap and was proud of it.

At the same time, I realized how ridiculous it was. Even if Hanson came down here, he'd have to step in exactly the right place at exactly the right moment for it to be effective.

But I wasn't counting on the trap injuring my opponent, only surprising him.

I hefted the sharpened walking stick.

Just let me get within five feet of him.

CHAPTER 28

The rain was starting to let up, though in the distance it was darker than ever. The time had come to lure Hanson in. My little trap seemed like such a long shot. His rifle provided an acute advantage. All he needed to do was point and shoot, and it was all over.

For me to succeed would take so many unlikely events to occur in just the right way that I wondered why I was even trying. The longer I sat next to my deadfall trap, the crazier it seemed. There were still hours of daylight left, probably the last hours I'd ever have, for once darkness came, there was no chance I'd be able to slip by my pursuers with their night vision.

How long could I keep hiding?

I was conscious of every breath, conscious of the wind on my face, aware of the scratches on my bare legs from the stiff material of the costume. I thought of old clients, of my friends, even of my crazy ex-wife. All the troubles I'd had seemed so unimportant now.

Maybe if I gave myself up, they'd let the others live.

The pain in my finger gave an instant lie to that thought. They wouldn't let me live, or any of the others, nor would they hesitate to torture me further to find the box. I didn't think it would come to that, however. I suspected that Samuels had probably given orders to shoot on sight. He was apparently willing to take the chance the box would never be found, wherever I'd hidden it.

Granger might find it someday and wonder what it was, but that wouldn't do me much good if I was dead.

A rock tumbled down barely missing my head, and I went

over to find my deadfall branch bending dangerously as water trickled over the sides of the gulch, loosening the soil.

I got to my feet, took a deep breath, and headed up the gully.

My plan depended on Hanson coming after me, but of course, he could lie back and wait. He knew that I was trapped. He could wait until nightfall when I'd be blind and he had night vision. He could wait until the elements or hunger made me reveal myself.

But I thought there was a good chance that Hanson would want this over with. The mercenaries probably never planned on spending this much time in the wilderness. No doubt they'd figured they'd have finished long ago. The longer I frustrated their search, the better the chance something would go wrong with their plans. Even a corrupt sheriff can't hide the truth forever. Granger was well liked in these parts. People thought he was weird, but he wasn't known for lying. He was considered a bit of straight arrow, the way only a reformed criminal can sometimes be.

The water now filled the bottom of the gorge, and I was forced to wade against the strong current, which threatened to lift me off my feet. The blunt end of the walking stick helped stabilize me, but for a few moments, I stood there struggling, feeling myself being lifted. I leaned forward, held my breath. Took another step.

I thrashed my way up the last few yards. I didn't have the time or luxury to worry about being exposed until I suddenly found myself standing in the middle of Deadfall Ridge. I turned toward Hanson, who was in sniper position, his scope pointing down into Butcher's Cut.

He must have heard something.

I needed to get his attention without being obvious. But I needn't have worried, for the moment I took another step, he swiveled the barrel of the rifle toward me. The shot rang out moments later, after I was already ducking away. A large, square lava rock near my feet splintered in half.

I dove for the entrance of the gully. My feet went out from under me, and I was swept away, slipping down the channel as if I was on a waterslide. Ice-cold water flooded the costume, which had the effect of weighing me down. I bounced along the bottom, trying desperately to grab hold of something. The nerves in my broken finger flared and pain shot up my right hand, making it nearly useless. As I was tossed from side to side, the stick in my left hand turned sideways, and the two ends caught against the sides of the gully, slowing me down enough for me to grab onto a jutting root. Just holding on exhausted me, and I was buffeted back and forth. With the last of my strength, I pulled on the root and made it into the hiding space I'd created under the juniper tree.

It was only as I leaned back, every muscle in my body exhausted, that I realized that my falling had been lucky. I would never have been able to make my way to shelter quickly enough, that is, assuming that Hanson followed me.

The denim rope I'd made lay limply across the front of the hole. The bottom of the branch had been lodged on a small ledge, but was it high enough above the current?

Was the deadfall still in place?

There was no way of knowing without pulling on the rope. The deadfall was below me, because that was the only place I could put it. I'd have to let Hanson pass my hiding place before confronting him.

Earlier, I'd pulled all the grass and brush I could find within the confines of the ravine. Now I reached behind me into the hole and pulled the stuffing out, placing it in front of me, covering the hole as best I could. Once it was in place, I realized how threadbare it was. Hanson would be on full alert. I had little doubt he'd hunted and killed men before. If I could see out so clearly, surely he could see me just as well.

I readied my makeshift spear. Surprisingly, the sharp point I'd carved remained despite all the abuse it had suffered.

A scraping sound came from above, as if someone had slipped and grabbed for purchase. I froze in the middle of putting another branch into my blind. All I could see was Hanson's legs and the barrel of the rifle, pointed forward. Hanson moved slowly and deliberately, but he wasn't hesitating, as if he expected me to have run as far as I could.

His thigh brushed against the blind, dislodging it half an

inch, but he was already ducking under the umbrella of dead branches and didn't look back.

I took hold of the end of the rope and counted the seconds. I'd figured it would take about five ticks for him to reach the deadfall. I counted down, knowing that I was probably counting twice as fast as I should.

I jerked on the rope. It rose but didn't come toward me. It was caught. I yanked again, hoping the knots would hold, and something gave way. I heard the clatter of rocks falling, louder and more threatening than I'd expected.

Maybe it had really hurt him. My heart pounded.

I waited. I expected a cry to follow, if not of pain, at least of surprise, of *something*.

Nothing. Not a sound.

I pushed the blind away, pulled myself out of the hole, and started down the gully. The water inside the costume unexpectedly slowed me down. To my own ears, I sounded like a rampaging cow. Hanson would hear me coming long before I got to him.

So much for an ambush.

I turned the corner, and he stood there, the rocks piled around his legs up to his knees. He didn't appeared hurt, or even all that concerned. He was facing away from me, as if he expected the attack to come from below. By some miracle, he didn't hear me.

The moment I came around the rock ledge, some instinct warned him, and he turned so swiftly that I was almost shocked into stopping. With a shout that sounded to me more like a frightened child than a warrior, I lowered the tip of my spear and charged.

The sharpened tip of my spear struck Hanson in the middle of the chest. He fired his rifle at the same moment. The bullet struck my side, twisting me to one side, blunting my attack. The point of the spear broke off, and I stood there stupidly, looking down at my broken walking stick. Only then did I realize that Hanson was wearing a Kevlar vest with a ceramic plate.

Hanson smiled, ejected the spent round, and ratcheted in another shell. I realized that the battered Bigfoot costume would buckle from a bullet fired from only inches away.

With the shout of a man who had nothing to lose, I charged again. The broken point of the walking stick struck Hanson in the chest. He fell backward, tripping on the deadfall rocks, trying to gain his footing. The water caught him, and he spun around, falling into the current. Silently, looking up at me with the expression of man who'd always expected to die in action, he tumbled out of sight.

I grasped my side, afraid of what I'd find. To my amazement, the costume had been torn open at my hip, but the bullet had taken Kevlar with it, not flesh. The pain was from the impact on the surrounding material and fading rapidly.

Without thinking, I grabbed my stick and made my way carefully down the last few yards to where the gully tumbled into Butcher's Cut. I looked down to see a raging flood where there had been only sand the day before. The water was brown with silt and topped with white foam, and there was no sign of Hanson.

Something nagged at me even amid my moment of triumph. By instinct, I looked across the canyon.

On the top of the hill on the other side of Butcher's Cut, Jordan kneeled, his rifle trained on me at a distance from which he couldn't possibly miss.

CHAPTER 29

That single second expanded to my entire life, everything that had come before erased, all my fears and hopes condensed into a single moment. It was as if I could see Jordan's finger tighten on the trigger, could watch the bullet flying toward my head.

The bullet came right at my eyes and then magically levitated, flying over my head by an inch and slamming into the rocks behind me. The sound of the shot followed. I dropped to my knees.

At the last moment, I'd seen something move behind Jordan, and now I realized the blur of white had been Kent's cowboy hat as he'd slammed into my would-be executioner's lower back.

Jordan whirled, slamming the butt of his rifle into Kent's forehead. Kent spun off, toppling over the edge and rolling down the hillside. The battered hat went flying. The horses whinnied in alarm. Jordan stood for a moment at the edge of the cliff and fired toward where Kent had disappeared. He must have emptied the entire magazine in his anger, for the roar of the gunfire was like rolling thunder.

The mercenary turned toward me, smoothly extracted another magazine from his belt, and slapped it home, bringing the rifle to my shoulder with a fluid speed that was paralyzing.

But my body finally moved, even as my mind reeled from the onslaught. I ducked out of sight, and the bullets sprayed the rocks at the mouth of the gully. A few of them ricocheted into the Bigfoot costume. Though most of their energy was spent, it was still as if I'd been punched hard several times.

The gushing water threatened to pull me down into Jordan's

line of sight but, again, the weight of the costume slowed me down just enough for me to recover. I grabbed the juniper's roots and pulled myself out of the stream.

A few moments before, I'd thought I was dead. Now, by some miracle, I was safe.

"Hey, Davis!" Jordan yelled over the roar of the stream between us.

I was about five yards up the gully, but even so, I shrank against the wall. There was no way Jordan could see me.

"I don't know if you can hear me, Davis, but I have to tell you, I underestimated you. I didn't think you had it in you. You're lucky. We didn't even consider bringing armor-piercing bullets. At worst, we thought we'd be up against a couple of civilians."

I had no urge to answer him. Maybe he'd think I was hit.

"By the way, you realize how much Hanson's rifle was worth?" Jordan continued. "Such a waste."

It was as if he expected me to answer him.

"All right, run away, Davis," he continued. "But it won't matter. Samuels will find you. The trap isn't just the Strawberry Mountains…it isn't just Oregon, or even just America. No matter where you go, you won't be safe."

It was clear he didn't have anything but taunting to offer. I pushed off from the rocks and started climbing.

"We've still got Conner, you know," Jordan shouted.

I stopped.

"It would be a shame if anything happened to him. He's some kind of idiot savant, you know? It's nothing fancy, but he's got a flair for cooking. So keep going, Hart. I'll try to talk Samuels out of doing anything to the kid, but I don't usually get too far with my boss."

I stood there, waiting for Jordan to continue, but he finished his bait speech.

I felt an overwhelming urge to sit, to close my eyes, to absorb it all, but I forced myself to keep going. The hillside was covered with loose, jagged rocks, as if an explosion had blasted them apart. The summit teased me, always seeming as though it was over the next rise. But there was always another hill, and another, until I was on top of Deadfall Ridge, the old Forest Service road leading to the narrow spot where Hanson had been lying in wait.

I trudged those last few yards. I looked up at the Widowmaker tree. Hanson's camp was just below it.

What good are you? I asked the snag, wondering why it couldn't have fallen on my enemies.

There, beside an extinguished campfire, was Hanson's gear. A heavy canvas backpack was propped against a pine tree. I grabbed it and unzipped the top.

The first thing I saw was a water bottle, nestled within an assortment of energy bars. I grabbed the bottle, tore open an energy bar and consumed it within seconds, then grabbed another bar and ate it. Part of it stuck in my throat. I frantically dislodged the blockage with some of the water and forced myself to slow down.

I could already feel the energy flowing through my body, as if I'd been dead and now returned to life. I rummaged through the rest of the pack. Another knife, wickedly sharp, a small flashlight, a compass, some matches, bug spray, Chapstick, other sundries, some maps, and a paperback Western. Nothing immediately useful except a flannel shirt folded neatly at the bottom.

Too bad there weren't any pants. Then I could have gotten rid of this Bigfoot costume once and for all.

But even as I thought it, I knew that I wouldn't have jettisoned the costume. Until I was safe, it was my suit of armor. I eyed the clean, dry flannel shirt, but to put it on, I'd have to take the costume off. The throbbing in my right hand warned me. I decided I couldn't risk it.

The dark clouds over Strawberry Mountain began to disperse. But at the same time, the sunlight dwindled. Another night would soon be upon me.

The way was clear. In the darkness, it would take at least a couple of hours for Jordan and the others to make their way down the slope and around the water filled Butcher's Cut, and another couple of hours to climb Deadfall Ridge. Meanwhile, once I reached the summit, I had a clear path, mostly downhill, for miles. There was no chance they could catch me now.

I felt guilty at the relief that flowed through me. Kent had given his life to save me. I was surprised. The laconic curmudgeon had never acted as if he liked me, or anyone, for that matter, except maybe Granger and Conner.

Conner.

I sat on the log Hanson had dragged to the side of his campfire and reached for another energy bar. I had a head start, but the mercenaries were fresher and trained for this. I couldn't wait around.

I didn't move. All the weariness and danger threatened to overwhelm me, for I already knew what I needed to do.

Conner.

If Samuels had taken Kent captive, there was no reason to think that he'd let Conner go. If I left now, I'd be leaving the boy at their mercy, and I doubted they had any. They wouldn't leave a witness alive, even a handicapped witness.

I slung the backpack over my shoulder, tightened the straps, and started walking downhill. The way I'd come.

"Wrong way," I said aloud.

The stream of water in the gully had receded, and I made my way down without mishap. At the base, I knelt and carefully poked my head around the corner.

Jordan stared gloomily into a roaring fire. Evidently, the mercenary had decided he'd done all he could, that his prey had made good on his escape. If Samuels had been there, I had no doubt that he would have ordered his man to get going, but it appeared that Jordan was done for the night.

The rifle was in his lap. If he'd planned to use the night vision scope, he wouldn't have lit a bonfire.

I climbed over the edge and down into Butcher's Cut.

CHAPTER 30

I could hear the water coursing through the ravine, getting louder with every step. There was no possibility that I could cross where I had before. It was getting dark fast, and even faster inside the canyon than on the rim. There were two large boulders upstream, with the flood jetting out from between. I thought there was a chance I could jump the distance.

The natural bridge was a hundred feet above where I'd emerged.

I scrambled from rock to rock, at several points needing to leap across offshoots of the main channel, but finally made it to the large boulder on my side of the river. I climbed it, slipping halfway down a few times and crawling the last few feet. Carefully, I stood up.

The gap hadn't looked this wide from a distance. Now I doubted I could have made it with a running start, much less wearing the Bigfoot costume.

I'd done my best. It was time to turn around, go down Deadfall Ridge, or better yet, go up the ridge and escape.

The longer I looked at the fissure, the scarier it became.

I jumped before I could talk myself out of it. It scared me more than anything else that had happened because it was of my own doing, not something that was being forced on me. I landed squarely in the middle of the other boulder, but the top was rounded, and I began to slip backward. I threw out my hands, clawing at the rough surface, and stopped my slide. Breathing hard, my heart pounding, I crawled the rest of the way up and lay face down, arms and legs sprawled.

Slowly, I regained enough courage to climb down the

boulder and pick my way across to the other side, staying above and parallel to the stream. It was only then that I realized I had a problem. The cliff was much steeper here, and I had to climb my way across at several points. The wet costume was ponderous, the gloves made it hard to feel, and Bigfoot's huge feet were clumsy. But I had no choice.

The cave I'd emerged from was hidden. When I'd come out, I'd looked back, and the cave entrance had disappeared. It hadn't seemed to matter then. I'd never expected to be back. I hadn't bothered to look for landmarks and I didn't recall any details.

I could see the waterfall from the gully where I'd fought Hanson about thirty feet upstream, which was about the location I remembered seeing it in. But damned if I could find an opening.

There was a large overhang above me. I climbed toward it. A small black hole appeared beneath the rocks, but I didn't remember the overhang or the cave being so high up the cliff. But it was the only cave in sight, so I poked my head into the hole. I had to at least explore it.

Hanson's backpack caught on the roof, and for a moment I thought I was stuck. I pushed my way forward. The pack lifted off my back, and with a jolt, it came loose. I went only a few more feet before I knew that this was wrong. This was a different cave. The entrance sloped downward, whereas I'd emerged from above. I started to turn around.

A snuffling sound came from only inches away. A foul breath blew into my face. The snuffling sound became a loud snore, but unlike any snore I'd ever heard, even when my wife had been drinking all night. It was more like a snarl than a snore.

I could smell the hibernating black bear even if I couldn't see him. He was moving, but I thought he was still only vaguely aware of my intrusion. I backed away carefully, moving a few inches at a time, fighting the urge to scream and run.

I almost made it. As my feet dangled and I tried to slide out of the cave, a rock came loose beneath my right hand. I grabbed for it, but my fingers wouldn't close, and it rolled away. It thudded down the passageway and stopped.

The bear bellowed, and I felt movement in the air. I scrambled the rest of the way out. I started to reach for my knife, realizing it was too late.

The walking stick was still in my hand. It didn't really serve a purpose any more, but it was what I had, and I didn't wanted to let it go. I backed away, pointing the broken end of the spear uselessly at the opening. In my fear, I hit the bottom of the overhang with the stick, and a chunk of rock broke off and tumbled down the cliff.

I swung the stick as hard as I could at what was left of the overhang, and it tumbled downward, at first a few loose stones, then a solid wedge of rock. I could hear the bear coming up the passage, and then, a loud *thud* as the top of the cave collapsed.

I almost fell backward, but instead spun around and sat down hard. I could still hear the bear roaring inside the cave. I was glad the creature had survived. I could only hope there was another opening somewhere from which the bear could emerge in the spring.

I stared up at an unexpectedly clear night. The moon was a sliver, and stars filled the sky. The clouds were gone, and without their cover, I could feel the temperature dropping again.

In all my years in the wilderness, I'd always been the hunter, not the hunted. I thought of myself an outdoorsman, so much so, in fact, that I'd felt like I could write about it for the local newspaper. But now I realized I'd always been cocooned by civilization, even when I thought I was roughing it. I'd always had a gun, and fire, and a tent. Most of the time, I had had company with me. The animals had avoided my clients and me, and I'd had to seek them out. That had been my talent.

It had never occurred to me that the opposite could happen. Without fire, without adequate shelter, without a weapon other than a knife and a sharpened stick, I had become the prey. The elements themselves were the most dangerous, the snow and the rain, the rushing waters, the freezing temperatures. Most of the time, over the last few days, I'd had no water or food. In my weakened state, I was vulnerable to animals who were truly wild, who survived in this world by tooth and claw.

In all my years out here, I'd only seen a cougar once. Once

I'd spied a mother bear and cubs across a meadow, and I'd seen a few others running away. I'd spotted coyotes, trotting unconcerned across pastures. I had heard rattlesnakes along the trail, and I'd had to kill one that had sought warmth in a client's sleeping bag.

But none of that had seemed threatening, not to anyone who knew what he or she were doing—until now.

I'd never thought to question my physical courage because I'd never been tested. Nor had I ever expected to be tested. The modern world protected me from even thinking about it.

I was still outnumbered by my enemies. I was still without a weapon that could even the odds. But I now knew I could survive by my own wits in the wilderness, with a little help from Bigfoot. More than that, I was part of the wilderness now. My enemies were still cushioned within the safety of civilization, no matter how badass they thought they were.

They wouldn't see me coming.

A small rock rolled past my head. I got up quickly. With the overhang gone, there was a chance that the rest of the cliff side could follow. I turned downhill. The cave had to be below me, and not too far away.

I looked back. The flames of Jordan's campfire, which I'd seen flickering for most of the time I was working my way downward, were now out of sight. I shrugged off the backpack and took out the flashlight. Shielding it as best I could with my body, I pointed the light downward.

There was nothing but rock as far as I could see. Not only that, it was too steep to climb, either upward or downward. I started to lower the flashlight in despair and caught sight of a black hole just beneath the surface of the rushing water.

With a sinking heart, I realized that the opening of the rattlesnake mine was now beneath the river.

CHAPTER 31

The flowing water barely covered the hole. All I needed to do was duck under the water and climb.

Like hell.

I needed to make my way back up Deadfall Ridge. Start a fire.

A voice came from inside. *You won't make it. You're exhausted. You barely made it over the creek.* It was my father's voice.

Hypothermia. I was starting to imagine things.

My father's acerbic voice would have none of it. *You aren't imagining how fucked up you are.*

"What if the water is too high?" I said aloud.

Then you keep swimming, said the other voice.

I was so tired I could barely stand. The thought of climbing Butcher's Cut, crossing the torrent, and ascending the ridge again was almost enough to make me give up. I just needed a little rest.

The nagging voice wouldn't let me. *If you sit down here, you'll die, son. You're shivering uncontrollably. That waterlogged costume is worse than useless. You need the shelter of the cave.*

I stared down into the raging torrent. "What if I get swept away?" I answered reasonably. "I can't swim."

And whose fault is that? said my father. *Besides, it doesn't matter. No one can swim in that.*

My laugh echoed in the air, and I wondered if I'd carried on the entire conversation out loud. Could Jordan on the bluff above hear me?

I waded into the water, breathing deeply, banking the

oxygen in my blood. I would push Hanson's backpack ahead of me. It was new, a good brand, and there was a good chance it was water resistant. If I wasn't in the water long, it was possible the contents would remain dry.

I remembered how surging water had filled the suit through the sagging gap around my neck. The suit had even more holes now.

I pulled the mask over my head and sealed it. I couldn't see very well, but it didn't matter. Once inside the cave, I was going to be completely blind anyway.

I looked down at the flashlight, wondering if it was water resistant. *Too late now.* I took one last long look at the location of the hole, and then put the flashlight away in the Bigfoot pouch.

This isn't swimming. It's just climbing into a cave.

I ducked under the water, grabbing for the rocks at the edge of the cave mouth. To my dismay, the rocks dislodged in my hands. As the water began to drag me away, I kicked and lunged for the side of the hole, and this time it held firm. The costume had shielded me from the freezing water at first, but now it poured in, filling the suit, dragging me back. I felt as if I was being pushed backward a foot for every few inches I pulled myself forward.

My arms weren't responding anymore, as if my muscles had turned to mush. I felt my fingers loosening. One glove caught in a sharp spur of rock, and I dangled there for a few moments, expecting to be swept away.

Don't give up now, you asshole, my tormentor said. I kicked and pushed against the side of the cave, scrambling upward. Within the lava tube, my head popped above water, and though the drag was stronger than ever, the knowledge that there was air above gave me strength.

I heard echoes and realized I was in the large chamber of the cave.

Climb a little farther, Father said.

I imagined the pressure of his hand on my shoulder, guiding me. I crawled on my hands and knees until there was a flat shelf of rock beneath me and collapsed.

Distantly, I sensed someone's hands feeling for the Bigfoot

pouch and pulling out the flashlight. I felt hands pulling off my mask.

Those are my hands, I realized. There was no one else here. I shook uncontrollably.

Get out of the suit, Hart. Hurry.

"When did you start caring, you old bastard?" I muttered.

You're going into hypothermia. You need to dry off.

I reached back and tugged on the zipper. I sat up, made a feeble attempt to pull my arm out of the suit, and stopped midway. I was done. I could hear my teeth chattering.

"I heard that shivering means your body is still trying to keep warm," I mused aloud as if it was a mere curiosity. "It's when you stop shivering that you need to worry."

As if saying it had made it happen, a sudden lassitude came over me. Somehow, I pulled out one arm out of the costume, and then the other. The pain in my finger felt as if it belonged to someone else.

I dragged my frozen carcass the rest of the way out of the costume, then took off my shirt. I was naked except for my shorts.

"How is this helping?" I asked.

Light flared near my head, and I turned my face toward the flickering glow, surprised to find the matches from Hanson's pack in my hands. I was bent over a pile of crumpled paper, pages torn from the paperback; a Western by D.B. Newton. I reached into the backpack and took out one of the maps, ripped it down the middle, and fed first one half and then the other into the flames.

The warmth bounced off my frozen body. It was as if I was encased in ice. I pulled the flannel shirt from the bottom of the pack and began drying myself off. My skin had no feeling at first. And then the prickling began, growing stronger, as painful as if I was being rubbed raw. I grunted.

That's it, Hart, Father said approvingly. *Feel it. Get those nerves working.*

The pain increased, and I groaned, but managed to get to my knees.

The fire died down. I tore a second map and fed it to the

flames. I stared into the fire, and it was as if the very sight of the flames warmed me.

As if watching someone else do it, I rose and wandered into the darkness, flashlight in hand. Near where the cave narrowed, there was a pile of old branches that had probably been washed into the cave long ago. They were so decayed that they broke off in pieces as I pulled on them.

I fed the rotted wood into the flames, one small sliver at a time. At first, all the fuel did was smoke, but then, little by little, with flames that were more blue than red, the wood caught fire. The light and the heat increased, and I scooted closer.

I don't know how much time passed before I thought to grab my shirt and spread it near the flames.

You're going to make it, Hart, my father's voice said, but it was distant, as if he was leaving me.

CHAPTER 32

The cave filled with smoke and heat, or at least the illusion of heat. A coughing fit woke me, and I checked my internal clock and guessed it was about three o'clock in the morning. I opened my eyes and for a moment I was confused. I was seeing stars in the sky. Had I dreamed about the cave? Had I gone outside in my sleep.

The stars were flickering in synchronization with the fire, which was dying down. I shivered. My shirt was still damp, but it was warm from the fire. I put it on. It was going to be a race between the warmth of my body drying the last of the dampness and the dampness cooling off my body.

The Bigfoot costume lay on the other side of the fire as if the creature had shed its skin. It smoked from the heat, and the smell of scorched fur filled the air.

If Moser had maintained his lookout on the eastern edge of the ranch, it was still too dangerous to show myself. The night scope would reveal me more than daylight. They might think I'd escaped, but they'd want to be certain. I'd have to wait until first light.

I built up the fire again, using the last of the wood. In the flickering light, I went looking for fuel, but all that was left were a few twigs and dried leaves. I added these to the fire little by little.

As the fire flared, I stared at the flickering lights on the roof of the cave. I realized I could reach one of them. I pried the shining lump out with the knife and took it over to the fire.

I already guessed from the weight, but the light confirmed it. Gold.

Well I'll be damned.

Not that it did me the slightest bit of good in my present predicament.

It was nearly dawn when the fire sputtered down to a pile of ashes. The smoke cleared from the cavern, and it began to get cold again. I felt the breeze on my hands and face. I didn't need to look to know that the water level of the stream outside had dropped enough for air to enter again.

I stirred the coals with the last unburned stick. The new breeze caught the small amount of unburned, buried material, and the fire revived for a short time. The paperback Western was still by my side, most of it unburned. Over the next hour, I fed the pages one at a time into the fire, stirring them, watching the cinders rise, glowing, in the darkness of the cave.

Bats fluttered above, squeaking. Maybe it should have creeped me out, but instead, the presence of other life reassured me I wasn't in some sort of purgatory, but still in the real world.

"Sorry about disturbing you," I said. The sound of my voice was startling, especially in the echoing silence.

When I was down to the last few pages and the cover of the book, I tossed them into the embers along with the stirring stick. In the last flickering flames, I turned the backpack upside down and examined the scattered contents.

The container of matches I put into the pocket of my coat. The rest of the stuff didn't seem important. All this was going to be over by the end of the day, one way or the other.

As I gave the pack a last shake, an energy bar came out of a side pocket I hadn't even known was there and dropped into the fire. I snatched it out, blowing on my fingers. My mouth watered at the mere thought of the chocolate and peanut coating. The water bottle was about a quarter full, just enough to wash down the food.

I smacked my lips, feeling almost safe. No caveman ever had it better.

A soft glow formed at the edge of the cavern. It was daylight outside, light enough for the sun's rays to reach the bottom of Butcher's Cut. Time to go.

I eyed the Bigfoot costume distastefully. No matter how

well it had served me, the last thing I wanted to do was put it back on. But even if I'd wanted to concoct some form of pants out of the flannel shirt and backpack, I couldn't do it. I needed the pack, and most of all, I needed the suit's protection.

I picked up the costume, almost dropping it because it was so heavy. Despite lying near the fire all night, it was still soggy.

It was unbelievable that I'd lugged this thing around for days. No wonder my muscles had turned to rubber. I pulled the suit on, feeling the dampness around my bare legs, the chafing around my ankles and knee joints. I put my arms in, saving my right arm for last. I was getting pretty good at maneuvering my broken pinky into the glove's finger hole, but it still hurt like hell.

I cursed as the last of the embers sputtered out and grabbed the flashlight from the floor of the cavern. Picking up the now-empty backpack, I made my way to the front of the cave.

In the light of the flashlight, the passages were even narrower than I remembered. If I hadn't already passed through them, I doubt I would have mustered the courage to push my way forward. The suit caught again and again on the rough rocks, but I pulled away, the fur scraping off patch-by-patch, leaving bare Kevlar gleaming darkly.

I could see the light from an amazing distance, as if the darkness wanted nothing more than to give way. It was a small glow in the air at first, almost an illusion, but eventually, when I turned off the flashlight, I could see the outlines of my gloves in the dirt.

I continued on, my eyes adjusting slowly to the light as it grew brighter.

The small cavern at the entrance, with the hole above, seemed intensely lit, though the day before, it had seemed so murky that I'd only guessed at what I was seeing. The odor from the pile of bat guano near the cave mouth was enough to make me gag, though I didn't even remember smelling it in my flight. Nor had I noticed the small insects swarming through it.

On one side of the entrance, the large rattlesnake that had attacked me the day before watched me, its tail rattling softly. To the other side was a mound of smaller rattlers, entangled together, looking dead. They were deep in hibernation. I scooted away from the bigger rattler.

"I don't want you, buddy," I muttered. It was almost as if it understood, for the rattling increased slightly, but it stayed coiled in place.

I opened the backpack and slowly approached the smaller snakes. I'd heard that younger rattlers were even more venomous than their elders. These snakes hadn't quite formed their rattles, and I figured they were less than a season old.

Fighting every instinct to run away, I grabbed a snake by the back of the head and tossed it into the pack before it could react. It slid down, squirmed a little, then seemed to accept its new surroundings. One by one, I grabbed the snakes and slipped them into the pack until it became heavy in my hands.

I didn't count them, but I figured I had at least half a dozen of them before I felt something strike my leg. A snake bounced off, slid down my leg, and rolled into the pile of guano. It recovered and slithered toward me.

Time to leave.

I wasn't sure I would have had the strength to pull myself out of the cave were it not for the thought of the squirming rattlers at my feet, all of them seeking a way to reach my bare skin.

I shuddered and jumped upward, my elbows reaching the edge of the cave mouth, and swung there, the costume threatening to pull me down. There was a sagebrush bush near the entrance, which had hidden it, and it was big and strong enough to withstand me putting all my weight on it.

I managed to get one knee up over the lip of the opening, and then the other. I rested for a few moments. The bag moved in my hand, and I sat up, making sure it was completely sealed. It was a heavy canvas bag. I thought it would hold them.

I swung it over my back. As I started descending the hill, I felt the snakes moving about even through the costume, and chills ran up and down my spine. Nothing, not even confronting the rattlers face to face, was creepier than this.

I looked over my shoulder and realized I'd strayed into Moser's line of sight. He wasn't there. I caught a glimpse of him heading down. I angled closer to the trees, jogging across the open areas, hoping that the mercenaries weren't still hunting for me.

But even if they were, I doubted they expected me to be hunting them.

CHAPTER 33

Five and a half hours after driving down the Strawberry Mountains, Samuels pulled up to the Airolo Corporation's private hanger at the Portland airport. The moment he passed Mt. Hood, the weather had turned nice. Just his luck; the weather in the rain forests of the valley, the I5 corridor, was beautiful, while the High Desert alternated between rain and snow.

Mathew Summers was waiting for him at the doors. Summers was of roughly equal rank, though it was sometimes difficult to tell the hierarchy of a corporation compared to the strict ranks of the military.

"You're late," Summers said.

"There was an accident in Warm Springs..." Samuels started to say.

"It doesn't matter to me," Summers interrupted. "What I should have said is, Mr. Crane complained that you weren't here to meet him."

"Right," Samuels said. He walked into the hanger, saw the private jet near the open doors, adjacent the runway, as if it was ready to take off at any moment.

He skipped up the steps, almost saluting the heavy security at the bottom. It reminded him of his last visit to Afghanistan. This was the big time.

The plane was empty but he heard a loud voice in the back. Barton Crane was sitting in a room with several rows of seats, where his underlings probably sat. Crane was alone. The seats to either side of him were full of work papers, but he was leaning back, talking on the phone, tie askew, thin white hair tousled. He had a round face, a round belly, and short legs. A bulldog. The President's bulldog.

"You tell the President that he of course has my full loyalty, but if I'm called before the committee, I will need to be completely truthful."

Crane looked up at Samuels, motioned to a seat next to him. Samuels lifted the papers, careful not to look at them, and set them on the next seat over.

"Of course, as a Supreme Court nominee, I will need to keep some things to myself, so as to not prejudice future opinions."

Again he looked over at me and shrugged, as if to say, *What can you do?*

Then he flushed and sat forward, papers spilling off his lap. "No, you tell him that my nomination is what is keeping me quiet. Yes, I know that's blunt, and yes I know we risk someone overhearing, that's why he'd better not change his mind."

Samuels couldn't hear the words on the other end of the phone, but he could hear the volume and tone, and it was loud and angry.

"I will not go down alone," Crane said calmly, as if whatever the other person had said reassured him of his control. "Nor had anything better happen to me like some of Putin's puppets. If anything happens to me, I guarantee the truth will come out."

He raised his eyebrows, lowered the phone and looked at it.

"Son of a bitch hung up on me," he muttered, before turning to Samuels and flashing the smile Samuels had seen on the cable talk shows. "I'm told you're a man who can get things done, Samuels."

As always, Samuels resisted the urge to ask what that meant exactly. Of course, that's why he was standing there instead of some other soldier, because he was willing to do what needed to be "done."

"Yes, sir," he said.

"Information can be both valuable and dangerous. For me, it's very valuable. For Mr. Russo, it's dangerous. I don't want Mr. Russo to make what I know become useless. Do you have things under control?"

"Within the next day or two," Samuels said.

"Good. I'm looking for a head of my private security detail, Samuels. I've heard good things about you."

Samuels tried not to react too eagerly. It was the cush job he wanted now, safe and boring. "It will get done."

"I want anyone who knows anything eliminated, you understand? If you can't solve the problem, I'll find someone who will."

Samuels was shocked. Not by the message but by its bluntness. Then again, they were alone in a plane, not on the phone where they could be overheard. Implicit in the message was that if Samuels didn't take out Davis and his friends he'd be part of the "problem."

"Understood, sir."

"Good," Crane said again. He reached over to the seat on the other side of him and lifted a notebook. Samuels realized he'd been dismissed.

It wasn't until he reached the bottom of the steps that he realized how pointless it had all been. *Crane thinks he's motivating me.* But if anything, it was alarming how unstable everything seemed to be. He'd just heard a Supreme Court nominee blackmail the president. The warlords he'd dealt with in Afghanistan had been subtler.

He saw movement toward the side of the hanger and several men standing and looking over at him. He walked toward them.

"Popov," he nodded.

The Russian looked like he was ready to salute. Then he caught himself and said, "Samuels."

"How many men did you bring?"

"Half my section. I was told to keep it small."

"Let's head out," Samuels said. "I want this finished in the next twenty-four hours."

CHAPTER 34

Granger had a spot above the ranch, along the trail, where he liked to spring his Bigfoot ambushes. It wasn't visible from more than a few feet away, a blind of trees and shrubs artfully arranged so that it could be seen out of, but not into.

I slipped into the space with the sun still low in the morning sky. It was a comfortable spot. Granger had placed a lawn chair there, along with a footstool and a cooler, and sometimes he didn't even emerge when it came time to do so, just stayed there and drank beer until everyone was asleep, then staggered home in his costume and crashed into bed.

It was a wonder that some of my clients hadn't spied him in the middle of the night. But then, Granger was aware of the danger. "Don't want to be taken for a bear and shot," he'd said when I'd asked him about the Kevlar.

"Or Bigfoot," I had offered.

"Or Bigfoot. Man, would they be disappointed!"

There was no one stirring at the ranch. I'm not sure what I expected. A lot of activity, I supposed—but the place looked abandoned. There were no cars in sight. The mercenaries must have cleared my burned Jeep off the road or gone around it.

I was surprised that Samuels hadn't left someone behind to watch the place, but then, if he'd cleared it of transport and weapons, he didn't have much to worry about. Granger had no phone, no Wi-Fi.

I crept out of my hiding spot and darted to the side of the house. In the shadows, I put my ear to the side of the building, but didn't hear anyone stirring. I shrugged off the backpack. The movement awakened the snakes, which thrashed about.

I almost lost my grip. I laid the pack carefully on the ground and worked the latch to the snack bin. The container was nearly full: Cheetos and potato chips, some Twinkies and donuts, other snacks. I pulled out some of the more nutritional nuts and cracker packs and put them aside.

I carefully unzipped the pack, keeping the top closed as best I could. Then, in one swift movement, I turned it upside down, feeling the snakes drop away as one. I slammed the lid of the box down and latched it securely.

The snakes banged so noisily against the inside of the box that I was afraid it would wake anyone who was around, if there was anyone, but as I picked up the snacks and put them in the backpack, I realized my heightened senses were magnifying the sounds, and in truth, they probably couldn't be heard from more than a few feet away. Even as I got ready to leave, the snakes quieted, no doubt reassured by the darkness and snugness of their prison.

If Conner was there, I doubted he would go near the snack box. He turned up his nose at junk food. I'd even heard him try to talk Granger into getting rid of the munchies.

"They can't taste the real cooked food," he'd exclaimed. "Their tongues are polluted!"

Granger had shaken his head. "Hell, kid, half of these guys come here to *get* polluted."

I climbed back up to Granger's spot and waited. I sat down on the lawn chair and lifted the cooler's lid. Three empty cans floated in the melted ice, but there was one can still unopened. I broke out the snacks and washed them down with warm beer.

Moser was apparently taking his sweet time getting down. It was clear they thought I was long gone.

I was so intent on watching the house that I almost didn't hear Moser coming from the other direction until he was past me. It was a good thing I was hidden. Not that the mercenary was paying much attention to his surroundings. His rifle was slung over his shoulder. It was obvious he thought his prey had escaped, that there was no need for vigilance.

"Hey!" he shouted, as he neared the bunkhouse. "Where is everyone?"

There was no answer.

"Shit," I heard him say. He removed his rifle and leaned it against one of the benches. Then he took off his pack and set it down. He reached into a side pocket and pulled out a walkie-talkie.

"Where the hell are you guys?" he asked.

I could tell the voice that answered was Samuels. I couldn't make out the words, but I could sense that he was angry.

"What's the point?" Moser answered. "He's long gone. I'd love to know how he took out Hanson."

Samuels's voice sounded a little more restrained, as if he could tell he was losing his man.

"What am I supposed to do in the meantime?" Moser asked.

There was a short, squawking retort.

"Yeah, I can do *that*," Moser said. He threw the walkie-talkie on top of the pack and sat down heavily. He dug around in his pack and pulled out a bottle of water. He drained it, then threw it into the remains of the bonfire. Muttering something under his breath, he got to his feet and ambled toward the house. I held my breath as he opened the outdoor refrigerator and removed a can of Pepsi. He turned around as if to go back to the campfire.

I cursed under my breath. Then he hesitated, turned around again, and approached the snack box. He leaned down and started to work the latch. Suddenly he stood bolt upright, as if alarmed.

Damn, he heard them.

"Goddamn squirrels," I heard him say. He got on his hands and knees, took out a knife, and threw the lid open.

A snake flew out of the box so fast I couldn't really see it. One second Moser leaned down, the next he had something attached to his neck. He shouted in alarm, the shout rising to a scream as he realized what it was. His voice cut off as if his throat was paralyzed. He pulled on the snake, but it wouldn't come loose.

Finally, he reached up with his knife and started stabbing. Red fluid splattered against the white refrigerator, and I wondered if it was all snake blood or if he was cutting himself as well.

In its death throes, the snake loosened its grip, and Moser threw it as far as he could. It landed on the benches, unmoving.

I wasn't sure how long the venom would take to incapacitate him. It was going to hurt, and it would likely do permanent damage, but if he got help soon enough, he would probably survive. What I needed was to get to his gun. If he was still agile enough to beat me to it, I was done. I prepared myself to make the attempt.

As Moser staggered around, the other snakes spilled out of the box. Most headed for the dark spaces around the house, but one crawled toward Moser and struck him in the leg. He lost his footing, stumbled backward, tripped on the first row of benches, and fell headfirst into the fire pit. I heard the *crunch* from where I was standing.

I emerged from the blind and ran toward the rifle, my eyes on Moser's twisting body. I reached the rifle and spun around.

Moser didn't move. He stared sightless at the sky, a pool of blood under his head. The snake on his leg wriggled off, as if it wasn't in a hurry. I watched it carefully, but it headed away from me.

I'd killed a man. The thought struck me like a blow, and I felt sick, almost dizzy.

You've killed two other men, my father's voice scoffed.

"But not on purpose," I answered aloud.

It was you or them, son.

It bothered me that his words made sense.

CHAPTER 35

As I reached down to grab Moser's backpack, the walkie-talkie screeched.

"Moser, come in, Moser."

I picked it up, debating whether it would be better to answer or to let Samuels continue speaking. When the silence stretched out, I realized that he was going to sign off.

"*What?*" I shouted, in an approximation of Moser's high-pitched, annoyed voice.

"Call Jordan down from the hillside," Samuels said. "I can't reach him. We don't need to guard the perimeters anymore. Sheriff Black has called in every cop within a hundred miles. Davis won't get far. Popov and his crew are showing up too." He didn't sound happy about that.

"Fuck Popov!" I shouted, hoping the walkie-talkie would distort my voice.

"Yeah, well, you boys didn't get the job done. We'll be lucky to get paid. Popov is bringing dogs and four-wheelers. But if we can get to Davis before Popov or the cops, we'll have done our job."

I didn't answer.

"Just do as I say, Moser. I'll be there soon."

Again, I didn't answer, but that apparently wasn't out of character, for Samuels clicked off without further comment.

I was full of nervous energy, but for once I had food in my belly. I knew the excitement would wear off, and when it did, I'd be drained. I grabbed both packs, the one I'd filled with snacks after dumping out the snakes and the one Moser carried. I'd investigate its contents later.

I hesitated at the corner of the house, wondering if I should go to my room first. I could check to see if the phone still had a charge, though I was pretty sure it was drained. I could also grab a change of clothing, but I knew from experience that getting in and out of Bigfoot took precious time.

Samuels had scared me. "I'll be there soon." It was the impreciseness of *soon* that had caught my attention. I also knew Samuels wouldn't be alone. It would take a good fifteen minutes for me to get to where I'd hidden the box and fifteen minutes to get back.

I trotted down the road, the Bigfoot costume chafing my legs with every step. I cursed myself for not having stopped by my room first.

Beside the road, the Jeep was turned on its side, its blackened carcass still smelling of burned metal and flesh. The grate had been dropped back down. All three gates had been left open. As I approached the highway, I left the road and climbed toward the trees. I made my way to the final gate from the side, watching for traffic.

The hole where I'd hidden the box looked undisturbed. Seeing and hearing no one, I ran the last few yards and dug up the covering. Inside, the box was where I'd left it, though the cardboard had half-disintegrated because of the rain. For the first time, I could see the contents. I pulled the knife out of the pouch and cut away the duct tape.

On top of the other contents, just beneath the soggy lid, was a revolver, which I quickly put into Moser's pack. Underneath that were piles of green. Packets of fifty-dollar bills. It was more money than I'd ever seen before. Hell, it was more money than I was ever likely to see in my lifetime.

Has this been all about money?

I don't know what I'd expected, but it had been something more than that. Money seemed like such an insignificant motive for all the murders. I tried taking a guess and figured it couldn't be more than a few hundred thousand dollars. Professional killers wouldn't be cheap. The operation seemed all out of scale to the reward.

By then, I suppose I had expected something out of a

Tarantino movie, a glowing yellow object of mysterious origin.

Something more than this!

I thought about leaving the money exposed to the elements. Let the squirrels use it for bedding, the sparrows for their nests. I didn't care.

I thought of Granger and Conner, the medical bills and the loss of income, and grabbed the packets and started shoving them into Hanson's pack. By the time I was done, the pack was bulging and heavy.

At the bottom of the box, nestled in the soggy cardboard, I saw something plastic. I pulled it out from under the almost paste-like paper and brushed it off.

A floppy disk. I hadn't seen one of those in years.

This was what they were looking for. The money and the gun, those were just to help whoever came for the disk get away.

I tucked the disk into my Bigfoot pouch, as if that made it safer. I turned and trudged back up to the ranch house. I headed to the kitchen. The lights were on, but Conner wasn't there. "Conner?" I whispered loudly.

If he wasn't in the kitchen, then he wasn't at Bigfoot Ranch. There was still no sign of anyone around, despite it being midmorning. I didn't know what had happened to Conner, but he wasn't there.

Still no sign of Samuels.

I checked my internal clock. About half an hour had passed. I decided there was enough time to risk going to my room to grab a change of clothing.

My bedroom looked undisturbed. The imprint on top of the bedspread from where I'd been napping, fully clothed, was still there. I pulled the phone from under the bed. As I thought, completely drained.

I went to my closet and exchanged Moser's rifle, which I wasn't even sure I knew how to operate, for my own hunting rifle. I grabbed my pack with its survival gear and ammunition, slightly smaller than the ones Moser and Hanson had carried.

At the back of the closet was a loose panel. Granger had once winkingly informed me that I could *hide* things there. I'd never seen the need—until now.

I piled the money in the hole, at the last second grabbing the driest packet and putting it alongside the disk in the Bigfoot pouch. I replaced the panel, turned around, and thought about what else I needed.

I turned Moser's pack upside down on the bed. Its contents looked similar to what had been in Hanson's pack. I grabbed the matches and the flashlight. There wasn't anything else in there that I couldn't improve on with my own provisions. I took Hanson's pack, now emptied of money, and stuffed it with dry clothing—pants, socks, shorts, a shirt, and a coat.

I thought about taking off the Bigfoot costume right there, but I knew it wouldn't be that easy. My broken finger had started to throb again, and I was afraid that if I tried the difficult maneuver now, I might be still changing clothes when Samuels arrived.

But even more important, I was leery of letting my protection go. The suit had become almost a talisman to me, a sign of my survival in the wilderness with nothing else but a knife. I felt like it was part of me now.

I caught a whiff of it as I zipped it up, and it nearly bowled me over. Talisman it might be, but when I had time, I'd take it off. Otherwise, people would smell me coming. But first I needed to get away.

I headed into the back hallway. For a moment, I thought I heard a voice from the front of the house, and I froze. I stood there for a long second, but there was no repeat of the sound.

Check it out? And what happens if it is one of Samuels's men? Another fight to the death?

I kept going down the hallway and out the back door, closing it quietly behind me. There were several old sheds dotting the back of the Bigfoot Ranch, most of them from pioneer days and nearly falling over. At the edge of the hill, among the trees, was a battered metal shed that looked abandoned from the outside.

I pulled open the door with a *creak* and looked down on Granger's Harley-Davidson swathed in a cloth covering. I reached over and pulled it off. I opened the sidecar lid and slid the backpack with the money inside. I was about to put my own pack on top when I heard a rustle behind me.

"Don't move, Mr. Davis."

CHAPTER 36

Martinson trembled, his red mustache squirming like a cat-erpillar. His rifle was pointed at my gut. From this dis-tance, he couldn't miss, and I didn't think the costume could withstand a direct hit this time.

Where had he come from?

His hair was tousled, the right edge of his mustache turned upward as if he'd been sleeping on it. Pretty clearly, he'd been left behind to hold the fort and had fallen asleep on duty.

"Hand over your rifle," he said.

"Sure," I said and reached up to swing the rifle around on its strap.

"Wait," Martinson said nervously. "Just let it drop."

I hadn't planned on shooting it out with him, but I did as he said.

Martinson sniffed and curled his lip. "Jesus, you stink."

I didn't respond.

He seemed uncertain about what to do next. I watched his finger, afraid he'd accidentally jerk the trigger in his jumpiness.

"Jordan called in last night," he said. "Said you got away. Why the hell did you come back?" He made it sound as if it was a personal affront, as if he'd thought it was all over and now here I'd come to spoil it.

"I came to check on Conner. I wanted to be sure he was safe."

"Why wouldn't he be?" Martinson said. "They only want you."

"That didn't keep Jordan from shooting Kent?"

Martinson seemed to lose the strength to hold up the rifle.

The barrel dropped a couple of inches before he realized it and brought it back up. "Why...why would he do that?"

"They aren't going to leave witnesses, Martinson," I said. "Whatever they're looking for is too important."

"Oh, Jesus, I knew it," Martinson said. His face was pale, the three-day growth of red beard showed brightly. He lowered his rifle, his finger coming away from the trigger. "Sherm warned me, but I didn't believe him."

I took a step toward him, reaching out for the rifle. He looked uncertain for a moment, then handed it to me. "I never wanted this. I never thought they'd kill anyone."

"What's in the box?" I asked.

"I have no fucking idea," he said. "How could anything that old matter anymore?"

"What do you do for a living, Martinson?" It was more obvious than ever that the little man didn't fit in with the mercenaries. "Why did they bring you along?"

"I'm just an accountant. I know we have some clients that aren't on the up and up, but what big firm doesn't? I mean, it wasn't any of my business to question it. But something changed a few weeks ago. Suddenly the bosses were all nervous about something. They asked me about Sherm, whether I'd noticed anything, and I thought it was a good time to get him out of there, so I made up some numbers."

"Some numbers," I repeated.

"That can't be what this is all about," Martinson said. "They just used it as an excuse to fire him."

"So you have no idea what they're covering up?"

The bushy mustache stopped twitching for a moment, as if Martinson had suddenly thought of something. "There were rumors about Sherm. That he was, like, an old-time soldier for one of the Five Families. I never thought anything of it. He's, like, an old fat guy, you know? But...well, I've been listening to Samuels and the others, and I think maybe I've been working for the same guys. Or worse."

"Worse?"

"I have an awful lot of Russian accounts," he said. "The figures they give me are always a little hinky. My job is to make them look good." His mustache stopped twitching and his eyes lost focus.

"You just thought of something, didn't you?" I insisted. "What is it?"

"Have you been paying attention to the news about the political scene?" he asked.

"Not much," I admitted. I tended to stay away from politics, other than to vote. I usually did my research about the issues the night before I sent my ballot in and then forgot about it.

"The new Supreme Court nominee, Barton Crane, they're saying he's in the Russians' pocket. But no one can find any proof."

"And?"

"Well, Crane was a high-powered lawyer for some of the big real estate deals in the nineties. Russian oligarchs buying up prime property. About the time Sherm handled all the accounts. Some of the deals were pretty shady, but enough time has passed that lost records can be explained away. I figured they probably whitewashed the books years ago...unless..."

"Unless Sherman Russo kept them," I said.

"So stuff no one cared about a few months ago suddenly becomes all-important. The Russians are about to have a man bought and paid for on the Supreme Court," he said.

"More than that. Crane was just the point man, the crooked lawyer who facilitated all the deals. He'd know all the guilty parties. Bring him down, and half of Washington goes with him," I pointed out.

"What are you going to do?" Martinson asked.

"I'm going to make sure the truth gets out," I said. "They tried to kill Granger. They murdered Kent and some hiker. I can't let them get away with it."

"You'd better get out of here, then," Martinson said. "Before Samuels gets back."

I nodded, looking down at the rifle in my hands, wondering what to do with it. I didn't quite trust Martinson.

I ejected the magazine and stuck it in my pack, then threw the rifle into the muck at the side of the shed. Slinging my own rifle over my shoulder again, I finished putting my backpack in the sidecar and latched it shut. I started to wheel the heavy bike out of the shed.

"What are you going to do about Conner?" Martinson said.

"Conner?"

"He's in the kitchen. Hasn't left it since you and Granger… disappeared."

I remembered the sound I'd heard in the hallway and realized why it had sounded familiar: it had been Pink Floyd. Conner probably had his earphones on full blast. He'd probably been in the pantry or the bathroom when I'd poked my head into the kitchen. Now he was likely cooking away merrily, unaware that anything was wrong.

I leaned the motorcycle against the shed. "Is he alone?"

"I think so," Martinson said. "Unless Jordan or Moser or Hanson have come back."

I unslung my rifle and put my finger on the trigger. "Stay here."

"Wait!" Martinson cried. I turned at the urgency in his voice. "Do you have it? Whatever was in the box?"

I didn't answer, which seemed to confirm his suspicions.

"Why don't you give it to me?" he said. He looked like he as trying hard to keep his face neutral, but I saw the gleam in his eyes. "In case something happens to you. I'll make sure the information gets out. I promise."

There was the smallest chance that I might have considered it, but Martinson's eyes drifted to the assault rifle on the ground. I went over, picked it up, and checked the chamber. It was empty, but it was possible that Martinson had ammunition squirreled away somewhere. Now that he'd figured out the stakes, I couldn't be certain that he wouldn't change his mind, try to play the hero for his bosses.

I turned the barrel in his direction and he held his hands up.

"OK, OK," he said. "But you gotta hit me or something. Samuels will kill me if he thinks I let you go without a fight."

I looked him over, and he mistook my inspection for hesitation.

"You got to make it hurt, man, or Samuels won't…"

I hit him over the head with the rifle stock. He dropped

without a sound and lay unmoving. The scalp wound bled profusely.

Shit. I killed him.

I dropped to my knees and felt for his pulse. He groaned, and without opening his eyes, he muttered, "Why'd you hit me so hard?"

"Stay down," I said, throwing his rifle as far as I could into the woods behind the shed.

My own rifle in hand, I walked toward the back of the house.

CHAPTER 37

Conner's voice echoed down the hallway. His voice was high-pitched, and he spoke distinctly, every word carefully enunciated. If you didn't know he had Down syndrome, you'd never have guessed it from how he spoke. Even so, he was blasting Pink Floyd at a high volume, and I couldn't make out the individual words.

Someone else spoke in a low tone. I couldn't tell who it was, but I was pretty certain whoever it was wouldn't be happy to see me.

I crept the last few feet to the door, wincing at the creaking boards, thankful for the loud music: *"Hey, teacher! Leave those kids alone!"*

"I can't hear myself think, Conner!" came a loud voice.

The CD was turned off.

"Thank you, man," Jordan said. "Now what were you saying?"

"I don't use butter on everything," Conner said. "That's cheating."

"I notice you don't use much salt either," Jordan said.

"There is always a better seasoning, Jordan," Conner said.

I was amazed. I'd never heard the boy address anyone by other than "Mister" or "Ma'am." I suddenly doubted if I could do what I was about to do.

Before I could change my mind, I stepped into the kitchen, rifle at the ready. Through the kitchen windows, I saw Kent's two horses grazing. Jordan must have ridden into the ranch while I was dealing with Martinson. Obviously, he hadn't seen Moser's body.

Conner and Jordan stood side-by-side, cutting vegetables. Conner's motions were a blur; the bigger man's motions were slower, if no less precise. They both turned as I came in.

Conner broke into a wide smile, and it looked as if he was going to come over to hug me. With a blank face, Jordan laid his big hands on the boy's shoulders, stopping him. Jordan still had the knife in his hand, propped casually near Conner's neck. I doubted Conner even realized it.

"What are you doing here, Mr. Davis?" Conner asked.

"You can call me Hart, Conner," I said. It was a strange time to feel jealous, but I couldn't help it.

"Yes, sir...Hart," Conner said. "Why are you wearing Mr. Granger's costume? He wrinkled his nose. "It stinks."

"Sorry about that," I said. "I haven't had a chance to take it off."

Jordan laughed. "Amazing. That's one thing we never would have considered, a bulletproof Bigfoot costume. Only reason you're still alive."

I didn't answer. I motioned with the rifle for Jordan to step away from Conner. He didn't budge.

"No reason to be unfriendly now," he said. "Samuels always was a little extreme, but none of that was necessary. If you just tell us where the box is, we'll go on our way. Leave you—and Conner—alone."

"Conner," I said. "Jordan killed Kent."

The boy looked confused, as if the words made no sense. "Killed him?"

"Shot him because he got in the way. He's going to do the same to you and me."

Jordan shook his head adamantly. "Not Conner. He doesn't deserve any of this."

For a moment, I believed him. But then I noticed that the edge of the blade was closer to Conner's jugular than ever.

"Put down the rifle, Hart," he said. "Let's discuss this man to man. Leave Conner out of it."

"I agree," I said. "Leave Conner out of it."

"We need to be on equal footing, don't you think? If you lower the rifle, we can talk it over."

"You'll kill us both without a second thought," I said.

"Your only chance is to leave now, Hart. Samuels is bringing in reinforcements. And if you haven't heard, you're a mass murderer. Granger is out of it. He's been given enough drugs to keep him quiet until it's too late. The cops are going to shoot you the moment they see you."

"Then I've got nothing to lose," I said. "Why don't you put the knife down, Jordan? Then we can talk. Or I'll tie you up and leave with Conner."

Jordan shook his head regretfully. "See, I can't do that. I'm paid the big bucks because I've never done that. It ain't in my nature. If I ever once give up, I'm done, and this is all I know how to do. So it looks like we have a bit of a stalemate, which is fine with me. Samuels will be here in minutes."

"No," I said. I took a step forward, pointing the gun at Jordan's head.

The knife came down on Conner's neck, and then stopped.

"Fuck it," Jordan said. The rifle barrel was only inches away from him. "I don't think you have the guts to shoot someone face to face, Hart," he said, pushing the kid away. "Get out of here, Conner. Now."

I had a clear shot, but I hesitated. Jordan came at me so fast I barely had time to pull the trigger. The shot went wide, hitting the countertop near where Conner stood, slack-jawed. I raised the rifle instinctively and heard the blade skitter down the stock. It struck the trigger with my finger on it, jarring the rifle loose.

Then I was on my back, the bigger man's weight bearing me down. The knife came at my eyes, and I flinched, moving my head to the side just in time. With Jordan's weight still on me, I couldn't use my rifle.

The point of the blade scrabbled across the wood floor toward my neck, where the Kevlar stopped it. I pushed upward with all my strength. Jordan didn't move an inch. I was immobilized, and Jordan still had a free hand. He lifted the blade over my head again, his eyes cold and deadly.

A jolt shot through his irises, and he grunted. The knife dropped toward my face, cutting into my cheek, but it was only the gravity of the weapon, without the force of Jordan's arm behind it.

He breathed into my face one last time. His head fell against my neck, and I felt nothing but dead weight.

I pushed him away and scrambled backward. From the middle of Jordan's back protruded the handle of the biggest butcher knife in the kitchen.

Conner stood over us, tears streaming down his face. I got up, went to him, and took him in my arms.

"I knew he was a bad man," Conner said, his voice muffled against my chest. "But I really liked him."

I heard heavy vehicles in the distance, coming down the ranch road. I held Conner out at arm's length. "You didn't do *any* of this, Conner, you hear? I did it. Remember that. It was me."

"Mr. Granger told me to never lie."

"You *aren't* lying, Conner. None of this would have happened if I hadn't come into the kitchen with a rifle. It was all me, Conner, no lie."

Conner looked uncertain, but I thought there was a chance that he believed me. I reached down to the handle of the butcher knife and rubbed off Conner's fingerprints, then made sure I left some good ones of my own.

There...they'll believe the evidence.

There was some blood on the kid's hand. "Wash that blood off, Conner," I told him. "We've got to go."

I left him in the kitchen and ran to the front windows. It looked like every emergency vehicle and cop car within a hundred miles was coming toward us. It had started to snow again outside, and the bright red, blue, and yellow lights flashing reminded me of Christmas.

This time, I didn't think the snow would stop. Once it hit the ground, it would stay until summer.

I returned to the kitchen, where Conner sat at the table, looking at anything but the body on the floor. "I'm going to leave you here, Conner," I said. "The police are coming. Tell them that Jordan and I had a fight. That's true, right?"

"I guess so," Conner said.

"You saved me, son. I will never forget it." I leaned over and hugged him tightly. If it had been only Samuels's men and the sheriff, I wouldn't have taken the chance of leaving Conner. But with so many witnesses, I thought he'd be safe.

I couldn't say the same for myself. Once I was in custody, there was no telling what would happen to me, especially if Granger was out of commission. One thing was for certain: the floppy disk in my pocket would disappear.

I was pretty sure Martinson would toe the company line, once I was out of sight. It would be my word against Samuels and the others, who had, no doubt, already given their versions of what had happened. That some of them were dead would only make their statements that much more powerful.

I had to get as far away as I could and make sure the information on the disk was released. Maybe then they'd have no reason to keep chasing me.

I went out the back door and trotted past the shed. Martinson was gone, his rifle still lying where I'd tossed it.

I got on the Harley, started it up, and headed into the hills. With my knowledge of trails and out-of-sight gullies, I had a good chance of getting to the summit of Deadfall Ridge before they knew it. Once I was on the other side of the Strawberry Mountains, they'd have a hell of a time finding me.

The only thing that worried me now was how fast the snow was coming down.

CHAPTER 38

Sherm knew exactly where Gina Simone lived. He'd Google-mapped her more than once over the years. She had a nice Craftsman-style house on a big corner lot, a neat garden, and a nice yard, just as he would have expected of her.

He'd thought of calling her when her husband had died, but he had doubted she'd want to hear from him. "Are you still one of them?" she'd ask, and he'd have to admit he was.

Though he was certain no one knew about her, he parked a few blocks away. As he got out of the Toyota, his knees buckled. He reached out for the car door and missed, slamming against the side of the car. The next thing he knew he was on the sidewalk, on his back.

The Toyota wasn't in sight. Somehow, he'd stumbled away from it, unconscious on his feet.

He sat up. The street sign on the corner said "Sprucewood Court," which was Gina's street. It had gotten dark. Dogs barked in surrounding yards, but no one came out to investigate. Anyone who saw him would probably think he was drunk.

Stumbling drunk in Salt Lake. That couldn't be that common, but maybe it wasn't unheard of. He got to his feet, feeling the dampness from the reopened wound running down his side, down his leg, into his left shoe. He squished as he walked.

The pain felt like it belonged to someone else, or perhaps another time, somewhere far away.

Gina's tan house was the smallest on the block, but the most kept up, with a white picket fence and a large spruce tree covering most of the front yard. He lurched up the steps and almost slammed his head into the red door. He knocked gently.

Gina opened the door.

She looked exactly the same to him, despite her white hair, despite the extra pounds. The wrinkles in her face only accentuated the kindness that had always been there. She didn't seem alarmed by the big man at her doorstep, merely curious.

"Can I help you?" she asked.

"Gina," he managed to say, and then fell forward. He felt her arms trying to hold him up, but failing, and he slammed into the floor. The pain in his shoulder exploded, like a star going nova in a distant galaxy, and then he drifted off into darkness.

Someone stabbed at his shoulder. Sherm awoke, one hand grabbing at whoever was torturing him. His fingers closed on a thin wrist, and he stopped himself just in time to avoid snapping the bones. Gina hovered over him.

"Be still," she said.

He was on his back on the floor, just inside the doorway. Sherm was impressed that Gina had managed to drag him that far. There was a pillow under his head and a blanket over the lower part of his body, and she had cut away the clothing around his shoulder.

"I'm sorry," he said.

She didn't answer, but kept probing his shoulder.

"I never wanted to bother you."

She looked at him with the steady green eyes he remembered, never surprised by anything, always in control. She didn't speak, however. She got up, and when he tried to raise his head to see where she was going, the pain immobilized him.

Gina returned a few minutes later and leaned over him. She had a cup of water and a handful of pills. She helped him lift his head, and he washed them down.

"What are they?" he asked.

"Some pain pills I had left over from when I broke my leg," she said. "I think they're still good. Says not to take more than two, so giving you four might be pushing it. But for what I'm going to have to do..."

"Just let me rest a little," he said. "Then I'll be on my way."

Gina didn't bother to answer. She knew he wasn't going anywhere.

"I'll be out of here by tomorrow," he insisted.

She snorted and shot him that annoyed look she always gave him when she thought he was being silly. It was as if the last thirty years hadn't passed and they were still courting each other, still learning each other's ways.

"I'm sorry," he started to say again, intending to explain his appearance, but her face grew fuzzy in his eyes, and the wrinkles and gray hair disappeared, and she was twenty-five again. Then she seemed to dissolve, as if she was an illusion.

"Angie," he said as she wavered like a mirage.

She was always an illusion, he thought, and then she disappeared, and he was alone in the darkness with his pain. He dreamed he was being held down and prodded by shadowy men; they had accents, but like nothing he'd ever heard. They laughed, and there were knives in their hands, and they stabbed him again and again, until he screamed.

He awoke to his own scream.

"Shush, you," Gina said in her calm voice. "You'll wake my neighbors. They already think I'm a witch."

The pain was even worse than in the dream, but at least Sherm knew where it came from. Gina dug into his shoulder with a knife and tweezers. He clenched his jaw and forced himself to keep from shouting, though a high whine came from behind his self-imposed gag.

"Got it!" she said, and then the shooting pain was gone. The dull throb that was left behind was almost pleasant in comparison. The pain pills she'd given him could handle that much, at least.

"When you think you can move, we'll get you into bed. In a week or two, you'll be ready to leave," she said.

"Thank you for not calling an ambulance," Sherm said. He wasn't going to stay for another day if he could help it. It wasn't just that he needed to get to Amanda, he didn't want to endanger Gina. He didn't think Samuels knew about her, but he couldn't be sure he hadn't left a trail of eyewitnesses to her door.

She said, "Didn't figure you showed up half-dead at my door because you wanted an ambulance."

He tried to sit up and found he could manage the movement, though vertigo almost dropped him again. He waited for the spinning to stop. "I think I can get to the couch," he said.

"Bedroom is closer," she said. "Give it a try, Sherm."

The sound of her voice saying his name filled him with regret, the same sad nostalgia he'd felt for thirty years. Sometimes he had wondered if he'd imagined that warm tone, that feeling that she was taking his clunky name and making it sound strangely wonderful.

"Angie," he said, his nickname for her. *I hate it when anyone else says that,* she'd told him, and so he'd kept it for their private moments.

She looked away.

Sherm tried to stand, his legs wobbling. He made it a few steps before falling to his knees. Before Gina could stoop down to help him, he got to his feet again and followed her the rest of the way to the bedroom, making it to the bed just in time to fall onto it. He lay there facedown for a few moments, waiting for the vertigo to stop, and then turned onto his back.

He was done. He couldn't move another inch, even though he was crossways on the mattress. Gina put a pillow under his head.

"Sorry," he muttered again. The softness of the bed was like another drug, dragging him under. He felt her hand run across his forehead, as if checking his temperature, and it was wonderful, and then he was out.

Sunlight blasted through the windows as if seeking Sherm out. He opened his eyes with a groan. The pain was still there, but he was clear-headed for the first time since he'd been shot.

What have I done? he thought.

Gina sat by the window, staring out onto the garden. Her profile was as he always remembered her: the long Roman nose, the high cheeks, the full lips. She was as Midwestern as she could be, but she'd always seemed exotic to him, like an ancient Greek goddess.

"I'm sorry about Howard," he said.

She turned to him, seemingly unsurprised that he was awake. In the daylight, he saw her true age. Her blue eyes were faded, and she had loose skin under her chin. But she was still Angie.

"Howard was a good man," she said. "I loved him dearly." She held his eyes steadily, but she oversold it.

Yes, and I loved Jennifer, at least at first, But I never loved anyone like I loved you.

Sherm threw off the covers and swung his legs over the side of the bed. The vertigo was gone; all that remained was the pain in his shoulder, and pain he could handle. He was still clothed.

"I've got to go," he said. "I've got to get to Oregon by Saturday."

Gina laughed.

"What?"

"Too late," she said. "Today's Saturday."

He froze, trying to figure out how that was possible. He'd gotten to Salt Lake on Thursday night.

"You slept through an entire day," she said. "You needed it. If you hadn't rested, there would be no way you'd be able to sit up today."

She rose from the chair by the window and approached him. She seemed so tiny, and her shoulders had a slight hunch to them. Even sitting, Sherm felt like an ungainly bear next to her.

"I'm not going to try to talk you out of leaving," she said. She nodded at his wound.

Sherm didn't answer. So much history was contained in those words Gina was saying to him, *I know you're still a mobster.* And for her, that was unforgivable. Had always been unforgivable.

He stood up and swayed for a few moments. He could smell his own sweat, but there was no time to clean up.

"You can't go like that," she said. "Howard's room is the way he left it. I think some of his clothes will fit you."

He followed her, trying to keep his stride steady and even, though it was as if he walked a tightrope. She led him to a small, dusty room. He immediately recognized it as an accountant's office. It had always seemed ironic to him that Howard had fallen into the same profession as him, if not quite with the same clients.

Gina crossed the room and opened a closet. There, as if enshrined, was the gear of another profession. A shotgun leaned against the back, a gun case to one side. A bulky, out-of-date bulletproof vest hung from a hook, along with a trench coat voluminous enough to fit over it.

"He couldn't completely let go of it," she said. She didn't sound disgusted as much as exasperated, as if to say, *Men!* "Take whatever you need, Sherm. The rest is getting tossed."

He opened the gun cabinet and found shotgun shells and ammunition for his revolver. He put on the trench coat, filled the pockets with ammo, and grabbed the shotgun and the vest.

"I need a car," he said, feeling ashamed for asking. The Toyota, with its stolen license plates, was too hot by now.

Gina simply nodded, went to the kitchen, and removed a key from a keychain. "This is to the Rav4 in the driveway," she said. "Marie, my daughter, has been trying to get me to quit driving for months. I've had a few fender benders recently. I think maybe it's time I admitted my age."

"Never," he said. *Angie will never grow old.*

As he walked to the front door, he felt almost like his old self. Not Sherm the mob accountant, but Sherman Russo, a soldier in the Family.

And there, as if to reprimand him, stood Gina Simone. It was the same choice as always: stay and forget his old life, or go.

But the choice wasn't really the same. He owed it to Amanda and Hart Davis to try to help. But most of all, he couldn't bring his troubles to Gina.

Assuming she'd even have him.

Sherm opened the door and looked out. There didn't appear to be anyone watching. He stood uncertainly on the porch. He wanted to kiss her—on the cheek, as a gesture of caring.

Gina stepped away. "Please don't come back, Sherm."

She closed the door softly behind him.

CHAPTER 39

Over the years, I'd built small cairns of stones or other markers at every mile point along the trails, so I'd know how far I was pushing my clients. Some clients I'd earmark for the easy one-mile trails, others for the more strenuous four-mile trails, and very occasionally, I'd take clients up the ten-mile trail to the summit of the old Forest Service road.

The mile markers passed by amazingly fast on the Harley, which handled the terrain and the slope easily. It felt wrong to be tearing up Deadfall Ridge, but being a scofflaw was the least of my worries.

Among the emergency vehicles, I'd spotted Grant County Search and Rescue trucks. They'd have four-wheeled off-road vehicles, but I doubted they'd be able to follow me, at least not at first. No one knew this area like I did.

The Forest Service had done their best to erase the old road from all their maps. There probably wasn't anyone alive who knew about it except Granger and me—and maybe Heffinger, but you couldn't pry two words out of the old man except with money or booze, and even then, he'd probably keep it to himself.

I was anything but quiet in my escape. Granger liked the full-throated Harley-Davidson roar. But I didn't think there was anyone up here, now that my pursuers were…inactive. I flinched from the thought that I'd been responsible for their deaths. In every instance, they had brought it upon themselves.

I'd been lucky. I wasn't a trained killer like my opponents, but I was familiar with the terrain. That and luck had made enough of a difference. But now, I needed to get out of the wilderness and among other people where I could blend in.

Once in civilization, it would be easier to hide. I had money in my pocket. I could afford to avoid my old stomping grounds.

Though the floppy disk weighed next to nothing, it was as if I could feel it pulling me down.

Who even has a floppy disk drive anymore?

Aaron would know what to do. I called my tech guy a wizard because what he did with computers seemed like magic to me. After watching him navigate the bewildering digital universe, I'd turned my website over to him, promising him a minimum and a percentage. Not counting what I owed my ex-wife, most of my debt was owed to him. Not that he ever bugged me for it.

I needed to get to Aaron and let him decipher what was on the disk. I'd have to approach him carefully, because it was possible that he was being watched.

But for that, I needed to get back to Bend. If I could get to Canyon City without being seen, I was pretty sure that Marty Bell or Candice Shuler would give me a ride to town, even if I had to hide in their trunk.

I drove under the big widowmaker without realizing it. Looking back, I slid to a stop. I propped the bike against a tree and climbed the hill to the base of the old snag. I pushed down on it, and it creaked. I pushed harder, and it gave way. It crashed across the narrow ridge, covering it from side to side.

There was no way around it.

I got back on the Harley and kept going.

As I passed the three-mile marker, which was the biggest ponderosa on Deadfall Ridge, a shadow passed over me. I veered into the shade of the tree and bent over the bike's metal chassis. The Harley was painted military green, but I wasn't sure how much it would flash in the snow.

The helicopter didn't slow down. It kept flying perpendicular to the road and out of sight. I'd caught the logo on the side: a Deschutes County copter, from three counties over.

I turned off the bike and listened to the sound of the rotors fade into the distance. I couldn't stop, even if they spotted me, but the longer I was in the woods, the tighter the cordon would get. I looked up into the darkened clouds.

"Snow harder, dammit, snow!"

Though I could barely maneuver in the snow, especially with the sidecar, I probably had more mobility than my pursuers.

The Fates were listening. As I passed the five-mile marker, a ribbon tied onto a juniper stump, the snow became a blizzard, coming down in huge, fluffy flakes that adhered to the fur of the costume. After another mile, I looked down and laughed.

I've gone from Bigfoot to the Abominable Snowman. I was covered in snow. There were so many holes in the costume that the cold air blew into it and swirled around, freezing my legs.

The snow wasn't melting, except for on my face, which was getting so cold that when I reached up to touch my cheek with my gloved hand, I couldn't feel. I stopped long enough to put on the mask, pushing it around until I could see out the eyeholes.

It wasn't just luck that had saved me the last few days. The bulletproof Bigfoot costume had made the difference more than once.

But enough was enough. I stunk, the Kevlar was rubbing me raw, and I was tired of dragging the Bigfoot carcass around. When I reached the summit, I would stop long enough to take it off and put on the warm, dry clothing from the backpacks. My survival kit had a windbreaker in it, rolled into a bag no bigger than my hand, which would keep the wet out and the warmth in.

As I got closer to the summit of Deadfall Ridge, more and more healthy orange bark showed beneath the blackened trunks of the burned ponderosas, and at their crowns were tufts of green needles. The Harley struggled up the last half mile, and I had to use my feet to help keep me upright for most of it, but with a final roar, it reached a wide clearing. There was an abandoned horse pen there, some metal grates where there had once been campgrounds, and, incongruous among the devastation, a metal outhouse, constructed on concrete and still functional despite being abandoned by the Forest Service.

From here the road was clear, two tracks looping down into the lowlands behind Strawberry Mountain. It was twice as far to Canyon City than using the highway, but it was all downhill from here.

I sat on the motorcycle for a few moments, suddenly reluctant to stop.

Or was I reluctant to take off the costume?

I laughed at the thought, but there was a part of me that wanted to push on, to ride into Canyon City in all my Bigfoot glory.

As I hesitated, I saw someone step out from the tree line into the middle of the road.

Nicole Nelson raised her revolver and pointed it at my head. She motioned with her hand across her throat, telling me to cut the engine. There was no sign of friendliness in her expression. It looked like she'd shoot me between the eyes if I didn't do as she instructed.

I turned off the Harley.

"Get off the bike, Bigfoot," she said.

CHAPTER 40

For a fraction of a second, I thought about accelerating toward her, throwing off her aim. From where I straddled the Harley, my toes barely reaching the ground, Nicole looked tiny. Barely over five feet tall, even in her heavy boots, she wore a thick parka and warm-ups and appeared almost round. Her blonde hair was longer than I remembered, tied in pigtails under a Tank Girl earflap hat. Her hand barely wrapped around the handle of the revolver.

But her finger reached the trigger, and her hand was steady. Her blue eyes were as cold as the snow. From what I knew about Nicole, she wouldn't miss. Could the Kevlar withstand a strike from so close, or would she aim for my face and the holes in the mask?

"Gods, you reek," she said. "I guess they weren't kidding when they said Bigfoot is a stinker. But no one ever said anything about Sasquatch riding a Harley-Davidson."

"It's me," I said, my voice muffled and meek behind the mask.

"It speaks!" she said with mock surprise. "Get off the bike, Hart," she repeated.

I dismounted from the Harley and stood there, uncertain what to do. I didn't think the kickstand would keep it upright, nor did I want to lay the machine in the snow.

"Lean it against the tree," Nicole said, motioning to a pine tree beside the trail.

I walked it over, almost slipping several times but finally getting the bike stable.

"Take off the damn mask, Hart. I want to see your face when

I talk to you. I want to know if you're lying."

I reached up and unzipped the mask around the neckline. Snow tumbled down my neck and melted around my chest and stomach, cold for a moment and then pleasantly warm.

"How did you find me?" I asked.

"Where else would you go?" she said. "Remember, I know these mountains as well as you do. Old man Heffinger showed me this road the first time I came up here."

"Are you going to turn me in?"

Nicole didn't answer right away. She kept her face blank. I searched her eyes and thought maybe I saw a smidgen of sympathy.

"I brought a client up to the Heffinger place a couple of days ago," she said. "A guy from L.A. named Nate Hamilton. A nice guy, wanted to take pictures of some birds, hoped to see some wildlife. I told him to stick around the ranch, but he went out walking while I took a nap couple of days ago. He's disappeared."

"Samuels's men killed him," I said.

I saw her glance at my bandaged finger as if she expected it to be moving. "Are you the one who buried him?"

"I tried. It's hard when people are trying to kill you."

I could tell she was almost ready to lower the revolver. "The animals were trying to get at him, but you did a good enough job," she said. "I spent a couple of hours building up the mound. The authorities don't seem to be in a hurry to recover dead bodies. They seem more interested in the person who made them dead."

"I didn't kill him," I said.

"If I thought you had, I'd have already put you down," she said.

"They thought he was me. It's me they're trying to kill."

"Obviously, but who are *they* and why are *they* trying to kill you, Hart? What did you do?"

"I didn't do anything wrong, Nicole. Amanda left a..." I realized the story didn't make any sense and broke off. "I can't possibly explain it to you now, but I promise if you let me go, I'll tell you the whole story when it's all over."

"Over Pappy's Pizza?" she asked with the hint of a smile.

I smiled back. It was clear she didn't know what was going on, but that she doubted I was the culprit. "Nicole, I've got to keep going. They're probably on my trail right now. They've got helicopters."

"Yeah, no worries. They're grounded because of the weather," Nicole said. She reached into her back pocket and pulled out a walkie-talkie. I recognized the brand as the same that Samuels's men were carrying.

My heart sank. There was only one way she'd know what was going on. Only one way she'd know the frequency. "So... you're with them?"

"Hell, no," she snorted. "I'm just not sure I'm with *you*, Hart. Not until I can figure out what's going on. I played along with Samuels, told him I'd help them find you. He offered me a lot of money."

"He's dangerous. Don't trust him."

"From what they're saying, it sounds like you're the dangerous one, Hart. You've killed maybe four men or five men, according to what the sheriff's saying."

"I wasn't trying to kill them. I just wanted to get away."

"Then why the hell *didn't* you get away?" she demanded. "Once you brought down Hanson, you could've made it out of here with no trouble at all. Instead, you turned around and attacked three more men."

"They killed Kent," I said. "I couldn't be sure they wouldn't hurt Conner. I went back for him."

She stared at me for a long moment, then lowered the gun. "I thought that might be it. Conner's a good kid."

"You can't believe Samuels," I said. "He's a professional killer."

"No shit. He's a real charmer, though. Luckily, I'm allergic to charismatic men. That's why I like you so much, Hart."

"Uh...thanks."

She laughed. "No, you're genuine, Hart. No bullshit. I like that."

"So you'll let me go?"

"Yeah, but I wouldn't advise continuing in the direction you were heading. They've got an ambush set up about a mile down the road where it loops around the cliff. You wouldn't stand a chance."

"Damn. How'd they know about the road?" I looked at her questioningly.

"Samuels has a map. Hell if I know where he got it. Every map I've ever seen of the area doesn't show the road, but the guy obviously has clout and a whole lot of money."

I went over to the bike and pulled it away from the tree. "I have to try anyway, Nicole. Maybe I can get by them. I mean, the deputies will be hesitant to shoot, right?"

"I wouldn't count on it," Nicole said. "Samuels met up with some rough-looking guys this morning. They're the ones who set up the ambush. They had accents. It was hard to tell for sure, but they sounded Russian to me. That's when I slipped away."

In the distance came the sound of revving engines, four-wheelers making their way up Deadfall Ridge. They stopped suddenly. They'd reached the fallen widowmaker.

Moments later, the slightly higher buzz of chainsaws floated up to us.

The tracks I'd left on the way up the hill were already full of snow, but it didn't matter. My pursuers knew about the road. If I tried to go off road, I might be able to ride the bike over the rough terrain for a while, but eventually I'd find myself trapped.

What little strength I had left drained away. It seemed hopeless. I'd been lucky enough to survive a game of cat and mouse with five trained mercenaries. But there was no way I could keep it up.

Sounding defeated, I said, "I'm not going down without a fight." I unslung the rifle from my back. I had a couple of dozen rounds in my kit. Chances were I'd never get that many shots off before they got to me.

I remembered the revolver in the Bigfoot pouch. I automatically reached down and began to pull it out. Nicole's fingers tightened on the trigger of her gun. Even now, she wasn't completely sure about me.

As I brought out the revolver, the floppy disk came with it and fluttered down into the snow.

I didn't have to get out, I realized. Only the information did.

"Nicole, you need to get away from here. Take this disk and give it to someone who can do something with it. Someone you trust," I said.

"*That's* what they're after?"

I nodded.

"Won't work," she said. "I think I'm probably in as much trouble as you are, Hart. The way Samuels put it was, 'I'm sure Ms. Nelson wouldn't think to warn him.' If I show up again, he'll be suspicious. I had a handler, who I ditched."

"How'd you do that?"

"I might have put a few Alprazolams into his drink. Either that or he can't hold his liquor. I might be able to get away with it, but Samuels doesn't seem like the trusting type."

"If he catches you, just give him the floppy disk," I said. "He won't have any reason to hurt you."

"You really believe that?"

My pinky twitched as if wanting to tap out a code. It hurt. Over the last few days, I'd come to ignore the pain in my finger. But it was always there, sometimes coming to the fore when I bumped it or when the rest of my aches and pains receded. I didn't want Nicole to go through what I'd gone through.

Samuels wouldn't take her word for it. He'd put her to the test.

"Then we're finished," I said. My voice sounded dead to me. Hollow.

Nicole looked genuinely surprised. "Not yet we aren't."

"We?"

She grinned. "If the back way is closed off, then *we* have to do something different."

CHAPTER 41

"Grab your stuff and let's go," Nicole said.

I decided to follow her lead, trusting she knew what she was doing. I was a few years older than her, but she was far more experienced in the woods.

I went to the sidecar and removed the two packs, regretting that I didn't have time to get out of the Bigfoot costume. First time I had the chance, I was changing. I didn't care how cold it was, I was going to give myself a sponge bath and get into some clean clothing.

Nicole walked west over the top of the ridge. I fell in behind her. We were above Butcher's Cut now, on a hilltop that was almost flat. To either side were rocky crags where the four-wheelers wouldn't have been able to follow us. But Nicole stuck to the level terrain. Apparently, she was more interested in speed than in hiding.

"Why don't we take the Harley?" I asked, stopping and looking back with regret. If I could, I would come back for the bike before it completely disappeared under the snows. It was Granger's pride and joy. "As long as we're staying on the flats, we can cover more territory."

"We'd just have to ditch it eventually," she said and kept walking along the plateau.

I glanced back at the trail we were leaving. "They're going to follow our tracks with the four-wheelers," I said.

"I hope so," Nicole answered without looking back at me. "I very much hope so."

After a few more yards, she stopped. There, directly in our path, was a rounded hole about four feet wide and a good three feet deep. Nicole shrugged off her pack and pulled out an old, moth-eaten blanket.

"I hate to lose this," she said. "My dad gave it to me. But if it has to go, at least it's for a good cause."

She spread the blanket over the hole and rolled a large rock on top of one corner. I searched the hillside for a rock of my own, and by the time I'd placed it on another corner, she'd covered the other two. She started dragging branches and loose sagebrush over to hide the symmetry of the rocks.

The snow was coming down hard. By the time we were done, the brown of the blanket was almost covered.

Nicole ran uphill a ways, then circled back, her fresh tracks leading right toward the trap. She jumped over it and kept walking. I joined her. After another dozen yards or so, she veered downhill where there was a jumble of lava rocks. She plopped down behind the cover they provided, and I joined her.

"We really should keep on going, but I can't resist," she said.

I knew what she meant. I wanted to see the coming misadventure as much as she did.

As we'd been hiking, the sound of the off-road vehicles had grown louder and louder until it seemed as if they were almost on top of us. Still, it was a surprise when two of the four-wheelers appeared. They careened down the trail, not slowing down in the least.

The driver of the first ORV must have realized that whoever had left the footprints had jumped for a distance, because he slammed on the brakes. Too late. The front wheels suddenly dropped, and the rider flew over the handlebars. The vehicle landed on top of him.

The other four-wheeler smashed into the back of the first one, and its rider somersaulted over the wreckage.

"I hope they're all right," Nicole whispered. "Those are the Halligan brothers...local boys."

We waited long enough to see both riders get to their feet. The first man held his shoulder, his left arm hanging uselessly. His brother looked as if he could barely stay on his feet and was groaning loudly enough that we could hear him

"*Now* we stay off the flats," Nicole said.

"They're going to know there are two of us," I warned. "They'll guess it's you."

"You want me to kill them?"

"Of course not," I blurted.

"Good answer," she said.

Nicole headed straight downhill, picking her way through the sudden drops by hanging onto trees and rocks. I had a harder time of it in my costume, and she had to stop several times to wait for me.

It was late afternoon, but in the snowstorm, it seemed darker than that, as if the clouds had swallowed the sun. I stumbled, almost losing my footing in the steep terrain. Nicole reached out and, with a surprisingly strong grip, held me steady.

"I forget," she said. "You've been doing this for days. I'm pretty impressed. It didn't look to me like Samuels and his men were amateurs."

"They are anything but," I said. "The only reason I got away is because they thought it would be easy."

"They underestimated you. To be honest, so did I."

I wanted to ask what she meant by that, but I was too tired to be insulted.

"Just a little farther, Hart. I know a place where we can get out of the snow," she said.

"Not a mineshaft, I hope," I muttered, though in truth, I would have been glad to get out of the freezing snow any way I could.

"More of an overhang," she said, glancing back at me with concern.

When next I was aware of my surroundings, I couldn't remember how I'd gotten there for a moment. The costume felt as if it was adhering to my skin, at least in those places where it wasn't rubbing me raw. I shook my head, and snow tumbled over me and down my neck, joining the growing puddles around my feet, which I only noticed because I could hear them sloshing. My feet were numb.

"Here," Nicole's voice broke through my fog. Her Tank Girl hat was in her hand. "Put it on."

"I can't take that," I protested.

"Just do it," she commanded. "I don't want to have to drag you the rest of the way."

I don't know how much warmth the cap actually provided, but the illusion of shelter seemed to warm me up, and I looked around curiously.

We had come down the western edge of Butcher's Cut. It was an area I rarely visited, too steep for most of my clients, with too few deer. We were walking along a path that ran horizontally across the steep incline. It ended at a hole in the hillside.

"It's only about twenty feet deep," Nicole said when she saw me hesitate. "There's a turn about ten feet in, and a small drop. We should be able to light a fire without being seen."

I followed her into the darkness, counting my steps, hitting a wall at about twelve steps in.

"Down here." Nicole's voice came from my right. I turned, walked another ten steps, and suddenly the floor went out from under me. The small drop Nicole had mentioned was bigger than I'd thought it would be, and I landed hard. Fortunately, it was on soft sand.

Nicole shone her flashlight into my face, and I winced. "Hold this while I go get some wood," she said. "I want to see if the light can be seen from outside."

I sat down, shining the light around the cave. It was bare, but it was obvious that people had stayed here before. The floor was flattened, a ledge was carved into the sand on one side, and there was a fire pit in the middle.

Nicole came back with an armful of branches and twigs. "Get the fire going," she said. "I'll get some more wood. And keep the flashlight beam low. I could see it zooming around."

Somewhere, she'd found some dry twigs for tinder. The fire started easily. I slowly fed the flames, adding the end of the largest branch when it got going. Nicole made three trips out onto the hillside.

"It's really coming down now," she said when she returned the third time. "Our tracks are getting covered."

I didn't respond. I could barely lift my eyes from the fire.

"No offense, Hart, but you are really stinking up the place.

You want to take that that thing off and get into some warm clothing?"

"Yeah," I said, but my arms and legs wouldn't respond. "In a minute."

I just needed to close my eyes for a moment.

"Wake up, Hart!"

I jolted awake at Nicole's sharp tone. I'd fallen asleep sitting up.

"It's time you told me what's going on," she said.

"In the morning," I muttered.

"No, now. I need to know."

I stared into the fire, trying to wake up. I began to tell her the story. My voice droned on as if it belonged to someone else, as if describing things that had happened a long time ago. When I got to the part where I'd been dragged to the fire pit and tortured, I heard her cursing under her breath.

"Jesus, Hart. I'd always heard you were stubborn proud, but that's crazy."

"I know."

"You dragged the others in with you."

The truth of it struck me like a blow. I had a vision of Kent flying in the air. Tears came to my eyes.

"Hart!"

I realized Nicole had said my name several times.

"Look at me, Hart!"

I lifted my head. In the flickering firelight, her blue eyes tender with concern. Her voice was soft. "Most people would have given in, but...I'm not saying you did the wrong thing."

You're not saying I did the right thing either.

"Tell me about what's on the disk," she prompted, gently but insistently.

I told her about Martinson's suppositions and my suspicions. My voice trailed off at some point, and I stared into the fire as if only it existed.

"Go to sleep, Hart. I'll figure something out," Nicole said.

I lay down next to the blaze, still in my Bigfoot outfit, trying to keep my eyes open. I was conscious of Nicole putting a survival blanket over me, and then another one that must have come out of her own pack. The warmth and the crackling of the fire were like a drug.

And then I was gone, dropping into a deep darkness in a dizzying spiral.

CHAPTER 42

I woke up alone. Nicole's pack was still there, and the fire was built up, so I figured she'd gone out scouting. I consulted my inner clock. For the first time I could remember, I had no idea what time it was.

I made my way up through the right-angle bend in the cave. Through a hole at the cave mouth, I gauged by the light that it was midmorning. I went back to the chamber, sat on the ledge, and wondered what to do.

Nicole could still escape. She could surrender, if need be, to the authorities. I was an alleged mass murderer, but she was merely an accessory after the fact. Once out of Samuels's reach, she'd probably be safe. She would take some convincing, but I was determined not let her dig the hole she was in any deeper. Everyone around me was in danger, all because I'd been too stubborn to let go of the box. No one else needed to get hurt.

For the first time in days, I was too warm. The cave held the heat, with an occasional breeze reviving the fire. I looked down at the blaze and saw a wide metal cup full of scrambled eggs and sausage. By now, my olfactory senses were so traumatized, I hadn't even smelled the food.

I reached down with my gloved hands, lifted the hot cup, leaned over, and inhaled the food. I must have chewed the sausages, but it didn't seem like it. Within seconds, just as my taste buds were coming to life, the food was gone. It was the best-tasting meal I'd ever had, and not nearly enough.

With the revival of my senses, I got a whiff of myself. The odor was stunningly acrid and sharp, as if I'd bathed in vinegar for days, overlaid by a stink that reminded me of gunpowder

and onion. I doubt smelling salts could have woken me any
more thoroughly.

Time to get out of the damn costume.

I reached over my shoulder, but it was as if the zipper had
disappeared, as if the costume had become my skin. My fingers
had almost no sensitivity through the gloves; I couldn't get a
grip. I stood up, cursing, trying to reach the zipper first with
my right hand, then, forgetting my broken finger, with my left
hand.

Pain flashed up my arm, and I sat down with a frustrated
grunt.

I *was* Bigfoot now. Food, water, warmth, and safety, that's all
that mattered.

Nicole returned as I sat there bemoaning my fate. She had
an armful of branches, which she dumped in the corner. I
didn't think it was for us, but a courteous gift to the cave's next
occupants.

"About time you woke up," she said. "It stopped snowing
over an hour ago."

"How long was I out?" I said. It was a disorienting feeling,
not knowing what time it was.

She looked down at me as if impressed. "From about five
o'clock yesterday afternoon until eight o'clock this morning. I
didn't think anyone could sleep like that."

"That's impossible," I said, but inside, my clock was
readjusting. I groaned. "Why did you let me sleep so long?"

"We couldn't have gone anywhere in the snowstorm
anyway," she said. She bent over the fire, grabbed the now-empty
metal cup, and wiped the last of the food out of it. "Besides, you
were out on your feet yesterday. A couple of times, it looked like
you were going to cartwheel down the slope. And you're too big
for me to carry."

I thought about that. We were safe enough, probably. The
snow was going to be tough on everyone. If we went to ground
long enough, maybe they'd even think I'd escaped and call off
the hunt.

"They're tightening the circle," Nicole said, as if reading my
mind. "They seem pretty certain we're still trapped. I figure we

have another couple of hours before they get too close for us to get out of here without being seen."

"How do you know that?"

She brought out the walkie-talkie and tossed it onto the floor. "I listened for about three hours this morning. At first they spoke English, then they switched to what sounded like Russian, and about half an hour ago, they stopped talking altogether."

"Which means they suspect that you're listening in," I said with a sinking feeling. Until that moment, I'd still hoped there was plausible deniability on her part.

"Yeah," she said, then shrugged. "Hey, at least they aren't underestimating us anymore."

"What do you mean?"

"Apparently, they're worried at least one of us knows Russian."

I couldn't help but laugh. "*Nyet*," I said.

"*Dasvidaniya, comrade. Privyet!*"

"I think you just said goodbye and hello, in that order."

"*Da*," she agreed.

"So what do we do now?" I asked. My brain felt sloggy despite, or maybe because of, the fifteen hours of sleep.

"First things first," she said. "We need to get you out of that damned costume."

"Oh, thank God!" I said. Just the suggestion filled me with gratitude. "Uh...can you help me with my zipper?"

Nicole laughed. "That's what *she* said." She motioned for me to turn around. She tugged on the zipper several times before it came unstuck. I quickly shrugged off both arms, then shed my coat and flannel shirt.

"Whoa!" Nicole exclaimed, stepping back a couple of steps. "And I thought you stank from the outside!"

"Sorry," I muttered. Apparently, there were a few nerve cells left in my nostrils, because the odor nearly floored me as well. I lifted my poor, scraped legs out of the costume and left it on the floor, looking like the carcass of a gorilla that had been lying in a swamp for months.

Nicole poured the contents of a water bottle into the metal

cup and began warming it over the fire. I couldn't wait, though, and used a bottle of cold water on my legs and arms, wiping them off with my flannel shirt. By the time I finished, the water in the cup was warm enough for my torso. I wiped off my armpits and chest, down over my belly, then became aware of the filthy shorts I was still wearing. It was fortunate that I'd had so little food to eat, because I'd only had to take off the costume once. Still, at least twice, I'd peed inside the suit.

I pulled out fresh clothing from my survival pack: a flannel shirt, underwear, pants, and glory of glories, a fresh pair of socks. I set my soggy shoes near the fire, hoping they'd dry out before we left the cave. My survival pack didn't have enough room for a coat. I hadn't conceived of a situation where I would have my pack but not any outer clothing. But there was the windbreaker, which would keep the warmth in.

I reached down to take off my shorts, hesitating until Nicole turned around and busied herself with the contents of her backpack.

I threw the dirty clothes on top of the reeking Bigfoot fur, resisting the urge to throw it into the fire, and quickly got dressed. With each article of clothing I put on, I felt more human. The fresh shorts equaled all the comforts of home. The shirt and pants were the very epitome of civilization. The socks were the most luxurious of all; I was certain no royalty had ever felt so pampered.

"Oh, my God," I said. "Can't we just stay here forever? Bring me a plate of eggs and sausage every morning and a fresh pair of socks every day, and I'll do anything for you."

"It's pretty bad when being a caveman is a step up in your living standards," Nicole said.

"You don't know the half of it," I answered. I would never be ungrateful for simple warmth and shelter again.

"Let me see your finger," she said.

The Bigfoot suit had kept the splint and bandage in place, but now they were loose enough for Nicole to pluck off. The knuckle was still hugely swollen, but the finger was pink, which meant blood was flowing through it.

"You were lucky," she said, reaching out gingerly and

touching the joint. I tried not to cry out. "I think they dislocated it, and you managed to get it back in place. Try not to move it."

No shit, I resisted saying.

I looked down at my pinky and willed it to move, but it was as useless as trying telekinesis on an inert object. When I moved the ring finger next to it, the pain was excruciating.

Nicole tied the splint back on. "You may not be able to use it again, but at least it isn't infected." She let go of my hand.

I stepped back, uncertainly. Her fingers had felt so soft and were so comforting that I wanted her to keep touching me.

Scooting as far away from the Bigfoot costume as I could get, I crouched near the fire and warmed my hands. The fresh clothing felt like silk rubbing against my skin.

"So...what do we do now?" I asked, then was surprised that I'd asked. Apparently, without my being conscious of the decision, I'd decided to let Nicole take charge. I had come to understand that survival wasn't just about toughness and strength, it was about whether you kept trying.

I was out of ideas. I had never wanted to kill anyone, but I didn't want to die. I was damned if I could see how I could have avoided the one without the other.

Nicole answered as if she'd thought it out. "If the back way is closed to us, then we need to go out the way they least expect: the front."

I said, "I'm pretty sure they're using Bigfoot Ranch as their base of operations."

She was undeterred. "I know they are, but I was thinking of the Heffinger Ranch."

"Heffinger hates me," I said, doubtfully.

"Yeah, but he *loves* me," Nicole answered. "He'll hold off shooting you long enough for me to explain what's happening...I think. Ernie isn't a bad guy once you get to know him."

"Ernie?" I'd never heard the old man's first name before. Somehow I'd expected Bart or Wyatt or something else that was quintessentially Old West. "If you say so. But where does that get us? We need to get to somewhere where we can get the information off the floppy disk. I'm not even sure how to do that. Aaron, my tech guy, probably knows, but he's in Bend."

"That's what gave me the idea," Nicole said. "Ernie is a little old-fashioned."

"You think?" I muttered.

Nicole ignored me. "He doesn't even have a cellphone. Landline only. But here's the trippy part. I noticed he still has dial-up, and that he's still going through AOL. Most important of all, I saw a floppy disk drive on his computer. Caked in dust, but I think it still works."

She stepped forward and put her hand on my arm, looking up at me with a smile. "We don't need to get to Bend. We can put the info online from here."

CHAPTER 43

"You ready?"

I nodded. "Let's go."

I resisted the urge to kick Bigfoot on my way out the door, afraid it would raise a mushroom cloud of poisonous gas. At the entrance to the cave, the hole in the snow had expanded since the last time I'd seen it. Water dripped down from the ceiling. Warm air instead of cold met us when we emerged.

The sky was clear, and the sun shined brightly. I could feel the warmth as if someone had turned up the thermostat in a house. It looked like it had snowed half a foot over the previous night, but the thick snow was already melting. Where rocks poked through the white blanket, the surrounding areas were thawing.

We hadn't gone more than a few steps before the first mournful howl of a hound drifted down to us, joined by another, and then what sounded like all the hounds of hell. It was hard to tell, but I guessed at least half a dozen dogs were in pursuit.

Nicole stopped so abruptly that I nearly knocked her down the steep hillside.

"You've got to put the Bigfoot costume back on," she said.

"What?" I didn't want to believe what I'd heard.

She was already brushing past me, heading back the way we'd come. I caught up with her at the entrance to the cave.

"What did you say?" I asked, just to be certain.

"You've got to put the Bigfoot costume back on," she repeated in the same tone of voice.

"Oh, *hell* no!"

Alarmed, she shushed me with a chop of her hand. "It's the only way, Hart."

"You've got to be kidding. I'd rather be shot."

"Hart, they're following your scent."

"Exactly! I don't see how they could miss it. I read somewhere hounds can distinguish seven different scents."

"But they can only follow one scent at a time," she said. "Trust me, I've got a plan."

I didn't move. It seemed smarter to me to make a run for it, unencumbered by the suit, make straight for the Heffinger Ranch, and upload the floppy disk. After that, the men who were after us would have no reason to chase us any longer. The word would be out, whatever it was.

"Please, Hart, just do as I say." Nicole looked up the hillside as if she could already see our pursuers. "I'll wait here."

"Yeah, you wouldn't want to have to smell me indoors," I muttered.

I ducked inside. It seemed as if I could detect the reek of the suit already, and the stench only grew as I trudged farther inside. The fire had diminished to coals, but the wind of my passage revived the embers. I leaned down and blew on them, and they glowed long enough for me to locate the suit.

It isn't like you're jumping into a volcano, I thought. But this almost seemed worse.

I picked up the suit, which was still damp. I expected to be knocked over by the stink, but instead, my nose was already becoming re-acclimated. Which kind of worried me. I wondered if my olfactory glands would ever return to normal.

I put first one leg and then another into the costume. It wasn't as bad as I remembered, if only because I was now wearing warm clothing. I inserted my arms, careful with my injured finger. It slipped into place as if it belonged there.

My shoes squished as I stood up, and I felt the water running down the shoulders of my windbreaker. It was at least partially waterproof, but when the flow of moisture reached my pants, I could feel the cotton soaking it up.

I started toward the front of the cave, and it was as if I'd gained a hundred pounds, as if I was carrying another entity on my back. I was Bigfoot again, and with that realization, the sense of normalcy and comfort I'd begun to recapture completely disappeared.

If I was going to be hunted as a wild animal, maybe it was for the best that I was one.

Nicole turned as I emerged, a large juniper branch in her hand. Apparently, she'd spent the time chopping it off with her bowie knife. She looked me up and down approvingly, managing not to wrinkle her nose in disgust.

She took off her backpack and rummaged around in it. "I'm not sure if I still have it," she muttered, then triumphantly lifted up a can of something. She walked over to me. Before I could object, she started spraying.

If I'd thought my nose was inured to anything by now, I was wrong. The odor was so strong I reared back instinctively. My back struck a tree, bringing down a cascade of snow. "What is *that?*" I cried.

"Quit whining," she said. "It's just a little bear bait."

I was stunned as much by the words as by the smell. Bear bait wasn't legal in Oregon. The last person I'd have expected to have some with her was the daughter of Cameron Nelson, the original *primitive* outdoorsman, who'd eschewed any artificial help in hunting beyond a rifle and a knife.

"When I have a photography client, it saves a lot of time," Nicole said, sounding slightly abashed.

She stepped back and looked me over. "That ought to do it."

"Yeah, they won't even need the hounds now," I said. "They can just follow their own noses."

The dogs suddenly got loud, as if they'd gotten the scent and were eager to chase down their prey for their handlers.

"Wait here," Nicole said. She ducked into the cave, leaving me there to listen to the approaching howls. She emerged with the flannel shirt I'd used to dry myself. She pulled out a plastic bag and put the shirt inside, sealing it. Only then did she stick it into her backpack.

I had a thought that gave me pause, even in the midst of everything else. "When this is all over, you're never going to want to come near me again."

"Don't worry," she said. "I like my men big and hairy."

I laughed. The fatalism that had threatened to overcome me from the beginning finally took over. What would happen would happen. "Lead the way," I said. "At least you'll be downwind of my stench."

She handed me the juniper branch. She had stripped away all the offshoots except for the bushy ends. "Step in my footsteps, Hart, and drag this behind you."

I did as she asked, looking behind me curiously to see what effect the branch was having. Our trail was clearly evident, maybe even more so thanks to the branch's regular contours.

"They'll still be able to follow us," I said.

"I've got a plan, Hart. Trust me."

We reached the end of the level trail. To my surprise, Nicole went upward toward Strawberry Mountain instead of down toward the Heffinger place. I almost spoke up, but I knew she'd just tell me to trust her vague *plan* again, so I stayed silent.

Within a few hundred feet, I realized I was going to have trouble keeping up with Nicole's pace. I stopped, breathing hard. She kept going for another dozen yards before she realized that I wasn't right behind her. She motioned me onward, but when I didn't budge, she came back to me. She stopped several yards away as if repelled by my smell.

"I've got a question," I said. She raised her eyebrows. "What happens if we run into a bear?"

"They might find you very attractive," she laughed. "Don't worry. I'm sure they're all in hibernation by now."

I just stared at her, alarmed that her laugh had seemed nervous, as if she hadn't even thought of the possibility.

CHAPTER 44

Within a mile, I was back in my own private hell. This time it was because of the heat instead of the cold. The temperature had risen, but the real heat source was the sun's direct rays. The black fur of the costume seemed to suck it in.

I was aware of Nicole and managed to step in the footprints she left. I continued to drag the branch, which got heavier with every step, but I'd retreated into the effort of moving my legs, of pushing forward and upward. My heart pounded and I began to sweat, which could be dangerous if it dropped below freezing again, which it was almost certain to do when darkness fell.

The skies were clear in every direction. Above was Strawberry Mountain and the surrounding peaks, which had been shadows against the sky a few days before but which were now clothed in white. The snow was so bright it hurt my eyes. Snow blindness was a new danger, one I hadn't even considered. I wondered whether to mention it to Nicole, then realized she was wearing sunglasses, which meant she was probably well aware.

I directed my gaze inward, almost closing my eyes, keeping them open just enough not to stray from the path. We couldn't hear the hounds, which was a good sign. Hopefully we'd lost them, at least temporarily.

The faint sound of helicopters buzzed in our ears. I almost walked into Nicole, who'd stopped abruptly and looked above us. She motioned toward the nearest trees, and we ducked under the canopy of a large ponderosa pine. We sat with our backs to the trunk. Nicole dug out some water and energy bars.

"The good thing about being in the mountains," she said,

"is that we can see them before they can see us. Helicopters are great if the people they're searching for *want* to be found."

"What if they have heat-sensitive equipment?" I asked.

"This is Eastern Oregon, Hart. What the hell would they be doing with high-tech stuff like that?"

"You don't know these guys. If Martinson is right and the Russians have a chance of getting their stooge on the Supreme Court, I don't think there is any amount of money or people they won't expend."

She stared at me as if trying to decide if I was serious. I remembered telling her about Martinson's suspicions last night, but it was as if she was only now realizing the implications.

"It's not just the Russians," I said. "I think organized crime is involved too."

"Not much difference these days, from what I hear," Nicole said. "Well, Russian Mafia or not, it will take them time to get the high-tech gear here. Hopefully, we'll be off the mountain by then."

"We have to get out of sight by nightfall," I warned. "They have night vision scopes."

She nodded as if she already knew that.

Our conversation had been interrupted several times by helicopters passing over our heads. They couldn't get too close. The winds in these mountains were notoriously treacherous. The helicopters circled twice over our heads, then headed west toward John Day.

I breathed normally by then, having recovered sooner than I would have expected. Despite all the deprivations of the last few days, I probably had more stamina now than when I'd started. Not so much physically, because I was more tired than ever, but mentally. I now knew I could push myself beyond what I'd thought were my limits, beyond the point where I once would have given up.

"Seal your mask, Hart," Nicole said, standing up and straightening her pack. "Tracking dogs are picking up on your dead skin cells, so the less they find, the better."

"You really think this will work?" I asked.

"Not in the slightest," she said.

It took a few moments for the words to penetrate. "What do you mean?"

"You can't outfox a good tracking dog," she said. "These are local dogs, probably, so there's at least a chance we can confuse them for a short time. But eventually, they'll pick up the trail."

"Then what are we doing?" I asked, the energy leaving my body. If it was hopeless, why not just wait here under the shade of the ponderosa?

"I said we can't outsmart the hounds, but the dogs are controlled by humans, and with those guys, we have a chance. We don't have to outrun the animals, we only have to outrun the handlers. If I'm right that these are local dogs, then Bill Johnson and Marty Hambly are probably running them. Both guys are over fifty years old, and both are carrying at least two hundred pounds of flab, not muscle."

"That's brilliant!" I exclaimed. "We don't have to outrun the bear, we just have to outrun the other guy."

"Exactly."

Nicole put her hand out and pulled me to my feet. "You ready for this?" she asked. "We're going to run them into the ground. We'll be going mostly straight uphill. Hell, we might even outrun the dogs. There's a reason marathon runners don't bring their pets along. That kind of thing can kill the poor animals."

"But if it doesn't matter, why don't I ditch the costume? I can go a lot faster without it."

"No, but it will still help confuse them. Besides, I've got a plan, remember? Just stick with me for a while longer, Hart." Nicole grabbed my gloved hand and squeezed tightly.

I couldn't believe how good that touch felt. I wanted to take her in my arms and hug her.

She retracted her hand swiftly, as if she could read my intentions. "I'd hug you, Hart. But I'm afraid I'd throw up."

"I bet you say that to all the guys."

She poured water over her hand.

How romantic, I thought. *I'm really winning her over.*

"Stick with me, Hart," she said.

She started straight uphill at the fastest pace yet.

For the next hour, we marched up the steepest hills Nicole could find. At times, I crawled up the slope on all fours, afraid I'd tip over backward, hanging onto shrubs and rocks. Somehow, we made it about halfway to the tree line.

Then Nicole suddenly shifted gears and headed horizontally instead of perpendicularly across the slope.

I didn't ask why, but my aching body thanked her for the reprieve.

After a half a mile or so, she abruptly turned uphill again. I groaned and followed. I was faltering, despite all my willpower. My muscles weren't responding anymore. My knees buckled at one point, and I felt myself falling over. Nicole slid down to me and grabbed me by the scruff of the costume's neck.

"Just a little longer, Hart," she said.

We were fast approaching the tree line, above which all the world would be able to see us. She turned sideways again.

"What...what are you doing?" I gasped. "Are you trying to fool the dogs?"

"Not the dogs. Like I said, that's impossible. But the handlers are another matter. They won't understand why the animals are suddenly urging them to go at right angles. With any luck, they'll overrule the dogs."

After another mile of circling around the mountain, she made one last turn uphill. We hit the tree line and stopped. Above, clouds rolled in again. The wind picked up, and I sensed it was going to either rain or snow. By my inner gauge, sunset was only an hour away.

"If Bill and Marty can follow that path, more power to them," she said. I was gratified that she looked tired.

"We'll set up camp in that hollow. That was my goal all along." She smiled at me encouragingly. "I'm pretty impressed, Hart. I didn't think you'd make it."

In no hurry now, we made our way to a small meadow in the middle of three rocky outcroppings surrounded by low, weather-beaten pines. The wind blew overhead loudly, but inside the hollow, it was almost pleasant.

If only it wasn't so damn cold. With the sun's disappearance, the temperature had plummeted. That plus the altitude had frozen the Bigfoot suit so much that it was getting hard to move in it. I dropped the juniper branch. All the green had been rubbed off the branches, leaving only raw splinters of wood.

Nicole set her backpack down and dug out a small plastic packet. Inside was a flimsy two-person pup tent. It was disposable, to be used only once.

Why is her survival kit so much better than mine? Some of my old rivalry with Nicole returned.

She threw our backpacks into the tent and went in.

I hesitated. The Bigfoot suit was rank. No way she wanted me in there with her.

Inside the tent, she turned on a flashlight. I watched her shadow as she took out the survival blankets and spread them out.

I sat outside, wondering what to do.

She poked her head out of the tent. "Take off Bigfoot and get in here."

CHAPTER 45

I had second thoughts about taking the suit off right outside the tent. Instead, I went to the far edge of the clearing. There was a small wall of squared-off rocks there, as if giants had laid them down. A couple of battered pine trees had driven their roots into the rocks, splitting the wall in half. I placed the costume inside the crevice, under the canopy of needles. Hopefully, it would be protected a little from the storm I was sure was coming.

What was I thinking? The damn thing *was* indestructible!

I knew it was a bad idea to have bear bait anywhere near where we were sleeping. Bears lived by their noses, and it was never a good idea to associate humans with food in their minds. Not that I wouldn't be carrying some of the scent with me, with or without the costume. Hopefully, Nicole was right and the animals were already in hibernation.

My windbreaker flapped in the cold wind. The sky was completely black, the moon and stars lost in the thick clouds. Though it was technically still fall, winter had arrived early.

I approached the tent slowly, wondering what to say. Nicole must have heard me coming. "Hurry up and get in here," she said, sounding irritated.

I unzipped the opening and crawled inside. The tent was on a slight slope, which was necessary if it rained. Nicole was on the upslope side, lying with her face toward the wall of the tent.

I scooted under the blanket, fully clothed. The blankets had Velcro seals along the sides. Not quite sleeping bags, but they would do in a pinch. I noticed that rather than sealing the two blankets, Nicole had put one on the ground and one on top.

The backpacks took up so much space at the base of the tent

that I needed to scrunch up my legs. I lay on my back, completely aware of the small, vibrant woman next to me.

We should cuddle. For warmth.

Before I could open my mouth, Nicole sat up, her head sliding along the top of the tent. "Jesus, Hart. I thought taking off the costume would at least make your smell bearable!"

She got out from under the blanket and pulled her pack toward her. She pulled out a tube of Chapstick and rubbed it thickly on her upper lip. Then she pulled something else out. She got under the blankets again, on her back, breathing through her mouth. I noticed that she was completely stretched out, her feet barely reaching the packs.

There was something boxy in her hand, and she fiddled with it. I heard a soft hum, and then felt a small wave of heat wafting over to me. She placed the little heater near the front of the tent.

Yep, her survival gear was much better than mine.

"Where did you get your survival kit?" I asked.

"Trade secret," she said. "But you're going to owe me a new one, Hart. Probably cheaper than fumigating everything."

"Sorry about that."

There was a short silence, then she said softly, "Not your fault. I made you put on the suit again."

There was a long, awkward silence.

"Did I ever tell you about my encounter with a skunk?" I found myself asking. I cringed a little inside. It was a story that didn't reflect well on me, and I'd rarely told it to anyone. My finger twitched at the idea of not telling the story now that I'd brought it up.

"Oh, are we exchanging life stories now?" she asked.

I tried to read her tone, to tell whether she was being sarcastic or warning me off, or was actually interested. Since I couldn't tell, I forged ahead. "Some friends and I were out by Hampton Butte, just kicking around. We came across a poor little skunk caught in a cage and decided to liberate it." I paused, wondering if I should continue.

"So you were *always* a kind-hearted idiot."

"But it was such a cute little skunk," I said. "We pulled up the trap door and let it out."

"Oh, dear," she said.

"In its gratitude, the damned skunk thoroughly drenched us on the way out."

"You were lucky," Nicole said. "Skunk spray can blind you."

"Yeah, it was pretty stupid. We started back home, and we thought the skunk was following us. We kept turning around, looking. Running, trying to leave it behind."

She started laughing.

"Seriously, it wasn't until we hit town that we realized that we were the ones who stunk. We had to throw away our clothes and bathe in tomato juice, and even that didn't really get rid of the odor. I swear that skunk followed me around for days."

"Maybe that's why you can bear to wear that costume," she said. "You've built up a tolerance."

"The irony was, it was one of my father's illegal traps. When the authorities heard from the other boys what had happened, they went out there and somehow connected it to him. So that was one of those times when he was gone on *vacation*, as Mom always put it. When he got home, he beat me to within an inch of my life." I tried to say it lightly, but it fell flat.

There was a long silence, and then Nicole said, "We should scrunch together, Hart, for the warmth."

She turned her back to me, and I tentatively reached out and held her. As tired and cold and stinky as I was, my body still responded to the closeness in the most predictable of ways. I could have sworn she pressed closer to me in response.

For the warmth.

Rain spattered down on the tent, and it was soothing at first. I wasn't sure if it was lucky or unlucky that it wasn't snowing until the first flash of lightning, followed by thunder that shook the ground under us. Nicole tensed in my arms, and I squeezed her tightly.

Somehow, I fell asleep.

CHAPTER 46

I stared distastefully at the Bigfoot suit marinating in a puddle of rainwater and its own slime. It wasn't that it was wetter and stinkier than the night before. In fact, a little of the bear bait had washed away, so it probably smelled a little less odiferous. But I'd escaped it, at least for one night.

"You have to put it on," Nicole said, standing behind me.

I'd woken first to find our positions reversed. She was behind me, her arms wrapped around my waist. I didn't dare move for what was probably an hour, soaking up the closeness. I realized how small she was when asleep. When she was up and ordering me about, she took up so much more space.

She woke up slowly, nuzzling me softly. Then she gave a snort, and her eyes flew wide open. She practically pushed me away, though it was she who was doing the hugging. Then she wrestled on her boots, pulled out some spearmint gum, and handed me a stick without comment.

She gave me an energy bar, and we sat there listening as the rain slowly tapered off until all that struck the tent was an occasional big drop. The heater had warmed up the tent to an amazing degree, though I could touch it without getting burned. Nicole turned it off, zipped up her pack, and looked at me.

"We'll head for the Heffinger ranch first thing," she said. I nodded, willing to let her take the lead again. "We can go down the canyon below Massacre Spring."

"Yeah, I used that ravine several times. It might be flooded by now."

"All the better. Are you ready?"

I nodded again, and she opened the tent. The ground in the

little clearing was sopping wet. The tent was perched on the only spot where there wasn't standing water, and once again I was impressed by Nicole's wilderness craft. She gathered up the tent, not bothering to fold it.

She either knew, or could smell, where I'd taken off the Bigfoot costume and headed straight for where it was hidden in the cleft of the rock wall.

"What's the point of wearing it now?" I said.

"Trust me a little bit longer, Hart," she said.

I lifted up the suit, and the water drained away, a sickly yellow stream of grime and sweat. I shook it a couple of times, needing both hands to do so since it was so heavy. Moments later, I was encased in my alter ego. It was starting to feel almost natural.

There was a reason I'd never been to this part of Strawberry Mountain. It was surrounded on three sides by cliffs. The wind never stopped blowing even at the height of summer. In the fall, the wind sounded like airplanes flying overhead, sometimes increasing in volume as if the plane was swooping down.

Instead of going back the way we'd come, Nicole led the way to the top of what appeared the steepest of the precipices.

"There's a path here that's traversable," she said. "I want to rope us together, though." Without waiting for a response, she shrugged off her backpack and knelt beside it. She pulled out a thirty-foot length of nylon rope. Her wonderful survival kit had come through again.

"Is that such a good idea?" I asked. I thought it far more likely that I'd lose my footing than that she'd lose hers, and I didn't think there was any way she could hold me up. With the Bigfoot costume on, I had to weigh a good hundred pounds more than her.

She didn't bother to answer but began tying the rope around my waist. She motioned for me to go first. I slid over the side on my belly, inch by inch, my legs swaying back and forth, seeking the path she had assured me was there. My right foot struck something level. I slid the rest of the way down, clutching the side of the cliff. Not looking down, I started to edge my way along the path.

"You'll have to go faster than that," Nicole said.

You're lucky I'm moving at all! I wanted to shout.

My every instinct was to hold onto the rocks for dear life and not move. But I knew if I stopped, I'd never move again, dooming us both. Thankfully, the path widened the farther down we went, and after what seemed an eternity, we reached a wide ledge about three-quarters of the way down.

Nicole tugged on the rope, but I was already sitting, thankful to feel safe for a few seconds. She handed me the last water bottle and two energy bars.

"Might as well finish up the provisions," she said. "Either we make it to Heffinger's or we don't, but we can't be out here another night."

"Knock wood," I said, looking around and seeing nothing but rock.

"So you're superstitious? Good to know."

"Only about that," I said. "Never tempt fate."

"That and the finger tapping," she said.

That brought me up short. I'd never thought of my tapping as superstitious, more that it was obsessive/compulsive.

She reached over and rapped me on the head a couple of times with her knuckles. "There. Satisfied?"

The rest of the way down was less steep but perhaps even more dangerous. Over the eons, huge boulders had broken away from the cliff. Time hadn't softened their jagged edges. It was difficult to get across them without sliding or twisting an ankle.

A small grove of junipers jutted out onto the hillside a short distance away. Nicole went over to them, jumped up, and grabbed a branch, dangling in midair for a moment before the limb broke off. She dragged it over to me. I took the branch without comment.

I dragged it behind me, still wondering why. *Just trust me,* I could hear Nicole saying.

From the base of the cliffs, we could see the entire valley. The aspen trees of Massacre Spring looked like tiny shrubs from here. Nestled in a small canyon to our left was the Heffinger Ranch, looking like a toy house, with the small town of John

Day in the distance. Overnight, the rains had washed away the snow, and the precipitation was seeking low ground, gathering force. To our right, a small waterfall tumbled over the cliffs, its spray catching the morning light in a rainbow.

The path to Massacre Spring was clear, and we started down it.

We hadn't gone more than a few feet before we heard the hounds. They were approaching rapidly from the east, closer than they'd been the day before. Nicole didn't even look in that direction. She broke into a trot. I struggled to follow with the branch seeming to snag on everything it touched.

Massacre Spring had seemed an impossible distance away just a few minutes before, but we ate up the ground rapidly. Behind us, the hounds yelped excitedly as they caught our scent. By the time we made it to the aspen grove, I was winded. I bent over, taking ragged breaths. The Heffinger ranch was still miles away. There was no way we were going to make it.

The wellspring within the grove had come to life. Where there had been muddy ground a few days before, there was a small pond, almost a lake. There was a rock island in the middle. The water spilled over the downhill side into Massacre Canyon.

"We can go down the creek," I said. "Lose them that way."

"They'll suspect that, especially if our scent just disappears," Nicole said. "Besides, you can't stay in the creek forever, and when you emerge, you'll be easier to track than ever. Instead of a few dry skin cells, the dogs will have a trail of water full of them."

Her expression was calm, her eyes worried but not frightened. What did she know that I didn't?

"Then what?" I asked. "I'm not shooting Marty and Bill."

"Of course not," she said. "This was all part of my plan, Hart. You've got to trust me."

"Don't you think it's time you told me your plan?

"You need to wade out to that island, Hart," she said calmly. "Hide. I'll lead them away."

Suddenly, I understood why she'd insisted on obscuring our tracks, on us walking in each other's footsteps. While we hadn't hidden our trail, it probably appeared to the trackers as though they were following just one person. With any luck, they'd think that one person was me.

Nicole set down her backpack and dug into it. She brought out the plastic bag where she'd stored my flannel shirt in, took out the shirt, and wrapped it around the stick I'd been dragging. She handed me her backpack. "Carry this to the island with you. I need to be unencumbered."

I looked down at her tiny feet. Even with her boots, it would be obvious that the footprints weren't a man's. "They'll never believe it," I said.

"My prints will expand in the mud," she said, but it was clear that the discrepancy was the one thing she hadn't thought of. "Besides, footprints always look too small on the trail. Have you ever noticed that?"

I look down at the Bigfoot footprints. "Not really."

"I'll drag the branch, at least for awhile. Once they have the scent, they're not going to stop to wonder."

"I can't let you do this," I said, shrugging off my rifle and checking the chamber. "We can fire warning shots. I doubt Marty and Bill will dare come any closer."

"They'll call for help," Nicole said. "They probably already have. It would only delay the inevitable. Even if we wanted a firefight, we wouldn't win one."

"Then I'll come with you," I said. "We'll keep outrunning them."

"I'm going to do just that. But no offense, Hart, but you're done running."

I couldn't deny it.

"If you don't hide, then everything we've done for the last day will be for nothing. I can lose these guys if I'm alone. I'll circle back, meet you at the Heffinger Ranch this afternoon. Hurry up, Hart. They're coming."

There didn't seem to be any choice. It was a lousy plan, but it was better than anything I'd thought of. As long as I was out of sight on the island and the dogs could continue to follow the scent of my flannel shirt leading away, it was at least possible that it could work.

There was no time to argue. It was time to either run or hide or shoot it out.

I waded into the water up to my knees, uncertain how deep the spring was. I had Nicole's pack slung over one shoulder, my own pack over the other. The rifle I held over my head. When I turned around, Nicole was gone. I barely caught of glimpse of her entering the trees above. I wasn't sure, but I think she waved her hand over her head.

Then she vanished, and I was in the middle of the spring, the oily residue of the Bigfoot fur polluting the clear water. I waded farther out, the water reaching my waist, then my chest.

The ground gave out from under me. Water filled the suit and, with a strangled curse, I went under.

CHAPTER 47

I let go of the rifle and tried to swim upward. The water weighed down the Bigfoot suit like poured concrete, and I remained firmly underwater. I shrugged off my backpack, but hung on to Nicole's.

I had to live. I still needed to find out the brand of her survival kit.

I pushed upward again and barely broke the surface, but caught a little air along with water. The air exploded out of me as I coughed, involuntarily taking in another mouthful of water.

In my floundering, my feet landed on something—a ledge, a rock, solid enough for me to stand on and raise my head above the surface. I desperately treaded water, trying to stay upright. The dogs sounded like they were on the shore, and I turned to look, nearly losing my balance again, but they were still in the distance.

The island was only a few yards away. I pushed off, reached out, managing to grab the top of a submerged tree and pull myself the rest of the way onto the edge of a rock. I wanted to just lie there, catching my breath, but I crawled upward, dragging Nicole's pack. When there was enough cover around me, I collapsed.

I lay there gasping, trying not to cough. It sounded as though the dogs were howling in my ears. I got to my hands and knees and peeked out.

Bill and Marty were standing on the muddy bank where Nicole and I had just been, obliterating our tracks. Marty gesticulated animatedly in the direction Nicole had run, while Bill stood stubbornly shaking his head. They both looked disheveled, their coats open, their hair askew. The dogs were pulling on their leashes.

All but one. The biggest of the hounds stared right at me

It raised its snout and howled its discovery. *There, boss! He's right there!*

I ducked under the bushes and listened.

"When are you going to train that bitch?" Bill said.

"She's just like all bitches, easily distracted," Marty answered. "Bettylou, come on, you. Let's go. Follow Clyde, dammit."

The yelping and howling receded, and I finally dared to look up. The dogs and their handlers were nowhere to be seen. Churned-up tracks covered the banks of the pond, leading away, following Nicole.

Nicole was right. Those good old boys had no chance of catching her. She'd run them into the ground. If I'd been along, we'd have already been caught. I stood, looking around. The other side of the island was only a few yards from the far shore. I jumped for it and landed in the water near the bank but managed to crawl up it.

Water was spilling over the side of the pond a few yards away. A rivulet ran down the middle of the canyon, enough to cover my tracks but not enough to pull me off my feet. I slid down into the water, feeling like I was almost home free.

I wasn't sure how Heffinger would greet me, but it seemed like a minor problem compared to what I'd already been through. With any luck, Samuels wouldn't expect me anywhere near there because the old man would have made known his low opinion of me.

The current grew stronger the farther down I went as side streams joined the main course. I looked back and saw that the opening of the pond had widened, that it was collapsing. I barely had time to register the flood before it came gushing down the ravine.

In the mountains, the last of the snows had melted in the fresh rainfall. The water had gathered in all the gullies and dry canyons, gathering speed, pouring down the cliffs until it reached Massacre Spring and then bursting the banks.

All aimed at me.

I had just enough time to reach out and grab the base of a four-inch aspen before the deluge lifted me up, dragging on Nicole's backpack and almost pulling my fingers off the tree. I let the pack spin away and disappear into the foaming torrent. I grabbed the tree again with both hands and held on.

With the last of my strength, I wrapped my legs around the tree. The sapling swayed alarmingly. I knew from experience that quaking aspen trees had stubborn roots, that it was nearly impossible to get rid of them, and that knowledge gave me strength.

The flood slowly subsided until I swayed back and forth instead of being tossed about violently. I swung my legs to the other side of the tree, still hanging onto the trunk, and onto solid ground.

What else could go wrong?

I knocked the side of the tree with my uninjured hand. "Knock wood," I muttered.

Too late.

I realized I was on the wrong side of the deluge to reach the Heffinger ranch.

Filled with a despair that robbed me of all strength, I lay on my back and looked into the sky, my mind blank for a moment. I was alone again. Nicole seemed like a dream. The clouds rolled overhead. As I stared up into them, something white drifted down. It was a single snowflake, caught by the wind, fluttering unerringly at me, and I lay unmoving as it floated down the last few yards and landed on my forehead.

It was followed by other swirling flakes, drifting downward, all of them seeming to be aimed directly at me.

"Oh, for God's sake," I said to the sky. "Make up your goddamn mind."

I closed my eyes and laughed. It occurred to me I was only half a mile from where it had all started, still wearing the Bigfoot costume, which was a little worse for wear. So was I. I was exhausted and ready to quit. If Samuels had appeared at that moment with a gun aimed at my head, I doubted I would have had enough energy to even raise my middle finger in defiance.

After a time, I sat up. I checked the Bigfoot pouch. The knife was gone. I tried to remember when I'd last used it, where I might have left it. It was probably in Nicole's pack, which I'd let the stream carry away. I found some soggy matches, which I now let tumble to the ground.

All that was left was the floppy disk. One corner was bent alarmingly, and to my surprise, I felt a stab of fear. Over the last few days, I'd become numbed to the stress and danger, but the thought that all of it had been for nothing terrified me.

I put the disk back in my pocket. Aaron would know what to do with it.

Staggering to my feet, I began walking down the side of the canyon, looking for a way across the stream, but if anything, it got deeper and wider the farther I went downstream. There was no chance of wading across. Rocks and branches tumbled beneath the surface of the torrent, any one of which would knock me off my feet, throwing me into the grinding maelstrom.

I heard the helicopter a long time before I saw it. It was coming down from the mountains above. I ambled over to a small tree and hunkered down in the shade, unwilling to hide myself any further. But it was clear that the helicopter wasn't searching for me, heading back to the base.

Some kind of insect scuttled into the suit and skittered down my arm. I slapped at it reflexively, hitting the Kevlar and missing the bug.

What did I need the costume for?

I couldn't think of a single reason to keep wearing it. As Nicole had said, either we reached the Heffinger ranch today or we were finished anyway.

And yet...

"*So you're superstitious?*" she'd said.

I realized that Nicole was right. When it came right down to it, I tended not to mess with what was working. The Bigfoot costume had kept me alive. There was no reason, really, to keep it. And yet I was reluctant to take it off.

I got to my feet and kept going, the costume rubbing familiarly against my arms and legs.

I was as close to the Granger ranch as I was to Heffinger's

now. I recognized landmarks: the huge old ponderosa trunk where a giant colony of ants had taken over; a rusted propane tank that had somehow landed in the middle of a ditch and that Granger kept saying he was going to remove but never got around to; the juniper that had split in half during the last windstorm.

One hill over and the top of Granger's bunkhouse would have been visible. It was a part of the ranch that wasn't used for much, but if any of Samuels's men were out for a stroll, I was done.

Only a hundred yards from the highway, I saw a way across. A big pine had fallen across the stream, its roots uncovered by the torrent. It was almost as if it had been designed to be a bridge, with branches jutting up on both sides and a clear path down the middle.

Nevertheless, the highway looked more inviting. I walked toward it. Moments later, the flashing lights of a sheriff's cruiser warned me off. I ducked down until it passed. As I watched, cars went by that weren't official vehicles so apparently the authorities had opened the road to traffic.

But it still seemed too risky.

I climbed up the tangled, muddy roots of the tree and began crossing the natural bridge. When I was halfway across, a station wagon passed by on the highway. In the back seat, three children were pointing at me, their mouths open, trying to get their parents' attention.

I looked down at the Bigfoot costume and laughed. With my tangled black hair and four-day growth of beard, I blended right in.

And thus the legend of Bigfoot grew.

CHAPTER 48

Sherm looked for a phone booth as he left Salt Lake City, but couldn't find one in any place he thought would have one; gas stations and quick marts. He spotted one out of the corner of his eye at a bus stop and looped back around to it. It was totally inoperable, the phone missing from the cord.

He drove on and finally found a working pay phone outside a Wal-Mart. There was even a young man talking on it. He didn't look at Sherm, nor did he say much more than "Yes... yes...no," before hanging up. He walked to the corner of the building and stood there, waiting.

Sherm plunked in all the change he had in his pocket and called the White Widow, letting the phone ring until it went to voicemail. He hesitated, then hung up without saying anything.

It might not mean anything. Amanda might be one of those rare people who neglected her cellphone.

But Sherm doubted it. There was too much going on. Unless he was an idiot, she would want to be available. Then he remembered how paranoid Anne Clarambeau had been. She'd probably tossed it.

The drive to Bend went fast. Sherm stuck to the freeway for as long as he could, driving at a steady eighty miles an hour. At the border, he turned onto Highway 20 and drove across the flat high desert almost as fast. His shoulder started hurting as the last of the pain pills wore off. He propped it against the passenger car seat and kept going.

Bend was a completely different town than he remembered. It looked as though it had doubled or tripled in size, and the traffic had increased by four times that. He slowed down as he approached the address he'd last memorized.

In the end, he decided that time was more important than stealth. Six days had passed since he'd last talked to Amanda.

He knocked on the door, his good hand on the handle of his revolver inside his coat. A young, dark-haired woman opened the door, a phone to her ear. She didn't stop speaking as she examined him. It took him several seconds to realize it was the White Widow. She seemed softer... almost domesticated.

"Yeah, they turned over the house. Didn't find anything, of course. I'm too smart for that."

She didn't seem curious or surprised to see him. She motioned him in, led him to the kitchen, and waved at a chair. She kept on walking into a pantry at the back of the kitchen, still chatting on the phone.

"I don't know...Russians, maybe. But they seemed more like private mercs, though. Mafia types. What do you mean, why would they bother me? They've been trying to track me down for years."

Sherm pulled out a chair at the narrow dining room table and sat down.

"Carrie!" Amanda suddenly shouted in admonishment.

The shout brought Sherm to his feet. Amanda was red-faced, angry enough to be spitting into the phone. "I told you what I used to do! I can't help it if you don't believe me! Fuck you!"

She clicked off the phone and turned toward Sherm, her manner completely transformed, a smile brightening her face. Sherm began to see her age. She was dressed young in a short, tight dress and white stockings, with heavy make-up covering the wrinkles around her eyes and mouth.

"Hi, Sherm," she said.

"Where's the box?"

"I put it in Hart's car. He's at his hunting ranch in the Strawberry Mountains."

She had been fiddling with something in the pantry, and now she turned around. She had a pearl-handled Smith and Wesson 9mm in each hand.

"What the fuck have you gotten us into?" she said, her voice low and menacing.

"I'm sorry, Anne. I had no idea this was going to happen."

She stared at him blankly for a moment. Then she quickly lowered the guns, turned, and put them away somewhere out of sight.

She hurried over to him and he flinched. She threw herself into his arms.

"Sherman Russo!" she cried. "I was hoping you'd show up!"

"You were?" he asked, puzzled by the shift in tone. He held her at arm's length. He could feel the wiry strength in her hands. She was vibrating with restrained energy.

"I didn't realize how important the box was. They had me on the meds at the time. I wasn't thinking clearly."

Ah...off her medications. That explains it.

Amanda continued, "They sent their goons the next day, but I didn't tell them a thing. I pretended to be the same ditz I've been pretending to be ever since I got to this town. I think they knew where Hart was anyway, though. I've been trying to get ahold of him ever since. Tried to convince those coming after us to back off, but that doesn't seem to be working. I'm heading to John Day first thing in the morning to get him."

"You know where to find him?"

"Of course!" she said. "I helped him set up the business. He hardly knew a thing about guns when I met him. I didn't tell him about my past, of course, not until later. By then, we'd been married so long that he didn't believe me. Which was good, you know? It was good that he didn't believe me."

The angry look in her glittering green eyes contradicted her words.

"What *is* your past?" he asked. "I mean, I knew you weren't part of the organization. More of loaner, I guess."

She laughed and, pointedly, didn't answer. "I told Hart to hide the box. Not to open it. He always was a trusting fool. Which is what attracted me. I mean, the shitheels I used to deal with..." She looked into the distance as if remembering a time long ago.

"So he didn't...?"

"What?" Amanda snapped, turning toward him with a motion so abrupt he tensed up.

"Open the box?" he said. "To find out what was inside?"

"No." She sat down at the table. "That's Hart. He's so afraid of being like his father that he is completely the opposite. Why don't you tell me what's in it, Sherm?"

He tried to get a read on her. Even sitting, it was as if she paced. She was frenetic, manic. He couldn't decide if, in her state, she would be a help or a hindrance. Did he have any right to bring her into this?

But really, he had no choice. He wasn't going to find Hart in the Strawberry Mountains by himself.

So, he told her an abbreviated version of what was on the floppy disk. To his surprise, she didn't interrupt once. She got up at the end of the story and went to the refrigerator, coming back with a bottle of cheap wine. She poured them both a glass. She drank hers down in a couple of swallows and refilled it.

"Poor Hart," said Amanda. She paused to drink more wine. "I *knew* he needed me."

"So you can find him?"

"We'll head out before dawn," she said, pouring herself a third glass of wine while he was still sipping his first.

Sherm let her refill his glass, feeling the wine blur his exhaustion and his pain. While he'd been driving, his injured shoulder had loosened up. Now, it felt almost normal. He suspected that in the morning, it would be stiff again.

"You'd better get some sleep." Amanda's sharp voice broke through his fog. She stood over him, pulling the chair out from under him. He stumbled to his feet, followed her to a dusty bedroom, and fell on the bed. When she left, he roused himself enough to get undressed and slipped beneath the covers.

He awoke to someone getting on the bed. He lunged for the gun in his overcoat, which lay on the floor.

"It's me," he heard a softened version of Amanda's voice say. Softened...and yet still intense. In the dim light, he could tell that she was naked. She was tall, well-formed. Not his type. Both Gina and Jennifer were smaller, and blonde.

But the proximity of a naked woman began to have an effect on him.

She reached over and turned down the covers.

"I'm old enough to be your father," he said.

She shrugged. "But it all still works, right?" She swung her legs over him and reached down to his crotch.

He took her by the waist and lifted her off him, somewhat surprised that both shoulders handled the weight. "I need my rest," he said. "You'll just wear me out."

"And I need to work off this fucking nervous energy," she said. "So shut up and lay back and enjoy it."

He debated with himself a little too long. Then she was on top of him again, and his resistance evaporated.

He'd been hoping this very thing would happen the previous night.

Angie, he thought, feeling vaguely ashamed but unwilling to stop what was happening.

CHAPTER 49

As soon as Sherm showed up on her doorstep, Amanda started counting the minutes. It wouldn't be long.

She couldn't believe her old comrade had lost so much edge as to show up in broad daylight. He had to know the house was being watched. Well, the younger Sherm she'd known would have been aware of that, she wasn't sure about this overweight old man. It probably didn't matter; she was planning to leave anyway. Things would have come to a head sooner or later.

To her surprise, they were left alone that night. She woke up with a whale beside her, but all whales were the same in the dark. She didn't regret it. It had been a long time since she'd held anyone. She had had a thing for Sherman Russo back in the day, and while they had made love, she'd held an image of that man in her mind.

"Better get dressed, Sherm," she said, shaking him. It was like nudging a boulder..

"What time is it?"

"Four o'clock. Unless I miss my guess, they'll be busting down the door any minute now."

"Right," he said, swinging his legs off the bed. He was surprisingly alert.

Maybe the young Sherm is still in there somewhere.

Amanda expected the knock on the door any second. It would be a mild knock, letting her think perhaps it was a friend. But when she opened the door, four or five guys would barrel in. It was the favorite tactic of good guys and bad guys all over the world: wait until the smallest hours of morning, when the target was most vulnerable. Which was why she could never comfortably sleep past 3:30 a.m.

"You got an escape route?" Sherm asked, pulling on his pants.

"Escape? Who said anything about escape?"

He turned his big head and examined her. "So that's how it is?"

"I've been researching your bosses, lover. I believe a point must be made. I'll need to change my identity again after all these years, and it kind of pisses me off. But I also want them to think twice about coming after me again."

"Seems unnecessary to me. Maybe a tad extreme."

"Well, I had a bit of a problem with them a few days ago. A couple of their guys are under the boat in the back yard. Looked for their bosses, put them down. But didn't manage to get any higher. They might not be inclined to let us go without making us pay for that."

"Why didn't they come after you before now?"

"They were waiting for you, Sherm. We were all waiting for you."

He put on an antique bulletproof vest, which made him look even bigger. Amanda never wore the things—they tended to make the wearers believe they were invulnerable. She opted for quick and agile, not lumbering around like a tank.

She'd drawn all the shades the night before, so she felt comfortable turning on the kitchen light and making coffee. They sat at the table, not saying anything, listening for the smallest sounds. Light began to filter around the edges of the blinds.

"They're waiting for us to come out," Sherm finally grunted.

"Smart. We'll be wide open targets." Amanda drank the last of the coffee and stood. "Change of plans then. I'm not sure I want bullets flying around the neighborhood. I like my neighbors… most of them. So we'll use the escape route."

Sherm sighed and lumbered to his feet.

She crooked a finger at him and went to the back door and peeked out the blinds. "They're there, all right." She grabbed her bugout pack from its spot near the door.

To the left of the backdoor was a laundry room. Amanda pulled on the dryer, moving it a few inches. Sherm got the message and pulled it the rest of the way out. Behind it was a small hole in the wall.

"I'm not sure..." Sherm started to say, but Amanda grabbed the shovel hanging on the wall near the door and started widening the hole. It was just drywall. White powder filled the air.

"Ready?" she asked after she'd worked on it for a while. She ducked into the hole without waiting for an answer. The crawlspace led to an old storm sewer line. Thankfully, it was empty of anything but dust and cobwebs. Amanda could traverse it by just bending over, but Sherm was forced to crouch, almost getting on his hands and knees. The residue of the sewer's former purpose still lined the bottom of the tunnel.

"I'd rather have shot it out," he muttered.

The opening on the far side was a simple plank of plywood, covered in turf. Every few months, Amanda visited her neighbor Liza Margolis's fabulous garden, making sure the hatch was unobstructed. She motioned Sherm forward and he put his shoulders to it. The grass held on for moment, then tore like rough fabric, raining dirt on Sherm's already filthy face.

He climbed out onto the lawn and brushed himself off. Amanda hopped up next to him.

"Bend down a little, Sherm," she told him. He was visible over the fence, though she doubted any of their enemies were looking this far away from the house. They had passed four houses in the cul-de-sac to reach freedom.

"My car is in the next block over," Sherm said.

"Screw that," she answered. "The only thing I'm taking is my Mustang."

"Where is it?" he asked, looking around.

"Back in my garage," she said, and opened the gate and started down the sidewalk. She pulled the Glock with its silencer out of her pack. Behind her, Sherm cursed, but she knew he'd follow and back her up. She'd figured out where the stakeouts were days ago, and they'd been too stupid to change them up. She came up behind two men in a 4Runner, one of whom was asleep in the back seat.

The other guy was awake, but barely. Amanda decided to save her ammo. Even with a silencer, a gun could be louder than she liked. She stopped at the back bumper and pulled out a knife. By then, the man in driver's seat had noticed her. He was staring at her as if he couldn't believe what he was seeing.

She took three strides to the open window and stabbed into the mercenary's neck three times, cutting off his cry. A hand rose to hit the horn, and she skewered it. The man gurgled. She stepped back from the fountain of blood. In the same moment, Sherm opened the backdoor and dragged the other man out of the seat, wrapping his beefy arm around the man's neck and squeezed. Amanda heard a snap.

She grinned. The thrill of the hunt came flooding back.

"I don't like this, Anne...Amanda," Sherm said, seeing the look on her face. "These guys are just soldiers, following orders."

"So were we once," she answered. "And this is how they treat us. Look, Sherm. They were going to kill us, and probably torture us first. Save your pity."

He sighed. "Where are the others?"

She pointed toward a white van in the driveway of the house across the street. It was so obviously a stakeout, she wondered how he'd missed it. Then again, he'd probably realized he couldn't reach the house without being seen and had discounted it. He would just have to brazen it out.

He started toward the van, while Amanda crossed the street to the house next door to her garage. The Andersons were in Oklahoma, visiting their son, but she'd seen movement behind the drapes.

For the last few days she'd dressed her most feminine clothes and done her most stereotypically housewifey chores—laundry, cooking, gardening. Despite their missing comrades, the men watching her had no idea what she was capable of.

Amanda walked up to the door and tried the handle. They were so overconfident they'd left the door unlocked. She walked in, weapon in hand. One man was asleep on the couch. She shot him twice in the chest. He never even opened his eyes.

The other mercenary was sitting on a tall chair near the window closest to her bedroom. He'd probably gotten an earful last night and thought the lovers were sleeping it off.

He was quick. He reached for his weapon, leapt to his feet, and dove to one side. Her first shot missed and shattered the window. Her second shot caught him in the leg, and her third hit him mid-torso. He got a shot off at her between her second and the third shots and she felt the bullet rip through the fabric of her blouse.

The man rolled on the floor and didn't get up. As Amanda walked up to him, he grunted. "Slut."

She shot him before the word was completely out. "Shut your filthy mouth," she said as the bullet went through the back of his throat and thudded into the wall.

She picked through his coat and found his cellphone. She heard two muffled shots from outside.

Sherm was waiting for her by the garage. Amanda hit the door opener and without a word, he squeezed himself into the passenger seat of the Mustang.

"Let's go get Hart," she said.

CHAPTER 50

I hesitated at the corner of Heffinger's house, wondering how and when, and if, to make my approach. Should I wait for Nicole? What was I going to do, knock on the door and say "Howdy?"

The door flew open, the screen door slamming against the side of the house. Ernie Heffinger stumbled down the steps, a shotgun cradled in his arms. He swayed as if he'd been drinking all day. He glanced over at me.

I froze.

"That gag gets *really* old, Granger," the old man muttered, opening his fly and peeing against the side of the house. Apparently, the front yard was closer than the outhouse in back.

"Granger's here?" I blurted, confused.

Heffinger turned, still spraying, and lifted his gun. "Holy fucking Christ!"

"Don't shoot," I said. "I haven't done anything!"

He glared at me, lowered the rifle and finished his business.

"They were trying to kill me—and Granger," I continued, encouraged that I hadn't immediately been shot.

He snorted and zipped up his pants. "Hell, I knew that even before Stevie told me." For a moment, the name "Stevie" didn't register, then I realized he was talking about Granger.

Heffinger continued. "You don't have the balls to do what they're accusing you of, Hart, even if I trusted those guys. Recognized the type from Nam, gung-ho killer assholes. They'd roust me out of bed when all I wanted to do was smoke my dope in peace, eager to kill gooks, as if any of it mattered, as if we had any fucking chance of winning the war. Same assholes have kept the wars going ever since."

"They wanted something from me," I said. "I couldn't give it to them."

"So you just haaaaad to drag everyone into your business," he said, "just like your father."

I wanted to object that I was opposite of my father, that everything had happened because I was trying to do the right thing. But he had a point. The end result was the same. Innocent people were getting hurt.

"I didn't mean for any of this to happen," I said.

"Yeah, well, you better come inside before someone sees you." Heffinger brushed by me, then recoiled. "Holy shit, Hart, you stink! No way are you coming in until you clean up. Go to the shed out back. We'll hose you off."

He clattered up the steps and slammed the screen door behind him.

It was pretty bad when Heffinger thought I was a mess. The old man was a hoarder. I'd only been inside his house once, if being in one of the narrow pathways between the newspapers and boxes could be called *inside*. Every room was filled with junk, from floor to ceiling. It also smelled, because Heffinger had God only knew how many cats, who considered the house one large litter box.

Because they couldn't stay out here at the ranch, Nicole boarded her clients in John Day, which was the only reason I still managed to compete with her. I had the advantage of on-site lodging. Otherwise she would have taken all my business a long time ago.

Well, that and the fact that I was male. Despite the fact that it was the 21st century, there were still plenty of hunters who thought that "girls" weren't supposed to be wilderness guides.

The shed in back housed a well, and I gave the handle a few tentative pumps. A trickle of water came out, then a full spurt. Satisfied that it was enough to wash with, I started to take off the Bigfoot costume.

For the last time.

I knocked against the wooden wall of the shed a couple of times, just to be sure.

Sorry, big guy, but it's time you went extinct.

I had second thoughts about taking it off inside the shed, however. Every rancher is forced to bear-proof their place, and I didn't want to be responsible for a big black bear breaking into Heffinger's pump house.

I walked ten feet away and let the suit drop to the ground. It seemed to fold in on itself, the mask and gloves and zipper disappearing, leaving nothing but a tattered pile of black fur, as if Bigfoot had shed his skin and walked away. I half expected to see footprints in the mud trailing away into the brush. I took off my clothes, which were almost as dirty and smelly as the costume.

Somehow, the water was colder than the snow-fed mountain streams I'd nearly drowned in. I grunted, but with every splash, I felt cleaner. The water running down my body went from brown to yellow to clear, my skin from tanned—in the old-fashioned sense of a tanned hide—to bright pink. I delayed dowsing my head until last, finally gaining enough courage to put it under the stream of water. I shouted, half from shock at the cold and half from exhilaration.

It was a baptism into civilization. I'd lived as an animal, and I'd survived. I doubted I would ever take the simple comforts of home for granted again.

"Want some warm water with that?" said a voice behind me.

I whirled, my hands out defensively, ready to charge.

Not quite civilized...yet.

A big ginger-haired man proffered a bucket of steaming water. I stared at him for a moment. "Granger?"

"Yeah," he said, sheepishly rubbing his short hair with one big hand. His face was rounder than I would have expected and who knew that he had a double chin?

"The jailors got way too much pleasure out of shearing me," he said.

"How'd you get out?" I asked. I was amazed that Samuels, with all his connections, would have allowed that to happen.

"They set bail at one million bucks. Bastards didn't do their homework. They didn't realize I could pay it."

The Granger I knew complained if my clients drank more

than one case of beer per visit and insisted on driving all the way to Costco in Bend to save a few bucks. I must have look surprised, because he said, "I had an interesting life before I settled down. You know that Harley sidecar? Well, you know, I designed it. Made me a bit of money."

I laughed. It seemed like every other Harley I saw on the road had the same make and model of sidecar. The image of his Harley leaning against the old tree at the summit of the pass, buried in snow, came to mind. I decided not to say anything about that for now.

"How's the wound?" I asked.

"Through and through," he said. "They kept me doped up, though." He lifted the bucket. "Better use this water before it gets cold."

"Pour it over my head," I said.

The warm water was the most pleasurable sensation I'd ever felt, or nearly. It washed away the last of the grime. Granger handed me the clean towel that was draped over his shoulder.

"You'll have to wear some of my clothing," he said. "A bit big for you, but you're used to that. Speaking of which, what did you do with Bigfoot?"

Reluctantly, I pointed behind the shed. Granger went to check. Moments later, he shouted, "What the hell did you do to him?"

I wrapped the towel around my middle and walked around the side of the shed.

Granger turned to me with wide eyes. He seemed more amazed than angry. "This thing absolutely reeks! Man, I never took my cosplay that seriously."

"I'll buy you a new one," I said.

"Nah, the prank was getting old. Time to think up a new one. Is that bear bait I smell?"

"Nicole thought it would disguise me."

"Nicole? So she found you?"

"If it wasn't for her, I'd be dead. She led the tracking dogs on a wild Bigfoot chase. She's circling around and coming back. Should be here any moment."

Granger kicked the suit tentatively and pinched his nose

shut as if it had farted. "I'd better burn this before some bear wakes up hungry from hibernation. Meanwhile, you're cold. Better get you inside."

I hadn't even noticed I was shivering. It had become almost normal. I let him drape his arm over my shoulder companionably and lead me to the back door.

"Conner will be glad to see you," he said.

"Conner's here?"

"He insisted," Granger said. "He won't talk about what happened. Gets tears in his eyes every time I ask him."

"It's my fault," I said. The magnitude of young Conner killing a man—for me—fully hit me. "He killed Jordan to save my life."

"I thought it might be something like that," Granger said.

I ducked from under his arm and turned to face him. "I'm sorry you had to kill Previtt, Granger."

"Me?" Granger snorted. "Don't you know? I didn't kill anyone. The 'Strawberry Mountain Killer' did all of the killing. Jordan, Previtt, the others, it's all on *your* head, buddy boy. I'm just an accessory, helped you get away."

"Well, that's good," I said as his words sank in. "I mean, better me than you. In fact, if they catch me, that's how it's going to be. No way am I letting Conner getting blamed...or you."

"You don't realize how famous you are, Hart. Those guys you killed had some pretty impressive resumes, special ops, most of them. People are figuring out that there is more to this story than some mad survivalist-type murdering bounty hunters. Hell, even the people in John Day are starting to come around, and we all know how they hate your guts."

"I hope I haven't ruined your business," I said.

"Are you kidding? Leaf House, that's history. But Bigfoot Ranch? I might as well give in to the inevitable. We'll be booked solid for years by crime tourists tracking the Strawberry Mountain Killer."

"Crime tourists? There's such a thing?"

"Little subcultures everywhere, Hart."

Granger walked up the steps, but I stopped short. "Bring me out a change of clothing," I said. "Maybe some food."

"Huh?"

"I've got to get out of here."

"What are you talking about?" he asked, seeming truly confused.

"I've involved you guys too much already. I didn't know you'd be here...or Conner. It's unfair even to old man Heffinger. I should have realized."

Granger stepped down next to me. He snagged the towel from my waist. "You ain't going anywhere, Hart. Unless you plan to go naked."

From the darkness behind us, Nicole said, "Granger's right. You're staying here, Hart. We're gonna figure this out."

CHAPTER 51

Granger handed me back the towel without comment. I was pretty sure that every part of me, from head to toe, turned red—a scarlet red that glowed. I wrapped the towel around my waist and followed Granger up the steps, conscious of Nicole behind me.

"Conner's in the kitchen," Granger said. "He's been trying to excavate the piles of trash and Ernie's been fighting him over every inch. I swear, we found pots and pans from the fifties with the stickers still on them. You know, on second thought, maybe you should try some of Ernie's clothes. He's more your size."

He led Nicole and me past the kitchen, where I could hear Conner and Heffinger arguing. I wanted to get dressed first. There was a narrow path through the junk to a closed door. Granger pushed it open. The room beyond was full of discarded clothing. I was pretty sure there was a bed under the pile of garments. This had been Sam's room.

"I can't go in there," I said.

"Why?" Nicole asked. "Oh, I get it…this was his Sam's room. Don't worry, we won't tell Ernie."

Granger said, "Hurry up. I'll go tell Conner you're here. He'll be eager to see you."

Most of the clothes obviously belonged to the old man, which made me feel slightly less guilty.

Why did I feel guilty at all? It was my father who had swindled these people, not me.

You could have stopped it, came the voice of my father.

There was a time when I would have accepted that. But I'd

been a twelve-year-old boy in the thrall of a sociopath.

It wasn't my fault.

The guilt dropped away for the first time in years. My sojourn in the wilderness had changed things.

I turned to Nicole, shrugging apologetically.

"Oh, right," she said, turning a little red herself.

She left the room and closed the door quietly behind her. I shed the towel and lifted the shirts off the jumbled pile one by one, trying to find one that didn't look too out of date. The trousers were all a little baggy, but that was all right. In a closet were dozens of pairs of old shoes, and I found a pair that fit and weren't too battered. Once again, I felt as if I was re-entering the civilized world, if a secondhand one.

I left the room and stood in the narrow passage between stacks of books and magazines and boxes. There were bottles of every size and shape, but predominant among them were the cheap vodka bottles that Heffinger must have bought by the case. Everywhere I turned, it seemed like cats' eyes stared at me suspiciously. I walked down the narrow path and heard claws scratching on the wood floor as the animals scurried away from me.

I hesitated outside the kitchen and listened to the voices and laughter. I was lucky to have such friends. My wilderness adventure had felt like it had taken half a lifetime, and in some ways, it had.

I should leave by the back door. Get away from here.

With a sudden start, I remembered Granger's threat to burn the Bigfoot costume and realized I'd left the floppy disk in the pouch. I hurried to the back door and down the steps. The sun was setting.

The costume was where I'd left it. I picked it up. The odor was familiar by now. The floppy disk was still there, no more bent than before. I pulled it out and hesitated.

It wasn't too late to get out of here.

But if I left, the contents of the disk might never see the light of day. If I got caught, shot, or put away for life, no one would ever know the truth. It would have all been in vain.

But at least Nicole, Conner, and Granger would be safe.

"You clean up nicely," Nicole said from behind me.

I turned with a smile, planning to return the compliment. The words caught in my throat. She'd changed clothes and was wearing a green silk blouse, a nice pair of slacks, and sandals. I don't think I'd ever seen her not wearing jeans and boots. Where did she find makeup? I wondered. Then I remembered that the Heffinger Ranch was her base of operations.

Nicole seemed to glow in the twilight. She stepped closer, and I wasn't sure what to do. She put her arms around me and laid her head on my chest. She didn't say anything. I returned the hug, and she felt so slight in my arms that it was hard to believe she'd outrun me, the hounds, and everyone else.

"I led Bill and Marty and the dogs in a big circle back to Massacre Spring," she said. "That's where they finally gave up. Last I saw of them, the old boys and the dogs were in a big pile, napping."

I laughed at the image, and she looked up at me, smiling. I almost leaned down to kiss her, but she broke away, gently, without rejection.

"Is that the disk?" she asked curiously. "I haven't seen a floppy in years."

"I hope it isn't...broken," I said. "Or however they say it."

"Don't ask me," Nicole laughed. "I'm a wilderness guide for a reason. Modern technology is a mystery to me."

"I'll need to talk to Aaron, my tech guy in Bend."

"Well, come eat dinner first. Conner's a little put out. Says we're going to ruin the meal."

The kitchen looked almost tidy, if you ignored the boxes stacked against the walls. Granger and Heffinger sat at the table, which—miracles of miracles—was mostly free of clutter, though the old man had a stack of newspapers in front of him as if already plotting his re-colonization of the room.

Conner was working at the stove, stirring something that smelled so good it staggered me.

"Hart!" he cried out and gave me a hug. I realized he'd used my first name, and that I'd finally joined the blessed circle of Conner's friends.

"Close the door!" Granger shouted. "We finally got this one

room smelling decent, but the rest of the house still stinks!"

"*Le dîner est preparé*," Conner said, speaking French with the same accent and tone that Granger always used.

I'd planned on telling them that dinner could wait, that we needed to deal with the disk first, but the look on Conner's face changed my mind; that and the smell of the food. My friends deserved a few moments of peace.

One hour wouldn't hurt.

"What is this?" I said, as the first mouthful went down.

Conner looked puzzled. "It's chili, Hart. It's all I could find."

"*This* is chili?" I exclaimed. "I seriously doubt any five-star restaurant serves a plate this good."

Conner beamed, his wide forehead blushing. "It's just chili," he repeated.

We spent the rest of the meal talking about anything and everything but what was actually happening in the world outside. It was strange to think that I was probably the most wanted man in the country and that CNN and the other 24-hour cable news networks were probably all talking about me. None of it felt real.

If I could get the information on the disk to someone who could do something about it, maybe it would all go away.

Heffinger had found a cheap bottle of wine and poured us each a glass while sticking to his usual vodka. He took a swig and put down his huge cup. "I have to admit it's nice to have company," he said. "I'll be sorry to see you go. By the way, your wife called looking for you. She's on her way."

I stood up, the chair bumping up against a cardboard box behind me. "Where's your computer, Ernie?"

CHAPTER 52

"The infernal contraption is under there," Heffinger said, waving his hand vaguely at the far end of the room. I could just make out the legs of an old rolltop desk and a wooden chair. "I hate the damn thing, but Sam insisted I get it."

Granger plowed into the junk, sending several cats leaping over the piles, hissing. He moved stuff aside until we got to the far wall. The desk was covered with stacks of *Rolling Stones*, documenting the magazine's ever-diminishing size and thickness. We followed him as if he hacked a path through the jungle.

When the *Rolling Stones* were stacked on top of the piles of *National Geographics* on the floor, it exposed an old desktop computer with a large black tower and an old TV-sized screen.

"Is this still hooked up to AOL?" I asked.

"I think so," Heffinger said. "I keep getting their shit in the mail."

I reached over and turned it on. The dial-up tone filled the room: *Creecch…dddinga…dddinga…creecch.*

Well, there was nothing wrong with the speaker system. I examined the black tower, looking for the floppy disk drive.

"Let me," Granger said, taking the disk out of my hand. He straightened the bent corner. I must have looked surprised because he shrugged. "I said I don't *like* computers, not that I couldn't *use* them."

"Do you think the disk is broken?" I asked.

"With any luck, it's only the shell that's bent," Granger said. He slid the disk in, and the screen prompted us to open a file.

Granger did so, and we sat and waited…and waited.

"It stinks in here," Nicole said. "I can't help you guys, so I'm going out back and setting up my four-person tent. Any of you guys want to sleep out there, you're welcome to."

Granger glanced at me but managed to keep his face neutral. "No thanks. Conner and I are used to the smell by now."

Nicole looked at me. I nodded, trying not to make too much of it. She left the room, letting her hand trail along my arm as she passed me.

"Now what?" Granger asked, looking up from his seat.

"I have no clue," I said. "I need to call Aaron in Bend. Where's the landline?"

"Can't use it," Heffinger said. "Not if you're hooked up to the Internet."

For a moment, I was stumped. We could turn off the computer, get instructions, then go ahead and turn it back on, but I knew instinctively it wouldn't be that easy. Aaron would spew a bunch of directions that I'd *think* I understood, then we'd disconnect and I'd be almost as clueless as before. But if there was no help for it…

"You can use my phone," Conner said. He brought out an iPhone in a bright blue case. He handed it to me, then realized that Granger was staring at him. "Sorry, boss. My mom insisted I have it."

Granger shrugged. "That's all over with, Conner. It's time for Bigfoot Ranch to modernize. If even old man Heffinger is connected, then it's time for me to join the modern world."

I called Aaron, hoping he was home. He worked by day in construction, which was strange because he was such a whiz online, but he'd told me once he liked keeping the digital part fun. He worked on retainer for a whole bunch of people as well as constantly helping out friends and family.

He answered the phone, and I could hear his wife and two girls in the background. It sounded like they were eating dinner. I quickly explained what I needed.

"Sure," he said. "You can probably attach the file to an email. It might take some time with dial-up, but if it's on a floppy disk, it won't be holding that much data anyway. What do you want me to do with it?"

"What's the quickest way to get it out into the world?" I asked. "I want it to have the widest possible distribution, and I don't want it squelched."

"I can put it on Reddit," Aaron mused. "Once it's there, it can never be called back. I suppose I could send it to fifteen friends, tell them to send it to fifteen friends, do a chain letter kind of thing. They all belong to other groups like Reddit, so it will get to anyone who is anyone. What's on it?"

I told him that I thought the file contained damning evidence on the current Supreme Court nominee, proving his connections to the Russian mob.

There was a long silence on the other end. Then he said, "Jesus, Hart, where did you get that?"

"I never expose my sources."

"Yeah, but I thought your *sources* were rainbow trout and mule deer. OK, I'll give it a nice click-baity title: 'Is Barton Crane owned by the Russians?' Something like that."

"Just as long as someone sees it who can do something about it," I said.

"You got it."

"Oh, and Aaron. Is there any way to hide where this came from? For your sake as well as mine?"

"I've heard of ways," he said. I could sense his smile over the phone. "I've been connected to the TOR network for years. You know, just in case."

"TOR?"

"The Onion Router," Aaron said. "Like what you saw in all those hacker movies in the eighties. It bounces the connection all over the globe, making it impossible to trace."

"Yeah, that," I said dryly, and hung up.

The old computer still whirred and clicked, struggling mightily to send the information, as if it was trying to digest something indigestible. Conner left to clean up the kitchen, and Granger and I waited companionably for the computer to finish.

Suddenly, the room was silent.

"That's it, I guess," Granger said, extracting the disk. He handed it to me, and I absently stuck it in my back pocket. "I guess they got no reason to kill us anymore. The shit's about to hit the fan."

Though thick curtains covered the windows, my internal clock told me it was dark outside. I could barely keep my eyes open. For days, I'd survived with one thought: unloading the disk. Now that it was done, it was as if my reason for doing anything had disappeared.

"I'm going to bed," I said.

"Sure, don't blame you. See you in the morning."

I started to turn away.

"Hey, Hart?" Granger said.

"Yeah?"

"I think Davis/Nelson Wilderness Tours is an excellent name."

"I do too, but Nicole would probably object."

"Oh, I wouldn't worry about *that*."

The tent was the size of a bedroom and nearly as comfortable. A thick rug covered the floor, and a thermal blanket was hanging overhead. Nicole had a battery lantern, and not just one, but two catalytic heaters going. It was toasty warm.

She was already in bed. I got undressed, keeping on my shorts, and lifted the blankets, expecting to find a sleeping bag. Instead, there were two sleeping bags zipped together. Nicole raised the covers, and I realized she wasn't wearing anything underneath.

I slid under the covers, my sleepiness disappearing, and she took me in her arms.

CHAPTER 53

I awoke with Conner standing over me, holding out his phone. He was trying not to stare at Nicole and me but had a strange smile on his face.

"Your friend is on the phone," he said. He handed it to me. "And breakfast is ready," he said, leaving the tent.

Nicole was still asleep. I sat up.

"Hey, what's up?" I said into the phone.

"*You* are up," Aaron said. I could hear his TV blasting in the background. "Or rather, your stuff is up, and it's up everywhere. And I do mean *everywhere*."

"What are they saying?" I said, not able to keep my voice down. Nicole stirred, rolled over, and looked up at me with a smile. I put my hand under her chin and smiled back into her eyes, for a moment forgetting the phone.

Aaron said, "At first, no one believed it, but the more they dig into it, the more people are finding things. They're finding corroboration in documents outside of what we posted, apparently."

"So, it's on Reddit?"

"No, it's actually everywhere *but* Reddit. The moderator removed the thread for some bullshit reason. But it was too late; by then, everyone else had it. Hold on…yeah, it just hit CNN. There's an interview with Senator Cartwright calling for congressional hearings. You did it, Hart. You sure you don't want to take credit?"

The thought of it horrified me, not only because I hated being in the limelight but because I wasn't so sure that Barton Crane was the forgiving type.

"Hell no," I said. "And don't get involved yourself, Aaron. This stuff is too serious for the likes of us."

"You ain't kidding. They're saying the information not only ties Crane to the mob but to the higher levels of the Russian government. Apparently, the digital data points to connections that are pretty indisputable. It not just Crane, either; they're saying some other high-level government officials are implicated, including a certain high-powered 1980s New York real estate tycoon."

I let that sink in. I'd wondered why it mattered if Crane was on the Supreme Court. What could he do, after all? But if the administration was involved, the lives of a few people in Eastern Oregon weren't going to matter much. I was surprised they'd only sent a handful of men to get the job done, but then they'd thought they were after one small-town writer/outdoor guide who didn't know what he had in his possession.

What they hadn't expected was to hunt me in a wilderness I knew and they didn't. They hadn't expected a bulletproof Bigfoot costume. And most importantly, they hadn't counted on my friends.

"Stay out of it," I repeated.

"If you say so," Aaron said.

"I say so. This is dangerous."

"All right, all right. But I'm going to get a kick out of watching all this!"

I turned off the phone, slid under the covers, and gave Nicole a hug. She whispered in my ear, "So it's over?"

"I hope so."

I felt myself melting into her. We were quiet, aware that the others were awake, and it was gentle and right.

We got dressed and went inside where Granger and Heffinger sat at the table and Conner was fiddling at the stove. We sat down. I started to tell them what Aaron had told me, but Granger interrupted. "Yeah, Aaron couldn't hold back. He told us already. We've been listening to the radio all morning. So I guess we did a good thing, huh?"

It suddenly struck me that it didn't change my situation at all. I was still a wanted mass murderer, the Strawberry Mountain

Killer. I'd have to find a way to surrender without getting shot on sight.

Granger must have seen my face fall because he said, "I don't think it's going to hold up in court, Hart. There are just too many holes in their story. And you got me and Nicole on your side."

"And me," Conner said.

"And Conner. Those were some bad dudes, Hart, and if it wasn't for Sheriff Black, I doubt anyone would have believed them. I bet a little digging into our sheriff's finances will find some interesting things."

Conner placed a heap of scrambled eggs and bacon in front of me. I took a bite, closing my eyes in pure pleasure. Granger was right. It was over. There was no way they'd be able to prove that I'd done what they were accusing me of.

If I had to, I would reveal the existence of the floppy disk, which I intended to hide in a very safe place with instructions to reveal it if anything happened to me.

That would shut them up.

I felt the tension flowing out of me for the first time in days. It was all out of my hands now. Let the media and law enforcement do their thing.

I was out of it at last.

Relief flooded my body, and I felt tears coming to my eyes. I stood up, the chair bumping up against the boxes.

"Are you all right, Hart?" Nicole asked.

"I'm good," I said, not looking at her. I went to the back door and out onto the path to the outhouse. I sat in there for a time until I regained control of my emotions. The next few months were probably going to be difficult. But even if they threw me in jail, the 'three hots and a cot' would feel like luxury compared to what I'd just been through.

I needed to tell Nicole about the money in my closet at Bigfoot Ranch. I might be able to afford a good lawyer.

It was going to work out. I was sure of it.

A car pulled up outside.

Amanda.

I felt a moment of panic, then I shook my head. Even the

thought of my crazy ex-wife arriving wasn't enough to bring me down. She might get weird when she sensed what was happening with Nicole and me, but I was pretty sure I could talk her down from the ledge, or talk her up, depending on where she was in the cycle of her mental illness.

Four car doors slammed, one after another, and I heard the jostling and whispering of more than two people. This wasn't Amanda and Russo.

With a sinking heart, I realized that it was probably the police. As prepared as I thought I was to surrender, now that the moment had come, I was reluctant.

I'd better get out there before my friends got in the middle of it.

"Come on out of the house, Hart!"

It was Samuels's voice. He didn't sound casually arrogant anymore. He sounded angry.

I froze, not knowing what to do.

"What do you want?" Granger shouted from inside the house.

"Is that you, Granger? Shit, man, you're always in the wrong place at the wrong time. You should have walked away from this."

"Hart's my friend," Granger shouted.

"And the wrong friend," Samuels said. "Aren't you sick of Hart hiding behind you? Whoever else is inside, you'd better come out too."

"Why?" Granger said. "You've lost, Samuels. The information got out. There's no point in killing Hart."

"I agree," Samuels said, shaking his head. "But my employer doesn't feel that way. He's always been a vengeful son of a bitch. He and his partners want Hart dead."

There was a long silence, and I could imagine my friends arguing about what to do. Heffinger would be heading for the door, Granger would be holding him back, and Nicole would have her arm around Conner reassuringly.

I doubted Samuels would leave my friends unharmed, whether I surrendered or not.

But I had to try.

The outhouse door creaked as I stepped out. No one looked my way. There were four men beside Samuels, all of them dressed in military gear, their rifles pointed at the front door of the Heffinger place. Samuels held a pistol down at his side.

I shouted out, "Here!" at the same moment Granger shouted "Fuck you!" and a shot came from within the house. A bullet hit the SUV's grill with a *plunk*.

Cats flew from behind every tree stump and rusted fixture. I think the movement confused the mercenaries for a moment, and they hesitated. It was obvious none of them had heard my shout.

Then they started firing, assault rifles at full automatic, spraying the house for what seemed an eternity but was probably only a few seconds before stopping and reloading.

I stood over the discarded Bigfoot costume before I was consciously aware of making the decision. I got into it with a practiced motion, barely noticing my broken pinky hitting the inside of the glove. It felt like I was returning to my natural state, my primitive self. The smell was almost reassuring, as if it was the stink and not the Kevlar that gave me mystical protection.

As I'd desperately donned the costume, several more volleys of automatic fire had erupted, along with a couple of loud booms from Heffinger's shotgun.

Then all the firepower came from one side.

The mercenaries would be expecting everyone to be dead. They were firing for the pure fun of it now. They'd think the rounds were shredding everything inside the house, finding every little hidden corner. Surely no doors or furniture or anything else in a normal house could have withstood such a broadside.

What the mercenaries didn't know was that most of the bullets had struck stacks of newspapers, magazines, and books, heaps of clothing, and old boxes full of every kind of useless thing.

There was silence.

Samuels's voice was commanding but unhurried. "Get on in there, Kolkov. Finish off any survivors."

The Bigfoot costume was finally on. I turned...and then froze.

A Mustang drove up behind the SUV. Amanda's car.

She didn't stop at the sight of the men with rifles, but drove right up to them. Behind the windshield, I could see Amanda's heavy makeup, her cat's eyes and bright pink blush, her tight and revealing clothing. Amanda was in full mania mode.

A big man got out of the passenger seat. It was a slow, deliberate movement.

For a moment, the mercenaries stared at the interlopers.

And then Samuels raised his pistol and fired right at the big man's chest.

I ran the last few yards downhill. As Samuels turned his weapon toward Amanda, I dove for him. He must have heard me, because he turned and fired, hitting me in the chest. My heart skipped a beat from the pain. I crashed into his knees. There was a loud *snap,* and he screamed. The pistol went flying into the air, and I went after it, expecting a volley of bullets to slam into my side at any moment. I doubted the Kevlar would hold up with that many men firing at me at such close range.

But Samuels's men hadn't bothered to reload after their last volley, and now they were frantically reaching for the magazines on their belts. Heffinger flew out of his house, faster than I could have ever believed the old man could move, his shotgun raised. He blew the head off the nearest mercenary. Granger followed, lifted his rifle, and shot at a second man, while Nicole fired a full magazine from her pistol into a third man.

The mercenaries were wearing bulletproof vests, but one went down. As he turned to clutch his thigh, a second bullet caught him in the back of the head.

I grabbed Samuels's pistol and turned around. Samuels was out of commission, holding his legs, both of which were bent at an unnatural angle.

I turned back toward the fight and found myself looking down the barrel of a rifle not more than five feet away.

Amanda emerged from the Mustang with a pearl-handled pistol in each hand. She raised them both, and the man with the rifle jerked backward and then shuddered as a barrage of bullets struck him in the chest, rising upward until one hit his exposed throat. Blood sprayed, and he went down.

A big shadow passed over me, and I saw Russo striding boldly toward the last of the enemy still standing, blasting away with a huge revolver. The mercenary held up his hands, but Russo shot him between the eyes, splitting his head down the middle.

Then it was silent but for Samuels's groans.

Russo stalked over to him, raising his pistol. I motioned for him to stop. The big man turned to me curiously, and I realized that he was looking at a man in a furry costume.

Samuels stared at me from the ground. "You think it's over," he said, "but it isn't. They'll never give up trying to kill you. *All* of you." His eyes flicked over to Russo. "*Especially* you."

Russo grunted. "You think I don't know that?" He opened his coat. He was wearing a bulky bulletproof vest, the kind they used to wear twenty years ago. He rubbed the area where Samuels's bullet had struck. "I knew Bart when he was a two-bit lawyer, and he was always a mean little prick. Why do you think I created my little getaway packages? Funny thing is, I probably never would have done anything if he'd just left me alone."

"They won't stop until you're dead," Samuels said.

"Who are *they*?" I asked. "Who's giving the orders? Crane?"

"Crane is a tool," Samuels said. "I'll tell you who's really in charge if you promise not to kill me."

I hesitated.

"I promise not to kill you," I said.

"The man you're looking for is Dmitry Kuznetsov, vice president of Airolo Corporation."

I turned to Russo, nodded.

Russo raised his revolver and stood over Samuels.

"Davis!" Samuels shouted. "You promised!"

I held up my broken finger. "I lied."

Russo fired twice. The bullets struck both of Samuels's femoral arteries. I stepped back from the flying blood. For a moment, I saw a look of fear in Samuels's eyes. It was as if he was a different man, a smaller man. Then his eyes glazed over.

It hadn't really been a lie. After all, I hadn't fired the bullets.

Amanda was staring out over the battlefield with a look of pure joy. She turned toward me, took a step.

I felt Nicole's arm go around mine. Amanda stopped short, her face going blank.

"Are you all right?" Nicole asked.

I nodded, realizing that it was true.

Russo leaned down and went through the dead man's pockets, pulling out the keys to the SUV. Then he turned to me. "Nice monkey suit," he said.

"Thanks. You must be Sherman Russo."

He smiled. "It's too bad you couldn't have held onto the information a little longer. It would have been worth a fortune."

I stared at him, but the anger didn't come. I'd chosen not to hand it over to Samuels. It was no one's fault but mine.

I said, "I still have the money from the box, if you want it."

"You keep it, kid. I've got plenty more squirreled away in a safe deposit box, if I can ever get at it."

"I think you owe me an explanation," I said.

Russo stared at me without expression. "All right, but only you, Davis. The others are better off not knowing."

We walked up an old hunting trail. I thought about taking off the Bigfoot suit, but decided I couldn't risk losing my chance to hear Russo's story.

So while we hiked upward, Russo told me his tale, from when he was a foot soldier in the Family to the moment when Barton Crane was nominated to the Supreme Court.

"Bart Crane orchestrated most of the big deals in New York real estate where the Russian oligarchs bought property," he explained. "The oligarchs were a front for the Kremlin, which is bad enough, but it also entangled a lot of big politicians in America. Believe me, Crane is just the point of entry. It leads upward from there."

"Upward?"

"All the way to the top," Russo said. "Crane is only the first to be exposed. This information was so important, I thought I could use it to ensure my safety. But then it became important enough to kill for. That's when my little escape kit became a death trap."

"A deadfall," I said.

"What's that?"

"A trap that's triggered when prey passes beneath it. Something heavy."

The big man didn't answer at first. I wondered if he was winded by the uphill climb, but he didn't seem to be breathing hard. "That pretty much describes it," he said, finally.

We turned around. On the way back, Russo told me about his trip across the country. When he reached the part where he met Amanda, he stopped in the trail. "She wants to go with me!" he marveled. "I've told her how dangerous it is, but that just seems to excite her more."

"Be careful," I said. "Amanda is fragile."

He laughed as if I was joking, then looked thoughtful. "I think I see," he said.

We got back to the Heffinger place. Someone had gone into the house, grabbed some old blankets, and covered up the bodies. I'd sort of expected to hear sirens if there were still police at Bigfoot Ranch, but apparently the sound hadn't carried over the ridge.

To my surprise, Nicole and Amanda were talking like old friends.

Russo walked over to the Mustang and looked back at Amanda. She passed by me, giving me a wink.

"Wait," I said. "What's your real name?" Hart asked. Not something an ex-husband usually asks after twenty years of marriage.

"Mary Celeste."

As in the frigate found adrift and abandoned? A typically mysterious answer from her. "So you aren't going to tell me?"

"I'm not sure...I don't know." Amanda turned and got into the Mustang. Russo was in the passenger seat, his bulk up against the dash. Her eyes glowed even more than usual. She didn't seem to notice when Nicole came up and put her arm around my waist again, this time possessively.

Russo leaned out the window. "For God's sake, take a bath."

I stepped back as Amanda started the Mustang and drove away.

EPILOGUE

We gave Bigfoot a proper funeral. It didn't start off that way. I mentioned that it was time to burn the damn thing, and Nicole insisted on coming along. By the time I was pouring lighter fluid over the putrid suit, Granger and Conner had joined us. Even Ernie Heffinger showed up, probably more out of curiosity than respect for the costume.

The biggest surprise was when Kent showed up after it was all over, his straw hat red with blood, but otherwise seeming unharmed. If he was any loopier from the blow he'd taken, with Kent it was hard to tell. He joined us and never asked what had happened.

I had come to regard the costume with fondness. It had saved my life more than once. Before we set fire to it, we turned it inside out and counted how many bullet impacts it had endured, and though it was not always possible to distinguish bullet indentations from other damage, it looked like Bigfoot had been hit at least a dozen times.

We placed the suit in Granger's fire pit and stood over it silently for a few moments. Conner was given the honor of tossing the match. The suit burst into flames, and a black, acrid cloud drove us back. Once again, Bigfoot proved that no stink was too much.

Several months had passed since my sojourn in the Strawberry Mountains. I had used the money Sherman Russo had left me to hire the best lawyer in the state. The charges against me were dropped rather rapidly once the mercenaries' unsavory history was revealed. It was Sheriff Black who was now under investigation. Though it wasn't mentioned in the papers, it appeared to be common knowledge in John Day that the whole incident was connected to the problems Supreme Court Justice Crane was having.

Instead of getting glares when I walked the streets, I received looks of curiosity and even the occasional thumbs-up.

The Harley spent a month under the snows of the pass before it could be recovered. I offered to buy Granger a new one, but he said, "Hell, I like tinkering with the hog."

I debated telling him about the gold I'd found in the cave. It was his property, but I also knew he didn't like the way the gold miners stripped the land. Someday, I thought, but not now.

Meanwhile, far away from the Strawberry Mountains, the revelations from the floppy disk had brought about the resignations of the secretary of state and the vice president, although the president looked as if he'd stay in office, at least until the next election.

The country was tired of the turmoil.

It appeared that Barton Crane was also going to survive the scandal. Enough of a shadow was cast on the information's legitimacy that the partisan Senate gave him the benefit of the doubt. He might always have a cloud over his head, but once in, he was in for life, unless something more damning was revealed.

"You think it's over, but it isn't. They'll never give up trying to kill you. All of you."

I tried to forget Samuels's last words. Surely Barton Crane wouldn't jeopardize his position now? But Samuels had seemed pretty certain.

I didn't care. I wasn't going to be like my father and run away from trouble. I would live my life in the open.

After Bigfoot's fiery Viking sendoff, Nicole and I drove back to my house in Bend. We were still in bed when the phone rang early the next morning.

"Turn on your TV," Aaron said, and hung up before I could answer. I did, and caught the middle of a newscast.

"...Barton Crane was sixty-five years old and had been on the bench for only three months. We have very little information at this time. What we know is this: a woman whom bystanders describe as black-haired and wearing heavy makeup ambushed Justice Crane as he walked to his chambers. The woman was armed with two handguns and fired multiple shots at Justice Crane, who was fatally injured in the attack. The suspect then fled the scene; authorities are continuing to search for her. They're asking for help from the public..."

I turned to Nicole, who looked confused. I'd never told her about Amanda's claim of having once been a CIA assassin. I still didn't believe it, at least, I didn't *think* I believed it.

But then, who would have ever thought that I'd be responsible for bringing down half the federal government? Who'd have thought I'd spend five days on the run in a bulletproof Bigfoot costume? Who'd have ever thought I'd be a partner with Nicole in Nelson/Davis Wilderness Tours? (She had resisted calling it Bigfoot Hunting and Fishing.)

"You think we're safe?" Nicole asked.

I slid back under the covers and wrapped my arms around her. "Safe or not, we'll handle it."

The future looked bright. Nelson/Davis Wilderness Tours was booked far in advance. It wasn't just curiosity about the Strawberry Mountain Killer (a name that I would apparently never live down).

A young family had posted a video of Bigfoot crossing over a raging stream on a log. A couple of other tourists swore they'd seen and smelled Bigfoot stomping around in the woods. Cryptozoologists were declaring it the best proof yet of his existence.

I had to admit, if I hadn't known who it was in the video, I might have been convinced myself.

ABOUT THE AUTHOR

Duncan grew up and spent most of his life in Central Oregon, the dry side of the Cascades, and whose terrain is featured in many of his books. He wrote several books out of college, including the heroic fantasy novels *Star Axe, Snowcastles,* and *Icetowers.* In 1984, he and his wife Linda bought Pegasus Books in downtown Bend, Oregon, which they still own and operate. They also ran a used bookstore, the Bookmark, for 15 years.

In the last five years, he's been able to get back to writing again, and found that he has a lot of pent-up creative energy. He's written numerous books for several different publishers, mostly in the horror or dark fantasy genres, though recently has been branching out into fantasy again, as well as thrillers.

Duncan grew up and spent most of his life in Central Oregon, the dry side of the Cascades, and whose terrain is featured in many of his books. He wrote several books out of college, including the heroic fantasy novels Star Axe, Snowcastles, and Icetowers. In 1984, he and his wife Linda bought Pegasus Books in downtown Bend, Oregon, which they still own and operate. They also ran a used bookstore, the Bookmark, for 15 years.

In the last five years, he's been able to get back to writing again, and found that he has a lot of pent-up creative energy. He's written numerous books for several different publishers, mostly in the horror or dark fantasy genres, though recently has been branching out into fantasy again, as well as thrillers.

Curious about other Crossroad Press books?
Stop by our site:
http://store.crossroadpress.com
We offer quality writing
in digital, audio, and print formats.

Enter the code FIRSTBOOK
to get 20% off your first order from our store!
Stop by today!